LOST IN A DREAM

R. E. Fury

Presst Publications

Advanced Praise For *Lost In A Dream*

An absolute masterpiece. ★ ★ ★ ★ ★

— *MY MOM* *BEFORE SHE READ IT*

I picked it up and just couldn't put it down.

— *MAN WITH GLUE HANDS*

What an absolute book.

— *ANONYMOUS*

I like it, and not just because we're engaged. I promise.

— *ANNIE G.*

I read it, then I just had to read it again.

— *MY EDITOR*

To my mother, a woman strong enough to love her silent son.

My father, also a writer, though in another language.

My wonderful Annie, who crafted a cauldron into which I poured my self-doubt, boiled the doubt away, and was left with a sense of self.

And lastly, two of my oldest fans: /u/akkiruk and /u/lordev0ldemort, who reminded me that people care about what I do, when I had so easily forgotten.

CONTENTS

LOST IN A DREAM

□

You are a world of your own.

That's not to say you're extraordinary, necessarily —you might be. Chances are you're more so than me, at the least, but that's not much of a feat. Rather, we are each little universes of thought; pioneers lost in our own minds. Every human is a wellspring of possibility and impossibility, every breath a wish for something greater as we run desperate from the impending dark.

We are, in a sense, prisoners to ourselves. Slaves to dreams we may well never grab hold of, working to the bone so that one day the schism between what we want and what we have might narrow ever so slightly. It is no surprise that every night we shut down for a brief reprieve, where we get a taste of the strange workings inside our heads. A glimpse into the potential we each have, raw as it may be.

When we aren't asleep, exploring our own dreams, we look to those of others. Snippets of what it's like to live in someone else's mind; pretty portals to vast, new, and often beautiful worlds, or ones so terrible and forlorn that anything seems tolerable when compared. Something—anything—to distract from the one that we're in. To feel greater than ourselves.

After all . . . isn't that why you're here?

·

Real

Is it greed to desire something grand?

I often asked myself things like that as I killed someone. Many lives have been forever reduced to similar questions that fade in and out like fireflies on a dark summer night—what's ironic is that putting a sword through a neck is so much easier than finding the answers. It shouldn't be, right? Just reach out and grab one of the little lightbugs and put it in a jar to study later . . . but every time I try, they vanish. All I get is a fistful of darkness.

By the time I was done thinking about all of that, there was only one other person breathing in the field before me: the man who had killed my family. My friends. My clansmen. I'd have cried looking at him if that well hadn't dried up so long before; screamed if there were any leftover rage to burn.

"You're strong, Kinghunter," Ilhor Drago snarled, a hulking man in shimmering ebony armor patterned with wispy typhoons of cream and ox-blood. He must've stood seven feet tall. "But this is my home, and I'll not die here like some flame you'd snuff out with a shovel of dirt."

He peered at me through two clusters of holes in a solid iron headpiece, describable only as a perforated bucket. The rest of his battalion littered the wood-lined meadow like smashed tin cans. They'd made quite a morbid medium for my art, shades of death tainting the lush, fertile forest around us, painting fern and flower slick with a contrasting crimson. In the holy glow of spring's sun, amidst a field paint-brushed with trampled fuchsia tulips and peonies that dribbled out of the treeline, the bloodied plants almost looked at home.

Ilhor charged at me, and I backpedaled toward the lake's muddy shore while keeping my sword raised overhead. Ilhor would be a challenge, no doubt—perhaps even worth three whole questions—but challenges are meant to be overcome, even if that challenge was once the most feared knight in any kingdom. A man known for cleaving children in two might terrify most, but I'd have fought God himself if that's what it would've taken to put an end to Hadrian's reign.

What will I do when all of this is over?

His footwork was perfectly placed with excellent tempo; he had the speed of a fox despite swelling with brutish strength, bowing the boundaries of human limits as if they physically couldn't contain his mass. Each swing of his enormous weapon left my own feeling heavier and heavier in hand, every metallic crack a seismic spasm that rang my soul like a church bell. I ducked and weaved through his razing, slowly backstepping to dodge; parrying had become too taxing on my aching palms. With each lurch forward, he churned huge piles of mud, flinging it around us. Though he was slowed, the length of his broadsword kept me from making a clean retreat.

Is there a place left in the world for someone like me?

Not only was I reduced to defense, but the stout cascade of steel he donned had virtually no openings, aside from under the armpits and a small gap beneath his helmet—one just big enough to slip a thin, thirsty blade into.

Another swing, another step, retreating further and further until I could avoid parrying no more and our swords locked with spark and screech. He grabbed me with a single hand that touched its fingers together at the nape of my neck, feet desperately reaching for the ground as he lifted me into the air. I must've looked to pedal myself airborne.

Why am I so damn good at this?

"Why did you come here?" Ilhor asked, though he didn't care to relax his grip. "I defected. I defected!"

My words barely squeezed out between his fingers. "Hadrian wouldn't let a defector live. Did you think an early retirement would save you?"

"How did you even find this place? He promised me it was safe!"

"Nowhere—" I punched at his giant gauntlets like a child, gasping. "—is safe."

He grunted twice; once at me, and once at the ground.

With our weight combined, he sank past his ankles into the soft, dense mud that lined the lake's western shore. He dropped me, hoping it wasn't too late, then yanked at them fruitlessly—an alligator has strength on the close, not open.

I lunged, but his sword slammed into mine and sent it flying further into the forest than reality should allow, nesting into the canopy with a grating *buzz* like a silver beetle. A pained screech and flurry of wings rang out, followed by a distant, wooden *thunk*. Before I could look back in disdain, his blade was thrusting straight at my heart. I ducked, twisting, and barely managed to get low enough for it to deflect off my mail, then grabbed his wrists and pushed forward with all my weight to outstretch his arms.

I only had a second before he'd overwhelm me, but that was all I needed. A small dagger, its polished gold hilt adorned with rubies, was partially hidden at his hip under a small flap of fraying linen. I let go of his off-hand, dropped even lower and grabbed it, then released his sword hand and pushed forward. In a blur of motion, I jammed the dagger into the thin gap between his helmet and breastplate just as his massive python of a left arm snapped at me again. A weary stumble backward was enough to escape his reach.

He struggled and sucked at the air, his words wet with blood. "I'm … not even … a king. …"

"How many innocent people did you kill for one?" I whispered, hacking off his head.

That was for you, Ophelia. For our little ones.

He plummeted into the coast, sinking into it a little bit. After a moment to collect myself, taking a few deep breaths, I was free to finally loot his body —a vulture hungry for the treasure I could smell on him. Out of a covered compartment at his right hip, I pulled out a golden scroll with reverence, cupping it in my hands and brushing my thumbs across its complex network of embossed vines. It was the fifth one I'd stolen, and it was every bit as mesmerizing as the first, glowing as though the sun itself had been laid out in my still aching palms. I knelt there for some time, drinking its glow, and aches melted to memory with each moment. Eventually, I found it within myself to forfeit worship and tuck it into a satchel at my waist.

My fugitive beetle-sword was stuck in a tree nearly twenty yards away, with traces of blood on and around it. Splintered branches and shredded leaves littered the area, but there were no signs of life—or death—anywhere. I yanked it out, apologized to anything I may have harmed in Dominaria Forest, and ran back to the lake's edge.

Hidden. No patrols, no shipments, no trade. Forest for miles on all sides. How ironic that your pet's hiding place has become mine, Hadrian. It'll need a little cleanup, to say the least, but maybe this can be somewhere my roots can anchor.

A place to belong.

As I approached the castle, stepping over bodies like they were nothing more than fallen branches after a storm, a light, playful voice caught me off-guard.

"What a shame—I wanted to kill him."

I spun, reflexively unsheathing my sword to flare wary steel. A woman emerged from behind bark, crossing her arms and leaning lazily against the tree she'd been using for cover. Her weapon was unattended, dangling with a laxness inherited from its owner.

"I was rooting for you to lose, but your fighting skills are impressive. You're not like the others I've run into around here," she continued, her gaze sharper than a blade fresh off of whetstone, her lips hinting at a smirk.

I smiled as a cool breeze slid through thick trees, relaxing. "Yeah. You seem . . . different, somehow. You seem real."

⚁

Caterpillar

"It does not do to dwell on dreams and forget to live."

—J. K. ROWLING

I refuse to accept that mentality.

Dreams are what drive us as humans; they're how we strive past what we are today in search of a better tomorrow. What is so fallible about getting a little lost now and again? Is the acceptance of a mundane path really a life worth living? I think not, and so I will continue to dream; I will get lost, and take my time finding the path back home.

Dreams are the dwellings where one's true self lives.

The corners of my lips curled up, like foxes cozying in a den, as I placed my quill back in its holster. A paperweight at each corner of the protesting parchment shackled it in place as it set. The smell of wet ink filled my nostrils, lingering there, and I basked in the scent of freshly written wisdom. Fresh morning sun spilled over the castle courtyard and in through dancing silk curtains, showering me with warmth, and I sighed with satisfaction.

"It's not a meal—you don't need to *savor* it."

I tilted my head backwards over the oak chair I was sitting on, and there she was: Maya, my beautiful, upside-down love, with her satin, chocolate hair contrasting flawless pale skin. She almost glowed in sunlight that crept through dancing silk curtains, gazing into my eyes through glimmering pools of deep blue with bursts of yellow around the pupils, like sunflowers floating in the ocean. She leaned in and cupped a hand on each side of my head. I tensed my lips somewhere between a kiss and smile but got a mouthful of rose-scented hair as she bit the tip of my nose and pulled back.

"You thought I was going for a kiss, didn't you?" she asked, words dancing in my ears. Her voice was like silk, smooth, rich and comforting, with a tug of temptation that could rival an apple stolen from Eden—when it wasn't overripe with sarcasm.

"Well, I certainly wasn't expecting whatever that was. I don't know where your enthusiasm comes from; the sun's barely risen and you're already so full of life. I hope you don't spend it all before the day starts."

She sneered at me. "I'm always full of life. I'm ready to take on the world! The question is: are you?"

A deep breath, then, "Yeah, I'm ready. I've been waiting years for something I now see on the horizon."

"There's no turning back from this, you know. We could take a little longer, branch further out and keep Hadrian off our scent."

I sighed, rising and walking toward the balcony. We slept in a central main bailey that served as both our personal chambers and a lookout station, at least fifty feet high, which made for a breathtaking view of our courtyard and the forest. Everything we'd fought for. "No, he must already suspect where we're hiding—he never did believe in coincidences. He sent Drago away, and now he's lost territories all around where he sent him to. I'd rather stick close and be ready for whatever might happen. Besides, I'm done playing games. I want to end this."

"I'm sure you do, Kingslayer."

Turning to her, I frowned. "You know I hate that."

"Oh, I know."

I approached her, feeling the faint shape of her waist beneath fitted mail. I was still in my robe, but she'd already dressed for battle—forest green pants and a tapered cream top, both of which were armored from the inside so they'd 'look prettier', in her own words. While certain parts of my mind drifted, I knew why she'd suited up so early. "Call me by my real name."

Her eyes danced across my face, and a wicked smile tempted me. "Reza."

That time, she leaned into my kiss, and we took a moment to savor it. Quicker than I would have liked, however, she slipped away and into the hall.

Following suit, I donned my armor. Pieced together from tough, white leather with an outer layer of gold scales on the torso and a black horn on each shoulder, it looked like the hide of an envied albino dragon. I'd never gotten around to decorating it with any accents or symbols; it was simple elegance from head to toe.

I slung a simple steel longsword across my back and stormed out the door, hoping Maya hadn't left me behind. Either it pleased her to be first, or my frustration made her giggle—likely some concoction of the two.

I descended a granite staircase lined with the finest embroidered rug in our possession, a tongue of crimson and gold, connected the main bailey at its base to the great hall. It was a long building, adorned with mementos of adventures past, that was intended to house dozens of a royal family. I couldn't help but feel satisfaction, despite having seen it hundreds of times, knowing that years of work were coming to a head. Tapestries and various treasures far from home littered the walls, hereditary plunders like the dual scythes of Tryst, dishonored by their relocation, or the Granymede royal crest carved painstakingly into jade. Jade was a fitting medium for the jaded old man they worshipped as God-Emperor, but it turns out he was more emperor than God. All power-hungry men are.

Chandeliers ten feet wide hung from the vaulted ceilings of each section. Rather than being fixed with crystal, we'd cut and shaped pendants from the armor of slain enemies, polishing the steel until it reflected walls so brilliantly it almost looked to be transparent. A few were ebony, or obsidian, or cobalt, demanding attention just as the men who'd worn them had. The way they glimmered in candlelight was truly a magnificent sight; a thousand metal fireflies reflecting off one another, flittering and recounting tales of war—tales of loss.

As I walked through the main hall, which connected the entrance hall with the dining room and great hall, something caught my eye: a small, ornate dagger on a marble pedestal, its blade and rubies stained with blood and dirt. Waves of nostalgia crashed over me again. Unfortunately, my moment of reminisce was short-lived, as it often was.

"You are so. Slow."

Two wooden doors that towered over me split away as I pushed forward, daylight spilling into the entrance hallway. Downhill, toward the tree-lined main gate, Maya was pacing near the armory. It was a fifty-foot tower sitting along the eastern edge of Lake Augr—yes, the castle courtyard contained a lake. A small one, perhaps, but a lake nonetheless, bound in a sandstone pavilion flanked by great pines and little brushstrokes of flora that popped under sunlight.

Maya called out to me again, jumping in the air and waving her arms. "Come on! I have a surprise for you!"

I approached cautiously, peeking my head into each of the archways that leapt along the coastline lest a "surprise" hit me in the face.

"Come over here already, child! You're gonna love this. I swear, I'm not screwing around with you. This time."

Inside the armory, she was standing near our forge. In her hands was a broadsword with a hilt of silver, its grip an oily sapphire blue—one that nearly matched her eyes but leaned closer to indigo. The blade was shaped from buffered obsidian, streaks of white swirling through it as if somehow smelted and laced with ivory, and a large onyx gem was embedded in the triangular pommel. Its crossguard was shaped to look like a bat's spread wings, intricate attention to detail placed on recreating the frail, finger-like appendages a real bat would have.

"Is that my surprise?" I asked, wondering if she somehow didn't know of my distaste for bats and other things that prowl in the night.

"No, silly, this is my sword. Why would I make something this amazing for *you*? I think I'm going to call it Vesper and take it out into battle today. Pretty sexy, right?"

"It's certainly well-crafted. Too flashy for my tastes, but it suits your style well."

"God, you take all of this so seriously." The words sounded harsh, but nothing in her features betrayed malice. Instead she was beaming, grinning with glee, and let out a little squeal of excitement. "I can't wait to go out and fight. Vesper is hungry for battle, and as its mother, I am obligated to feed it! How'd you like that line? Maybe I should be the one writing."

"The closest you'll get is *riding* me about being too slow. Anyway, is that all? If so, we should get going. It's already quite late."

Her lips pursed as she clearly fought back a smile, bobbing up and down, ever so slightly shifting weight between her toes and heels. I stared her right in the eyes and raised my eyebrows. *Does she really think this is subtle?*

After a few moments, she burst out with a giggle. "Okay, okay, I'm not that mean. I made something for you, too—I know you mentioned disliking fun, but we're badasses, and a badass needs a unique look. Besides—I think you're gonna like it. I tried to tailor it to you."

She pulled a longsword out from behind the stone hearth; it was sheathed, but even the hilt caught my eye. It was a stunning gold, with accents of forest green running over its grip in a crisscross pattern of emerald vines. The cross-guards curved toward the blade up until the tips, which redirected sharply in the opposite direction. At each end sat the head of an ancient Chinese dragon. The detail was painstaking; sets of miniature teeth, nostrils with pearl tendrils hanging from them, scales running down its back, and eyes of ruby.

My eyes were glued to the work of art before me. "Maya, this is amazing. You made this for me? The detail you put into it . . . this must have taken you forever."

"I did make it, just for you. It took a little while to design, yeah, but I had a feeling that you'd fall in love with it. Unsheathe it, silly."

I drew the blade from its pitch-black sheath, a sharp, metallic screech bouncing between stone walls and lingering faintly for a moment before silence fell. The blade looked like jade, layered and marbled shades of green with streaks of cream—yet, somehow, it kept the metallic sheen of steel. I broke the silence with a gasp as the blade caught sun, drinking light like a parched desert traveler before refracting it across the room.

"Too flashy, or do you think you can live with it?" she asked with a sly smile. "C'mon, take it out into battle with me today."

My gaze shifted from the sword to Maya for a moment, before returning it. "I think that, for this, I can make an exception to my rule."

"Yes!" she hissed, pumping her fists. "By the way, that blade has a special function. You see those little red buttons where the cross-guard meets the grip on each side? They're hidden a bit, so you don't accidentally hit them."

"Yeah, I think I see them. What are they for?"

"Well, hold the sword away from your face

and push one."

"I feel like I should know what will happen before pushing one, for . . . basic safety purposes?"

"Stop complaining and press one of the damn buttons."

I held the blade up cautiously. "Does it matter which one?"

"They do the same thing, I only put a button on each side so you always have access to one."

I squinted my eyes, pulling my head as far back from the sword as I could.

Click.

A needle-like blade sprang forth from the jaws of each beast, and I jolted at the feeling. My reaction prompted stifled laughter from Maya, ever amused with herself. The blades were narrow, but long—they extended about eight inches out.

"Okay, that is definitely the kind of flashy I'm not a fan of. I suppose it could come in handy, but it seems like a risky addition." Maya stuck her tongue out at me. "How do I get the blades back in?"

She squinted her eyes and sheepishly laughed, rubbing the back of her head. "Well, you see, uh, I haven't really had the time to get that far. You kinda have to push them back in with a stick or something. I swear, I'll work something out later!"

I sighed, grabbed a scrap of wood off the floor, and stuffed the blades back into the beasts' mouths. "We don't have time now, but tomorrow I'd rather you remove the feature than continue to work on it. I swear, if I lose an eye to this thing. . . ."

"Hmph. Well, as long as you don't suck enough to point it at your own eye and press the button, you'll be fine. Give it a spin today, and if you really hate it, I'll take it out."

"Fine. I really do appreciate the work you put into this, though. Let's get going so I can test it out."

"I'm so glad you like it!" She smiled, placing a hand on my shoulder. "I love you."

I met her eyes for a moment, then looked away. "We should get going." Pulling away from her, I tossed my old sword into a trunk by the entrance and slung its replacement on my hip. The weight was nice, and it felt at home. I could feel her eyes on my back, but tried to ignore it.

"By the way," Maya said, a hint of disappointment in her voice, "what're you gonna name it?"

"I don't name my swords, you know that," I said, turning back to her.

She scoffed. "Right, too good for fun—I forgot. Come on, just name it. Think of it as your payment for all my hard work."

Hand ruffling through my short beard, I mulled over it for a moment. "How about Lóngsword?" I suggested, chuckling.

"What a stupid name! Why would you name your longsword 'Longsword'? That's actually the worst thing I've ever heard you say."

"Not 'Longsword', *Lóngsword*. 'Lóng' is Mandarin for 'dragon'."

Maya stared at me blankly, each slow blink a statement of her displeasure. She raised Vesper toward me, one eyebrow lifted well above the other.

I raised my hands to surrender. "Okay, okay, sorry . . . I guess I'll name it Somnior."

"What is that, Mandarin for, 'I suck at naming things'? Whatever, enough chit-chat. Let's get out of here."

I let out an exasperated sigh at the floor, then grabbed a map and ran after her. *Yeah, let's not forget this and get lost in Zoxum, of all places. I swear, what would she do without me? Waltz into the sun, probably.*

Lake Augr was an oil painting, the sun's scattered reflection across its soft, rippling surface. A hint of green lurked deep within, just enough to give it life. *It's almost noon if I can see the sun without much stretch to it. We really need to get moving.*

Maya was waiting at the main gate, forcefully tapping her left foot against the dirt so I would hear it.

"Don't give me that look. Though I admit, we're running late today." I glanced toward the midday sun.

"Oh, good! You brought the map. I totally forgot about it."

"Did you, now?" I unrolled the parchment, its corners resisting me, revealing a detailed layout of the world, including topology. The map had one additional function: it showed who controlled each region. Typically, when in control of a scroll, the owner puts a drop of their blood on the parchment, sealing their ownership. When the owner dies, the blood vanishes, and another may claim it. I never claimed them, only stole them, so there was a series of missing names in an elongated crescent around where our castle would be. Zoxum was claimed by Brego Corvir. "Anyway, their eastern border is about six miles from here. If we pace ourselves well, we can get there in under two hours."

"Well, let's get going then! You navigate and I'll keep an eye out for danger." She smiled at me, though it wavered ever so slightly.

Dominaria Forest was an expansive sea of thick, knotted trees and flora that rustled with the movements of diverse wildlife. It stretched out as far as the eye can see, in some directions. Thankfully, our castle sat right on the eastern edge of it, still protected by its thick foliage without needing to traverse it for more than a few miles when heading at least partially north.

Compass and map in hand, we waded northwest through grassy woodlands dusted with cyan moss, hacking at dense, prickly brush that brandished tiny orange scimitars at us, and swatting away insects that glimmered like frantic gemstones caught in a whirlwind. Overhead swayed a canopy was an eternal spring, the tree's leaves were caught in a transfixing dichotomy of youthful greens and aged auburn. Most of the wildlife had mild temperaments, scampering and scurrying up trees and into shrubbery as we stomped by. For this, I was thankful. Wasting our energy in the forest would become a handicap later.

Please, please *tell me she's sleeping right now.*

"Hey, Reza?" Maya asked. There was an unusual tinge of hesitation to the words, where normally everything about her is full-speed ahead.

I knew what she was going to ask, and wished only for a way to distract her from it. "Yes?"

"How come . . . well, you know. Why don't you say it back? It's been years, now."

I sighed, cutting through brush as though it were the source of my problems. "We've talked about this, Maya. You know the answer. It's nothing to do with you."

"It's kind of hard to believe that after all this time."

I slowed to a stop, sighed, then sheathed Somnior and turned to her. The look on her face was unbecoming of her usual tenacity and fire. "It's not fair to think that way—not to yourself or to me. Hadrian killed everyone I'd ever loved in the world. He stole love from me, that night, and I never got it back. That doesn't mean I don't care about you, I just . . . it feels wrong to say the words."

She shook her head. "He didn't take it from you, Reza, you buried it to avoid the pain."

"How can you say that, knowing what he's done to me?"

"Because you know damn well you're not the only one that's suffered at his hands. Stop pretending like the only person that psychopath has ever hurt is you. I know what he did to you, and you know what he did to me—we're in this together. We're taking him down, bit by bit, to avenge the people he stole from us, but if you let him stop you from feeling love then you're giving him more power instead of taking it away."

I pinched the bridge of my nose. *I can't deal with this right now.*

As if the trees could read my thoughts, the canopy overhead shifted, the sunlight poking through gaps in leaves no longer swaying calmly against dirt and roots. Maya and I quickly drew our swords and looked up, following the rustling intently.

"Do you think it's *her*?" Maya whispered to me, her eyes maintaining focus on the treetops.

Before I could answer, a shadowy blur fell toward the dirt in front of us with a loud *thud* and a dusty wave of leaves. I raised Somnior, adrenaline coursing through me. Its back was turned to us, and I was not going to waste any time.

"Wait!" Maya screeched as I advanced toward the beast. "Don't hurt it, or I swear, I'll kill you!"

I tensed, falling to the ground as my momentum suddenly halted. Shock is extremely unpleasant when you're pumping with adrenaline and fear, like dumping baking soda into a bowl of mixed acids. Not twenty feet away from me stood an enormous brown bat.

"Why did you stop me?" I spat with venomous anger. "I had an opening!"

"Shut up, you'll scare it! Oh my goodness, oh

my goodness. Okay, calm down, Maya." She slowly walked over to the bat, which stood at least a full head higher than her. Its black, slightly furry body was now turning around, slowly rotating to face us.

You've got to be kidding me.

It shrunk back slightly as Maya approached it, despite having the size advantage. She held her hand out, coaxing and cooing it with a soothing voice, then reached in her pack and pulled out something that was a shiny red.

"Hey, buddy, you want an apple? You look like a fruit bat, you want an apple? Come on, go ahead and have it!"

It looked at her with massive eyes, glossy black like the polished obsidian of her pommel, and a furry face snouted in the same manner a dog or fox would be. There was a long slash of striated, sheen skin running across its dark, matte belly, a twisting of lighter flesh knotted like vine.

"Careful, Maya—it's seen battle and survived, that's no defenseless animal."

The bat slowly craned its head toward her extended hand, and Maya continued to encourage it. "Yeah, come on big guy. Just a little closer. There you go!"

It bit down on the apple and pulled back, grabbing it with claws the length of my palm and nibbling ferociously with complete disregard for its seedy core. Within seconds, the apple's existence was erased. Maya approached the bat further, and it slowly dropped its head down to her. She giggled as a long, pink tongue lurched from its mouth and lapped at her fingers and face.

"See? Not everything new is scary, Reza. This is just a cute fruit bat! Look at his sweet face." She turned toward me, still petting the bat. "Apologize right now. You almost killed him!"

"Well he dropped from the sky, and you know what lives here. I was startled, you can't blame me. Besides, what if Hadrian had sent it after us? What if it's a scout?"

Maya was giving me that blank stare again, slowly blinking in waves from one eye to the next. This time, her left eyebrow was raised, and her arms were crossed. It's amazing how many physical variations of 'annoyed' she could conjure.

I sighed and threw my arms up. "Okay, okay. Sorry, *bat*. As for you, try to stay attentive and alert moving forward. Let's get out of here before something worse shows up."

"See, Mr. Bat? He's so mean and grumpy, but you're so cute and fun, yes you are! I have to go now, but you stay safe out here, okay?" She patted its head again, laughing as it licked at her fingers.

We set forth into the dense greenery once more, increasing our pace. After a few moments, I turned back to find the beast watching us fade into the thick, twisting underbrush, a curious head slightly cocked as if to ask what the rush was.

"Hey, Maya," I said, pulling ahead of her. "Maybe if Vesper's hungry, you should feed it an apple."

The heat of her glare against me made my hair stand on its end, and I sped up to avoid being stabbed. "Just because I want to protect wildlife...." She continued to grumble angrily, the words out of earshot; I didn't have the gall to slow down and find out what they were.

Awakening

If God is real, why did He create bugs? A loving creator—a loving Father—would not be so cruel as to breathe life into such disgusting creatures. I wonder, if He is real, and He did make bugs ... what was He thinking? What would possess Him to make a six-legged, slimy, filthy, buzzing demon that refuses to die and can lay eggs in your ears? Do they find some instinctual joy, as they zoom around through the air, trying so hard to lodge themselves in my throat? Why—

Something rough and hard slammed into my face, disrupting thoughts and balance alike. The earth was fertile beneath me, as it should be in an eternal spring, and a quick brush of my hands left kitten scratches of dirt across my palms that dried almost instantly. The scent of mineral, leaf and dampness filling the forest, like cold air, was collected closer to ground level and stung my sinuses.

"I thought you said to be attentive and alert." She forced one eye shut, a true parody of a wink, before continuing forward without even bothering to offer a hand.

Upon regaining my posture, the extent of my spill's repercussions became apparent. There were brown smears across the whole of my left leg, and a chunk of soil had wedged into the scales on my chest, ruining its regality. Without thought, I raked a careful hand against my chestplate, only pressing the mud further into the scaling, leaving me with a fistful of dirt and an emblem of shit on my chest. I was a self-proclaimed king of refuse.

In the mountain of filth that had re-accumulated in my hand, something poked out of it, as an old woman might hobble out of her front door to wave a flock of pesky children off with a broom. The mud catapulted as my inner monkey came forth, disregarding where it might land, and I let out a disgusted half-grunt, half-shout. My arms flailed and I swatted at my body, every bead of sweat suddenly feeling like the mucus of a living creature gliding across my skin.

Maya noticed my helpless shouts and ran to me, sword raised. I matched her sword with a palm.

"I'm fine, it was nothing. Must've been my imagination."

She halted, sheathing her sword, and gave me a narrow-eyed stare. Her arms went up in defeat.

"You threw a hissy-fit like that for no reason at all? I don't believe you." My eyes shifted to the slight bobbing of pink on the tree next to her, and she poked at it with her finger. A little, pink worm was wriggling around in it, confused by the state of its new, airborne home. "Wait—are you scared of bugs?"

"No. Of course I'm not. They're just tiny little insects. They can't hurt me. I know that. What does it matter?"

She twirled it around between her fingers. "Wow, look at the size of that clitellum. Meow."

"Excuse me?"

"C'mere, take a look at it!" She gently pulled the worm from its home, once again upturning its world, and approached me with it on her hand.

Despite my best efforts, I recoiled in disgust. "Get it away from me!"

"Well, *that's* good to know. I can't believe you've hidden this from me for almost two years. Here, I'll get rid of the worm—but now I know your true weakness, Kinghunter. You better not piss me off, or I'll stuff your pillow full of maggots and centipedes."

All I could muster in response was a weak croak. It took everything within me not to retch as an image of the little slimy noodle inched across my mind, squelching and stretching, stretching and squelching.

I really, really didn't want her to know about that....

Maya cast the worm aside and for a brief moment, it soared through the air, experiencing flight as the bird that eats it would. With a tiny splat, it landed on a pile of mud, abruptly ending the adventure of that clueless worm, whipped up in our storm. I eyed it as it inched around, trying to make sense of its new home, and for a moment I empathized with it—before the disgust set in.

She rolled her eyes at me before continuing forward. "Come on already, stop being so dramatic and keep walking. We're almost out of the forest."

I straightened myself and looked overhead. It was hard to see past such a thick canopy, but I was able to make out roughly where the sun was by a concentration of yellow poking through the matted net of rust and emerald. *She's right, it's probably six hours until nightfall. We need to work extremely quickly once we get to Zoxum.*

Once I caught up to her, I left a bit of space to mitigate any awkwardness, knowing that she still might have been sore from our conversation earlier. After a few minutes, I heard a distant sigh, and she slowed to let me catch up but didn't turn back to face me.

"Look," she said, trying to catch a gold beetle buzzing near her. "Forget about what I said earlier. I know you're probably on edge given that we're getting closer to him than ever before, and I shouldn't have pushed it. Let's focus on taking out the Zoxan king for now. Someday soon, when all this is over and we have our revenge, we'll talk more about us."

I nodded, though she couldn't see it. "Good plan."

Thankfully, we cut through the rest of the forest

with ease and a pleasant lack of interruptions. Dominaria's tangling of vegetation ends rather abruptly, withering into a vast ocean of sand dotted with blue cacti and arid trees that stretches to the horizon—very aptly (and somewhat unimaginatively) named the Endless Desert. We're still not sure how a forest can exist right along the edge of a wasteland, but one thing is certain: trying to cross it on foot would be suicide. Which is a shame, because legend has it that, at the other end, there are mountains frosted with pink snow and exotic fruits so sweet you'll fall asleep after a few bites.

And at the nexus of these two biomes, a fault between blossom and wither, lay an oblong skull at least twenty times the size of our castle grounds. Time had weathered the bone to a dirty brown, dulling the teeth and flattening the eye sockets. Inside it was a city, and as for why anyone would live in the bones of a monster, I cannot say. Perhaps they were the dying thoughts of a stubborn Titan desperately clinging to the world.

The skullcap was shaved thin, looking like parchment stretched over the city, letting the sun's light in with less heat. There was a thin black line wrapping the bone, like a hairband stretched over it, dotted with red. It was an uncomfortable, eerie sight, and to further the mystery, there were no other bones around it.

Luckily for us, Zoxum's dead keep was built with its snout kissing the forest—or, maybe, that was how the behemoth had died, burning under the sun and snapping at the treeline for a bit of shade. The forward wall stood twenty feet high, sealing the creature's slightly opened jaw, but there were also entrances at the north and south borders —since the west faces the Endless Desert, perhaps they saw no need in making it accessible. *Or maybe they ran out of resources for another gate.*

I motioned to Maya, beckoning her to follow me, approaching Zoxum's southern edge. There was a watchtower guarding the east, short, erected in the nasal cavity. It did not look sturdy, made of bound logs instead of stone. *Either they're really confident, completely vapid, or they ran out of resources. It's hard to tell with these guys.*

As we neared the seam between sand and wood, I grabbed Maya and pulled her behind a mossy boulder, finger pressed to my lips. My eyes motioned toward the scouting party returning from deep within Dominaria Forest. There were five, all covered from head to toe in absurd, red and black armor. *Yeah, I'm beginning to think they're just lacking for intelligence—which is a resource, in a way. What kind of camouflage is that, when you live in-between a forest and desert? And black armor, under this harsh sun . . . no, quiet your thoughts. Focus.*

"We can use this as an opening. Let's take them out swiftly, drag them out of sight, and use their equipment to masquerade as the survivors of an ambush. They'll let us in, and we can work from there," I whispered to her, keeping an eye on the scouts.

A huge smile swept over her face, and we slid from behind the rock back into the forest, hooking behind them. We each took to one side of the group, slinking low with swords drawn until within ten feet. In the distance, the massive stone gate ground against sand as it swung. Our eyes met, and a synchronized nod set us in motion.

Like a receding hairline, the forest thinned nearing the desert. Before the party could get there, we leapt forward, each hacking the head off the two rear guards. Crumpling armored bodies alerted the three further up, but by then, our blades had skewered the throats of two more, streaking the brilliant blades with streams of black blood. The final warrior dropped his sword and ran like a frightened deer, Maya immediately giving pursuit.

"Maya, you *have* to kill him or he'll alert the town," I whispered as forcefully as possible. She continued toward the forest edge, gaining on him, slipping into leaping distance, then . . . stopped the pursuit and turned to me, shrugging.

"He got away," she said with a sly smile.

"Maya, the *entire city* will know we're attacking now. Their king will throw everything at us, you know that right? It was an insane mission to begin with, but this. . . ."

"It'll be fine! It's more fun this way," she said in a playful tone. "I hate sneaking around."

I lifted my face from the cup I'd made of my hands. "You—you *let him go?*"

"Yep! You're so boring and stealthy, I hate it.

Sorry, but you're gonna have your work cut out for you today, mister."

I sighed deeply, looking to the ground and locking eyes with a mouse taking cover under a bit of shrubbery. *You seem like a nice mouse. One that wouldn't try to make my life more difficult than it needs to be.*

The rodent scurried across my boot, leaving behind a thin streak of urine.

"Well, we've come this far already. If we retreat, they'll just build their defenses even further, so I guess I have no choice now. Damn it, Maya. Let's go."

She giggled, jogging backwards ahead of me. "Count how many you take down. I bet I'll beat you."

I rolled my eyes without a word, but she knew I'd participate in the contest. I detested losing a challenge with her—she's an insufferable winner, but a quiet loser.

The eastern entrance was blocked with a massive stone gate that swung out from a single hinge; one massive slab reaching toward the forest just enough for patrols to get in and out. *They must've only had the resources for one.*

"We need to slip inside before that gate closes, or we're not finding an easy way in," I shouted to Maya as we closed in on the entrance. The gate was swinging shut now, inky soldiers atop the wall cranking as hard as they could to the shouts of a hidden master. Somewhere deeper in the city, a booming, brassy horn blared that made my skin tingle.

Maya leapt through the opening with ease, but I struggled to fit myself into such a tight space. In went my left leg, left arm, then my head and torso, and finally my right arm. My right boot, however, was caught in the door. Fearing a pancaked foot, I yanked as hard as I could, pushing against the door with my arms. As the gate squeezed shut, crushing the metal like a piece of parchment, my foot popped out of its boot and I stumbled free. Looking back, I saw the faint, flattened remnants of it sticking out from between the gate and wall like a freshly minted coin and let out a nervous chuckle. Maya shook her head in disappointment at the sight of my now bare foot, protected only by a sandy sock dangling from my toes.

Why does the ground have to be so hot? I hate sand. It's so coarse, and rough, and . . .

Damn it.

Paying too much attention to my searing foot, I failed to notice how many soldiers were gathering in the courtyard. Zoxum was a rather bland keep on the inside except for its creepy, milky bone sky. The city itself was of plain sandstone buildings laid out in repetition from edge to edge. It had been designed around an enormous tree with thousands of matted branches fanning out from a single, stocky trunk. It was like a wooden mushroom from the underside, topped with green needles that let no light through. Twelve main roads stemmed out from it, like tick marks on a clock. A myriad of cookie-cutter structures filled the spaces between roads in straight, even rows. We were in the eastern courtyard, a massive and wide open stretch of sandy flooring with nothing to hide behind. It looked more like someone had taken a bite out of the cityscape than it did a place to gather and relax.

"Well, Maya, I hope you're satisfied," I said under my breath, looking in every direction as a tornado of black and red swirled around us.

"They kinda look like bugs, don't they?" Maya joked to me, our backs against each other.

"Are you trying to kill me before the fight even starts?"

"More for me."

We were rotating slowly, backs touching, scanning the rooftops and doorways as soldiers jeered and gestured at us. They almost seemed to be crawling, the way they circled around us.

"Don't get cocky, now, Maya. This won't be easy like it was when we conquered the castle at Garavax. I can't even count how many soldiers there are." She was too busy howling back at the screeching swarm to pay me any mind.

The swirling stopped, and the soldiers quieted. A chilling silence set in over the city of sand and bone, one that made hairs stand up on my neck. Nobody dared move—not us, not them, not even the wind.

Finally, one rushed toward us, the others waiting in the distance. Maya started to turn and face him with me, but I outstretched my arm to block her. "It might be a distraction. You have to watch our back."

She grumbled but obliged, and I braced myself, gripping Somnior tight. Once close enough to swing, I could hear the soldier snarling and growling like a wild beast, and it fought like one, too. We were about the same height, but the attacker moved with animalistic, unnatural anger; a starved predator on the scent of blood. Whatever it was, it was fast and swung hard from above in a very telegraphed motion. I blocked it easily, but it was in some kind of mania, and swung at me over and over so quickly I couldn't do much to respond. The pure brute force of it nearly overcame me, but as the beast grew tired, I managed to slip below its strike and shear an arm off.

No other soldiers descended upon us; instead, they howled and screamed, clutching at their heads and writhing. They swirled around us again, not closing in, but stirring as if in restlessness, then came to a sudden stop once more. No longer swirling, the hurricane had ended, and we were in the storm's eye. The sun had crept well past its zenith, judging by the brightest smudge overhead. *We have another four hours at best to get back. Crap.*

We braced ourselves, but still, they did not come. They did not shout or growl or stomp their feet. What had once been a swirling black turned into stillness, like the night descending upon us. I gulped, tightening my grip on Somnior, which was lamenting the lack of sunlight to bathe in.

I pushed my back against Maya's to get her attention. "Get ready—they're coming. Break for the building to my left and we'll try to control a rooftop, forcing them to funnel into us."

She didn't get a chance to respond.

The tension snapped so hard you could hear it, like a twig crushed underfoot.

A pile of soldiers blocking off the eastern entrance launched forward. We broke off toward the building I'd pointed out, barreling at the entrance. I slammed my shoulder into a Zoxan trying to intercept me from the right, casting him to the ground and tripping the incoming soldiers behind him. Maya lowered and twirled, threading her blade through the throats of two blocking the doorway.

We shoved inside, hearing a sea of footsteps pounding the ground behind us. There was a stairway just ahead, and another Zoxan came stumbling down it. I merely needed to sidestep him and he crashed into the ground behind me, leaving us with an opening to scramble upstairs.

There were five on the rooftop, somehow caught off-guard by our approach despite seeing us enter the building, as if we'd died the second we left their sight. Steel clanged as the brutish beasts clumsily tried to swing their greatswords from their sheaths. Getting around their blows and slipping our blades through the gaps in their armor was a simple task, leaving five more dead. We quickly piled their bodies into the stairway, hoping to slow the incoming swarm.

I think that's four for me, and three for Maya. I better pick up the pace or I'll lose again.

The bodies jammed into the stairway exit clinked around as Zoxans below tried to force past them. My right foot was throbbing now, raw—even the sock I'd had on was gone.

"Thank God they don't have ranged weapons," Maya joked. "We're sitting ducks here. A few terrible archers could pick us off."

"Thank God they aren't better swordsmen," I replied. "They have numbers, but I swear each one puts up less of a fight than the last."

"True. It's a little boring, to be honest. What kind of army is this?"

We pressed our backs together once more, staring out into the restless sea of swirling soldiers running through the city like an obsidian flood. Watching the journey of ten thousand ants, faintly glimmering in the muted, high sun.

"Ready?" Maya asked me.

"No," I replied, my mail clinking against hers, looking down at my sad, exposed foot. "But I'll do it anyway."

Ninety-seven. Nice, I managed to skewer the guy behind him. Ninety-nine. God, they're weak, but there's so many of them, like a swarm of gnats. This may take far too long.

I glanced up to a milky sky. The sun smudge was halfway down the skullcap's rear, leaving us with approximately two hours left in Zoxum to get home comfortably, perhaps three if we sprinted.

"Maya, we need to pick up the pace. Do you see the King anywhere? He's probably hiding, but there's a chance he'll come out and watch the battle," I shouted, removing my sword from the armpit of a Zoxan.

"Give me a second! Cover me," she hollered back. After decapitating the one in front of her, Maya ran to the corner of our building and stacked several dead bodies on top of each other, standing on them.

"I'm going to be a bit occupied over here, so let me know if you see something. Try and make it quick, please."

As gullible as ever. One hundred and thirty-three, one hundred and thirty-four....

It was getting hard to maneuver around the dead bodies littering our rooftop arena. We'd been trying to push as many off as possible, but with the constant refreshing of soldiers it was impossible to keep up. I began to fumble, my bare foot being caught and cut, burning on the tiling of black armor that was sucking in sunlight like a garden of iron Black Cat Petunias. I was slaughtering the Zoxan forces with suspect ease, but the dead were finding a way to fight back.

I was forced back to the ledge, near Maya's little corpse outpost. From a perimeter viewpoint, it became clear that the roof was sagging slightly in the middle, buckling under the weight of a hundred dead men clad in mail and plate. I glanced right, down a row of homes and markets arranged like stepping stones, each building no more than eight feet from the next. The obsidian river of soldiers continued to flow, though it had become spotted with matte blues and whites.

"Any sign of the King yet?" I asked. A blur of blue came from behind the body of a soldier and I reacted on instinct before reality set in. Somnior split the side of a civilian open, possibly a woman given the dull teak gown. She had been wielding only a small kitchen knife, but attacked with the same frothed anger those before her had. I felt sick to my stomach, but couldn't spare a second longer—the horde continued filing in.

Maya kept her vision focused, squinting hard beneath an unnecessary hand on her brow. "I think I see him. There's a caravan about four hundred feet away, to the right of their central tower. I can't see it well, but it looks pretty fancy from here. We should head there first."

"Well, we better get moving *now*. They're starting to come through faster than I can fight them, and the roof's giving out. And Maya—the King is sending civilians after us, too. Be careful."

She shot a concerned glance toward me, hopping down to help. Several more barely-armed men and women mixed in with the soldiers, and we did our best to disable them without entirely lethal force. "Why are you doing this?" she asked them. "There are so many soldiers. Why risk your lives for no reason?"

They did not answer. In fact, the concentration of civilians grew, injured ones even rising to attack again, and horror melted across Maya's face. "Reza, something is terribly wrong, here. These people are not okay. We have to move."

"I have an idea—this time, I'll need you to fend them off a bit while I work."

She nodded.

Well, there goes my lead . . . though she may not be keeping track anymore.

I moved closer to the center of the building while Maya did her best to manage the civilians and the soldiers. "When I tell you to, jump over to the building next to us. You might want to sheathe your sword—it's not going to be an easy one."

I hopped to the center of our rooftop, lifted my sword high into the air, and plunged it straight down with all my strength. It was only enough to cause a small crack around the point of impact, but with tons of dead Zoxans pushing down on it, that fracture quickly expanded. Within seconds, it was branching out like a flash of lightning, cracking like thunder, and I signaled to Maya for our retreat.

She knocked back her foe, fumbled with something on the ground, and we bolted across the rooftop, bouncing from Zoxan to Zoxan, before leaping to the next building.

Of course, Maya had not sheathed her sword before making the jump—and, of course, she cleared the gap with little issue. I, however, slammed my chest into the ledge and barely managed to cling on. A chorus of howling came from below me as Zoxans piled against the wall and tried to hack at my dangling toes.

"Maybe next time you should try jumping with your sword out," Maya said, looming over my dangling body. Thankfully, she didn't gloat for long before dragging me up.

"I lost my footing, since I'm missing a damn boot." I looked down at the naked foot, crusted in a mixture of blood and sand that almost looked like footwear.

Maya nodded, beaming with pride, holding up a red boot. "You owe me one."

"Oh, thank you!" I took the boot from her, surprised by its weight—until I saw it was still being worn by its previous owner. She giggled as she left me behind to empty it.

My foot sang a song of salvation as I slipped the boot on. I stood up, shifting around to settle it in its new home. The current of Zoxans shifted toward us, but some were still pouring into the previous building. Five, ten, fifteen more rushed in, and with the thunderous crack of stone splitting, the roof imploded. The dead came crashing down upon the living, along with a hundred tons of rubble. The sides of the building blew out and toppled over, which couldn't have been any worse a fate for the tightly packed stream of Zoxans around it.

A cloud of debris and sand kicked into the air, rushing over us at our new outpost. I shot Maya a satisfied look, hands on my hips, and chuckled. "What is that? Probably at least a hundred, right? Damn, I'm good. I should win because of that alone."

She scolded at me with her eyes. "Shut up, Reza. There were civilians in there, too."

"They're mixing in with the soldiers and trying to kill us. We'll die if we try and save them all, you know."

"Are we any better than Hadrian, then? These people are barely putting up a fight."

"Don't you dare compare us to him, Maya. They're not sleeping or having tea, they're trying with every fiber of their being to kill us. We'll try our best, but there's only so much we can do."

She sighed. "I know. I just—I don't know. I swear some of them looked like they were crying."

The clamor below us grew loud as the river flowed upward, into the stairwell. "Well, what now?" I asked.

"They seem to struggle with rooftops, so we should try to hop across this row of buildings for now, then cross over to the next row once most of them fall behind. Try not to fall and die along the way, will you?"

"I think I can manage, now that I have this new boot."

We took off, soaring through the air between stony buildings. I was barely making each jump, wobbling and stumbling as I tried to find footing on the ledges with a sore sole and loose boot, but I was getting by on my own nonetheless.

One Zoxan actually had the foresight to try and cut us off, climbing onto a building we hadn't yet reached. Still, he was no match for me—I slid down and swept his legs from under him without losing much momentum, taking care of the problem without wasting any time. A pained howl cut through the air as his left arm hit the ground palm-first and inverted at the elbow, his sword flying into the street below.

"We're getting closer, but we shouldn't jump down until the horde is further behind us," Maya shouted over her shoulder, hair whipping behind her. "Follow me."

After leaping across three more buildings, Maya dropped to the ground, buckling her knees, rolling across the sand and springing back to her feet. I followed suit, albeit far less gracefully and with added crashing. I stumbled, regaining my bearings with a groan, and we ran into a building two rows over.

Up the stairs we climbed, through the roof, and we were once again jumping from building to building. With my semi-heavy mail, the fighting, leaping, and heat were starting to slow me down. I stopped for a moment to look back, hundreds of Zoxans swarming in between buildings, plunging from rooftops to be trampled in a stream of their own allies.

I wonder, is all that black staining the earth of this city armor, or blood?

The caravan was soon close enough to see

clearly; a series of elephants with canopies on their backs, fashioned from silver and dressed in exotic tapestries of green, donned with gold frills and blue gems. The poor creatures had their tusks serrated, and the largest of them was dead center in the caravan.

"Maya, let's hop onto the nearest one in his row and cut through to the center. If we're on equal grounds with him, no one can stop us."

"Good plan, I'll try to swing around from the other side if I can," she shouted, bounding over a building. "Oh, one more thing."

"Yes, *dear*?"

She made a sloppy heart shape with her hands and smiled as wide as she physically could. "If you hurt the elephants, I'll kill you."

I sighed and left the safe stability of solid ground, landing on a bobbing animal, its rough skin speckled with thin, wispy hairs that were damn near invisible. Its back was the size of my personal quarters, a spine thick and knurled like an oak root raised and splitting it in two sections. Though it had nearly no forward momentum, each step was accompanied by a crash and sway that carried through my body. There was a rhythm to the beast's gait, as if it were the beating heart of a stone giant long since lost to the world. Jarring as it was initially, I quickly adapted to the ebb and crash and flow, dancing with vectors as I charged the Zoxan crew aboard.

Warriors manning each elephant were clad

in black garb with crimson, leather plate atop it, matching Somnior's slick coating. On each chest piece was a swirling sun as black as their blood, and bladed quarterstaffs replaced ordinary broadswords. They looked magnificent, menacing and powerful, but they charged at me like children wielding sticks and fell in mere seconds.

It's pathetic how poorly trained these soldiers are, down to the rear guard. It's like slaying children.

I jumped onto the caravan's heart, slicing at the tapestries hanging between me and the King. Two more grunts charged, armed with double-sided staves taller than me. A challenge had presented itself at last, and it was welcome.

Just as the excitement settled in, I heard the familiar war cry of an overexcited Maya explode from behind them. Turbulence kickstarted with a trumpeting cry as weight shifted to the beast's opposite side, knocking me flat on my back and sending the two guards stumbling forward. They tripped over their obscenely large staves, dropping them in panic to free their hands. It didn't take long for the quaking to end, and when it did, two defenseless soldiers scrambled toward me without even grabbing their weapons. I cut through them much like I did the room's exterior cloth.

"How disappointing," I sighed.

Ahead, there was a lavish bed the size of a small room, lined with disheveled, silk textiles of red and gold. Black, velvet body pillows were strewn across it and the surrounding floor. Beyond that, there was nothing.

Did he see us approaching and run?

"I've got you now, King!"

I frantically ducked as a bat zipped over my head with blistering speed. Maya stumbled forward, pivoting abruptly on her left foot before spreading her arms and falling onto the bed as though that were the intention to begin with.

"Don't kill *me!*" I half pleaded, half spat.

"Oh, sorry. I got kinda carried away there." She let out a light chuckle, then sat up and looked around the tent. "Aww, did you already get him? Boo."

"He's not here; there were just a couple guards, like every other tent I cut through. This one actually had fewer men in it, now that I think about it."

She chewed on my words for a moment. "It's probably a decoy, then. Clever guy, this King. You think there's another caravan on the other side of this city?"

A blazing trumpet blared through the city air, lingering like kicked dust as a definitive answer to her question. We ran out of the tent and hopped back onto the buildings for a proper view.

Oh, my. . . .

There was an ocean of Zoxan knights standing at attention, a black hemisphere immediately behind the city's center tree. After several moments of silently gazing at the sea of glimmering death, Maya and I nodded to each other and set off for its shore.

At its forefront stood a man, taller than the

rest, leaning against the towering trunk—but as we approached, it became increasingly clear that it was not a *man*, per se. Thick, black fur fanned out from its body, with a facial structure similar to that of a mountain bear. Thin streaks of red accentuated tufted cheekbones, running vertically from eye to jaw. It was wearing a bright robe that looked like the tapestries we'd seen atop the elephants, with a gold crown that was spiked the way a serrated knife would be. A large steel greatsword with a dark orange handle and pommel shaped like the sun was pointed into the ground, the King shifting away from the tree and leaning into it like a walking stick.

Wind struggled to whip sand through air thick with tension as we stood not thirty feet away.

"So you're at the front line, eh? I expected you to be cowering in a tent, surrounded by guards. I'm not sure if you're bold, arrogant, or just a fool." I threw my words at it like daggers, set to gash even the tough hide of a King's pride.

"A good leader should lead, no?" he responded with a thick, growling voice, heavily weighted with an unfamiliar accent. "You will battle me, not these measly drones. Clearly, even with numbers on their side, they are too stupid for the Kinghunter and his bitch; slaves have a limit to their purpose, I suppose."

"First of all, I've killed a few kings of my own, you mangy stray." Maya contorted her face, taking a step forward. "And slaves? You call your citizens— your soldiers, dying for you—*slaves*? What's wrong with you?"

"Silly girl, these are beasts bound to me—not some troop of free men. They do as I say, without hesitation or regret; they are nothing but my will made real. Watch, if you don't believe me." He pointed to a soldier behind him and snapped his fingers.

The Zoxan skewered a soldier to its right, opening a spigot from its neck. Not a soul stirred in the battalion as the slain soldier crashed forward without a single yelp or groan; an army of stone men carved hollow.

Maya was gritting her teeth, fists clenched and shaking. "Then we'll kill you and set them free. People like you don't deserve power."

The king let out a hearty, bellowing laugh that filled the city streets. He stepped forward from underneath the tree's near solid canopy, out of the shade and into reddening light that left his face-lines blazing.

"Let me ask you something, girl. What is 'power'? Is it merely something temporary, whether handed to you or plundered with force, or is true power something much deeper than that; something that can't be taken, or subdued, despite all efforts?

"Is 'power' *truly* power if it can be stolen, like a chest of gold or fine, silk sheets? I think not. These men aren't bought or broken and trained. Their very existence is owned. I am their God, and nothing you do will change that. I—"

With a massive squelch, roughly three liters of a viscous, chunky liquid rained down on the King, drenching his robe and soaking into his soul. He remained frozen, mid-speech and mouth agape as if the words were stuck in his throat, choking him.

The stench ... it's nauseating, even from here.

"For a guy that talks a lot of shit, you sure don't wear it well," I quipped at his unmoving body, statuesque like the army of slaves he'd bred.

"Reza, look! Up there!"

I traced the path of Maya's finger. Two bats were circling overhead, looming above us like swirling stormclouds. As they passed in front of the low sun-smudge, orange light punched through the thin membranes of their veiny wings, exposing all the bones in their arms twisting and gyrating with each wild flap.

Well, I guess I can't complain. That's some serious aim on their part, though.

The bats swooped down and began plowing through the crowd, scattering soldiers all about. They couldn't drag any of them very far, but the commotion brewed chaos amongst the once serene soldiers. After a few attacks, the bats began grabbing debris from the building we'd downed and dropping it on the army, poking holes in their ranks. Their formation was crumbling like a smashed sandstone building.

The back of the city-skull was painted a reddish-purple, bruised on the horizon. Before I could urge our attack, Maya was already in motion.

Swords drawn, we approached him with no trouble at all—he was vomiting, desperately trying to wipe the guano from his eyes and nose. After a venomous glare at us, and a glance back at his suddenly chaotic army, he ripped his sun-sword from the dirt. The blade shimmered the burnt orange of sunrise.

It was something of a dance, the way Maya operated when burning with fury. Twisting, she threw a dagger directly from her hip, then whipped another hand at him in a cyclone of graceful wrath. The King unsheathed his sword from the dirt, slicing the dagger out of the air, only to be caught in the chest by a second.

He let out a wet cough of sticky blood that unraveled into crazed laughter. "You think these people are yours to take, to free, but they are not. I am their leader, silly girl—their *only* leader. Not even Hadrian can control my people. In death, I will show you what real power is.

"*It cannot be taken, child.*"

He plunged his sword deep into the tree's heart. It glowed in his bloody hand, sending pulses of light coursing through the trunk and up into a thick matting of branches. Like a struck match, brilliance pooled in the canopy, aqueous and shifting, then sank down. The tree turned to charcoal, collapsing in a tsunami of smoke.

When all settled, where once a pillar of life stood, only a pile of swirling ash remained. It blew across the open courtyard and into the city's veins.

A single needle was all that was left, its green a sliver of life on dead sands. Every Zoxan within the sight had fallen on their swords, staining the sand like upturned inkwells, and the King was singed and crumpled. Maya cringed, the vicarious sorrow of ten thousand lost souls in her eyes; that look of sadness, however, was quickly swallowed by burning anger. I barely managed to get out of the way as she led with Vesper towards the King's body and hacked at it with heaving wrath, leaving a furry head spurting blood several feet away, its hairs melted and curled.

"You sick bastard," she muttered amidst labored breaths. "I wish I could kill you a thousand times."

"It was genocide and cowardice, but I don't think we could've fought the rest of them."

"Yeah, but . . . damn it all, I wish I could have stopped him."

"I know. But we're one step closer, now. The end is near."

She sighed, hands on her hips and head hung low.

I wiped Somnior clean with a muffled gag. "Hey, Maya, would you want to take the scroll from him? I, uh, need to go check something out over there."

When she turned to protest, I'd already pulled off her signature move—leaving her to deal with the mess. Her eyes rolled back to the King, and she used her sword to part his filthy robes, revealing a small ornate box at his hip. I inched closer as it clicked open, revealing the gold and ebony scroll we'd come for.

"Let me open it up and read it, just to make sure," I told her, holding out my hand. The parchment stretched about a foot long, with a few words in large font.

> *He who holds this scroll,*
> *Has irrefutable evidence,*
> *That he claims this land, ZOXUM,*
> *As his own.*

"You know, the language in these things could use some work, because a 'she' just killed his ass," Maya said, pulling back from her perch near my shoulder.

I retracted the scroll, handing it to Maya for safekeeping. "We can add an 's' here and there for you. Now, the problem is: how do we get home in time? I don't think it's possible to run fast enough through that damned forest."

She looked longingly to the sky as muted sunset light caressed her bloodstained face.
"I have a feeling our new friends can help us out," she replied with a visage carved from stone.

The two bats hovered low, gently grabbing each of us with a leathery claw. I glanced at Maya, making no effort to conceal the fear in my eyes.

"You'll be totally safe, Reza, but . . . it'll be a bumpy ride. Their wings connect all the way down to their legs, so as their wings beat, we're going to get kinda kicked around. It'll be fine if you don't struggle."

"Lovely. I'll make sure to turn toward you when the time comes for me to vomit." My gaze turned to the setting sun and the milky, purple-orange work of art it created through the skull-cap. "I *really* hope you can direct these things back home...."

Without warning, the bats took flight, dragging us through the skull's nasal cavity. I screamed at nothing but a desert graveyard and ten million insects crawling in the forest alongside it.

I wonder, is this how that clueless worm felt as it flew through the air? My only hope is that my adventure doesn't also end with a splat. I don't think I could survive the fall....

It only took a few minutes to become familiar with the bat's flight pattern, which made the jerkiness mildly more tolerable. I watched as miles of forest passed below us, a blur of green and auburn staunchly contrasting the violet sunset haze attempting to engulf it.

So this is what the canopy looks like from its other side. I could get used to this. It's amazing what a little change of perspective can do. The forest has never looked so beautiful.

I shouted over wind that whipped with fury. "Hey, Maya. I thought bats use echolocation to see. How are you communicating so easily with gestures?"

"Fox bats don't use echolocation, they see

with their eyes. Most bats can see out of their eyes, they aren't there for decoration."

I'll take that as a cue to shut up.

Somehow, completely unbeknownst to me, Maya directed the bats to our keep. They let us down gently within the castle walls, and Maya gave them both fruit from her pack. It was much easier to see them in open space, and they *almost* looked cute in dusk's light. Brown, furry bodies and black leathery wings acted scarily like human arms as they embraced her. I expected them to dramatically fly off into the sunset, but instead, their claws latched to the stone beam above our main entrance and they draped down like curtains—kicking their feet up after a hard day of work, I suppose. Maya squealed a little, hopping and clapping hurriedly at our new drapery.

I motioned inside. "Come on. The sun's about to set."

Back up the stairs we ran, stripping our armor and weapons along the way. Maya handed me the scroll and I placed it in a chest near our bed, alongside the twelve others we'd collected, each embossed with patterns of different stone and color.

A faint breeze grew louder into beating wings, and a raven landed on the windowsill. I detached the parchment from around its leg and read it while Maya jumped into bed. *It's finally happening.*

"What's it say?" she asked, her voice low.

"Yuurishmen are marching on us from the east. Probably no more than a day away." I tossed the parchment into a wastebasket.

"Looks like Hadrian figured it out."

"Told you. He already knew, it was just a matter of time before he caved and sent his own army on a hunch. He's scared."

I joined her in bed, pulling an amethyst-like gem from beneath my pillow.

"Good night," I said, placing the gem into a keyhole above our headboard and twisting. "See you tomorrow. It's gonna be brutal."

I leaned in for a kiss, but her lips didn't move much in response. Her eyes didn't meet mine, and she rolled over, pulling the quilt tight. "Sorry, it's been a long day. Good night."

With a sigh, I closed my eyes, letting darkness settle in around me.

⚭ ⚭ ⚭

An alarm went off, buzzing in my ear like a particularly persistent fly. I sat up and swatted at it, rubbing my eyes, yawning with a deep stretch. My body ached from the previous day's particularly intense session of doing nothing, and I rolled around trying to loosen the muscles—what little of them there were on me, anyway. The clock read 7:00 a.m., meaning I had no time to snooze and get a few more minutes of laziness in, and I groaned into the dark.

I don't want to get ready for work. Why can't I just lie in bed and sleep forever?

⚃

Déjà Vu

Maybe tonight, I'll go to bed early and work on a vehicle to traverse the Endless Desert. I could also use the extra time to prepare for Hadrian's siege . . . either way, I should fall asleep at 8:30 instead of 10:00 and get there before Maya. Per—

"Hello? Jackson? Are you even paying attention?"

I shook my head with a sharp inhale. Sitting up, straightening my lopsided collar, I tried to force a smile. "Of course I am, Ms. Henderson. Please continue with the slideshow—it's riveting."

The group stifled snickers, trying to retain poignancy. Henderson took it in stride, though, continuing her lecture without a hitch. Good sport.

"Well, exactly for this purpose, media campaigns need to be more enthralling—*captivating* and *enrapturing*. Too often are they cookie-cutter or bland, resulting in people like Jackson sleeping through them. That's our purpose here at Medialive.

That means I need you guys to care when campaigning."

I nodded and agreed with a look of appeasement carefully crafted through the years, as if I appreciated listening to a woman making five times my salary drone on over being enthusiastic about cold calling strangers. Our titles are 'Marketing Experts', but that's just so we'd sound professional when making calls—the more apt term would be 'telemarketers', or, alternatively, 'those people you wish would trip and stumble onto a high-speed freeway'.

Henderson continued with her lecture, and I continued to draw a grin on my face, bobbing my head up and down, up and down, with slightly staggered offsets to emulate an attention span—as if I have one of those.

Oh, look, a squirrel.

When the meeting was over, I shuffled back to my cubicle and pretended to be swamped with work to avoid the coworkers in my biome—I don't know how I ended up with the Gossip Girls around me, but I did. I guess people are more receptive to strange female voices than male, but they couldn't have women comprise the entire department or it'd look degrading. Which, it is, obviously—there was nowhere near the same concentration of women in any other section, but they can't have it *blatantly* look that way. That's basically what I got paid for, if you can even call it getting paid.

Face buried in a computer filled with empty

words, I lightly swung my letter-opener around as if it were a sword, slicing through mail of paper and imaginary steel. The exhaustion wasn't helping me get any work done; I'd spent too much time dreaming, leaving me lethargic and unmotivated. Well, more than usual, at least—it's not like I ever had much energy, given that I'd have probably died if I ever set foot in a gym.

That's what happens when you barely make it back before the sun sets. I wonder, if I pick up the phone and talk to myself, would anyone even know I'm faking it?

"Don't work too hard, Jackson. You might hurt yourself at this rate."

Startled, I instinctively snapped a hand at my work phone, missing and knocking aside the receiver. It clattered across my desk, slipping into a gap between it and the wall, and I yelped.

"Oh, it's just you, Mike." The words came out as a sigh of relief. Mike Fonsetti was a man far too focused on his appearance, everything tidy and clean-cut, and perhaps persistent at worst, but easy to stick around in a workplace. Also, he liked me for some unknown reason. That's always a plus.

He was cracking up at my clamorous fit. "Sorry, Jax. You're too easy to screw with, always zoning out and getting caught up thinking about whatever it is you think about. What *do* you think about, man?"

"Oh, nothing really. A nice vacation in the forest, beautiful women, and adventures. Typical stuff.

All I really know is that anywhere, even somewhere in my head, is better than this dump."

"Amen to that, brother. Although—women? How risqué. I wouldn't have expected you to say that, since you never come out when I invite you." He falsely gasped, hand shooting up to cover a gaping mouth. "Maybe you've had a change of heart? I'm telling you, man, those happy hours are a lot of fun."

I shrugged and maintained a taut smile as my eyes shifted towards the floor. "Maybe some other time, Mike. I always appreciate you inviting me, but I don't really feel up to it."

His lips twisted down, and his eyebrows up. "Alright, Jax. Whatever you say, man. But I'm telling you, if you're sitting around daydreaming about having fun at work, you should do something besides work. Live a little, before you're too old and get a hangover from the smell of wine."

"To be fair, the smell of wine already gives me a hangover—blech. But thanks, Mike. I'll take you up on that offer someday."

His hand tapped my cubicle wall twice, signaling his departure. I decided to buckle down and get a few calls out of the way so I wouldn't get fired for failing to meet weekly quota.

"Hello Mr. Gano, my name is Jackson with Medialive, and I'd like to take a few moments of your day to—"

"No." The line clicked, to my relief.

Thank God for people like Mr. Gano. They didn't bring me any closer to earning a monthly bonus, but most of the time, I just didn't care.

At 11:30AM on the dot, I decided to take my lunch break and get some fresh air—it's a bit claustrophobic being stuffed in a cubicle for hours, the grey walls of it slowly closing in and crushing me. I always got lunch at Harry's Deli, this great little hole-in-the-wall shop that makes a beautiful Rueben and the best fries in town. Far from healthy, but I never cared much about things like health, especially since I've always been the kind of tall thin guy that eats horribly without gaining any weight.

"Hey, Jax," the cashier greeted me cheerfully. I have no idea why she was always so happy. "The usual, right? That'll be $6.74."

I handed her a worn ten dollar bill. "Yep, you got it. Thanks, Clara—you can keep the change."

"Aww, you're so nice! Enjoy the meal!"

"You t—" I caught it before it came out. "Take care now."

That was a close one.

I waited by the counter for my food, staring into the refrigerated display case full of baked goods; a rainbowed myriad of cupcakes and cookies decorated in vibrant colors, lush cakes and brownies. They looked delicious, but I knew I wouldn't be able to eat one after a sandwich and fries, so instead I stared at them and drifted. I thought about work, and Hadrian, and why sandwiches are so appealing—perhaps it's because they are the perfect representation of man; slowly, piece by piece, day by day, we're slapped together into a hodgepodge of bad ideas, anxieties, and lunch meat.

A voice echoed in my head, ripping me from the daydream. "Jackson? Jackson? Hello, Earth to moron. Wakey-wakey."

At first, I thought an annoyed employee was trying to hand over my order, but there was no one behind the counter; the noise's belligerent source had crept up beside me, a short woman with vaguely rose-dyed hair browning at the roots, which was a stark contrast to her pale skin—it didn't glow so much at looked transparent.

"Hey, Diane. You here to get lunch, too?" Smooth, as always.

"No, I just enjoy the smell of deli meat," she retorted, elbowing my side. "This place is a favorite of mine."

I ruffled my hair, chuckling at myself. *Do I rib her back? No, right? That's weird.* "Yeah, of course, I don't know why I asked such a dumb question. How are you? How's Caleb doing? I heard he's been sick lately."

"He's holding up, thanks for asking. We're all positive about his remission, and he's a fighter." There was a slight hint of uncertainty in her downcast eyes, but she truly seemed to believe the statement.

"That's great to hear! You look really tired, by the way. Long night?" I asked with a bad wink and playful tone.

"Very funny. No, actually, I went to bed at a normal time, pretty boring night. I just had some pretty crazy dreams and slept like crap."

"Huh. Story of my life. What kind of dr—oh, my sandwich. Sorry, one second."

Hugo—the main chef at Harry's, a real nice guy—handed me a wrinkled brown bag with my Reuben and fries, smiling like he always did. "Here you go. Fresh for you."

His accent was thick, but clear enough to understand—what baffled me was not his English, but how jovial he always seemed despite working in a deli at forty or fifty, handing people grease-soaked bags of food like they were actually bags of gold and he was a stocky, Portuguese leprechaun. I thanked him with less than equivalent enthusiasm and turned back to Diane, who was second in line to place an order. I tried to come up with something to say, but she punched my shoulder and broke the silence for me.

"Go, Mr. Lazy Bones. You've got important things to do."

I smiled. "Yeah. Not a bad call. Don't want to piss the boss off. Again."

The air outside was brisk, yet not painfully cold, as winter was on its way out in the Virginian equivalent of spring. There wasn't much of a walk to enjoy the weather, and within minutes I was back at Medialive—*where the ads are livelier than the employees.*

The rest of the day was excruciatingly uneventful, dragging by like a dog's ass on carpet; every bit as shitty, too. I made my quota and drove a battered '07 Civic home, mind churning with what I'd set up for the night. There was little else to look forward to.

Within the bleak, greyish walls of my one-bedroom apartment, the pungent smell of frozen, two-dollar enchiladas being microwaved filled my nostrils; simple, but cheap. Mediocre, but damn near effortless, and it's not like I could do any better myself. Best to save the money and time for more entertaining things. As I watched the little tray spin round and round, my phone flashed with life:

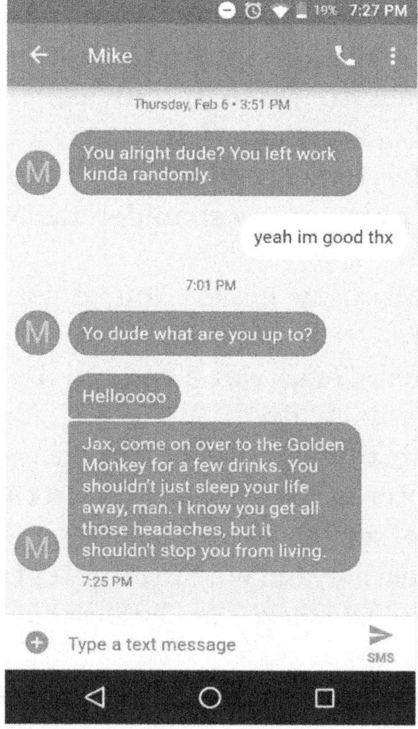

'Sorry, Mike, but sleeping my life away isn't all that bad' is what I wanted to respond with, but I opted to simply thank him and say I'd take a raincheck. I felt bad for lying about the headaches, but I had work to do—and it's not like he'd believe the truth, anyway. No one would.

My enchiladas were downed within moments, the sleeping pills quickly following suit. I haphazardly tossed my plastic spoon atop the piling trash, brushed my teeth, and hurried into bed. One last time, I glanced over a few notes I'd laid out about siege defense, scribbled amongst pages of ideas and rough sketches. It was a sort of reverse dream journal that held my world in its binding, with all kinds of notes and mediocre sketches, things to pass the time and help me plan out what would come next.

It became difficult to read after a little while as the pills kicked in, and I lobbed the notebook onto my nightstand, tossing a few times in bed. What I thought of in the waning moments of wakefulness was not of sieges and starlight, but the stupid question I'd asked Diane earlier.

"I just like the smell of deli meat."

It was a funny retort, but why did I always fumble with words around pretty girls? Or, honestly, with basically anyone? My head heavied, swallowed by a down pillow, and darkness overcame me.

Falling asleep is the best feeling in the world.

∞　∞　∞

It's nice waking up to the kiss of sunlight rather than the slap of an alarm clock.

Even though dreaming was as natural as being awake, if not more, it was still a little strange opening my eyes so soon after closing them. There's a peculiarity to the mind being awake while the body is sleeping, a sort of tingling, ghostly presence in the back of my head. Thankfully, occupying myself was always enough to override the feeling and fully immerse myself—but the act of waking never felt right to me.

I sat up and stretched, silk sheets floating off my body and down to the bed as warmth spilled upon me through huge windows lining our bedroom wall. As usual, I hopped out of bed and spread the bi-folding glass doors separating our bedroom from an expansive balcony adorned with potted flowers of every color. Butterflies fluttered around in the true spring air, their wings a stunning blur of onyx, orange and ocean blue. It was such a lovely day, warm and absent of humidity, a light breeze ruffling through my hair and soft, billowy clouds floating through the sky without a care in the world.

Perfection.

After a few minutes spent reveling in relaxation, I clad myself in armor and strapped on the belt that housed Somnior. Down the staircase, through the entrance hall and out into the court-yard, a sudden commotion caused me to start. I approached the scratchy sound, following it to the main entrance.

Ugh, I forgot about them.

Disgruntled and still on edge, I stormed off toward the outer gate, continuing my journey as two bats flapped wildly through the air around me like thunderclouds born of my annoyance. I examined the outer wall's perimeter to the erratic soundtrack of beating wings, scanning its weaknesses and obvious points of entry—the most blatant of which was a dip in the wall, to the castle rear. Thankfully, both the armory tower and our personal chambers have a trebuchet of sorts sitting atop them to fight off initial combatant waves—assuming that Maya doesn't just open the front gate and invite them in for tea and slaughter.

Once I'd returned to within the castle walls, I ascended the armory tower, onto the roof, and peered around in search of any signs of Yuurishmen marching in the distance. To my relief, not even a single leaf was rustling suspiciously in any direction. It would have been a disaster if the siege had started before Maya arrived. Not because they'd destroy me, but because *she'd* destroy me for fighting without her.

Bits of straw sailed through the air as I hacked at a pell with a wooden training sword, over, under, and cross-slashing it while keeping my footwork swift. Once it had been sufficiently beaten and broken, I returned to our chambers, where a piece of parchment waited on my writing desk:

Dearest Reza,

I can't believe you missed me on your way down to the armory. The bats definitely have better vision than you.

Get your shit together, Mr. Lazy Bones. We have important things to do.

Sincerely,
Batwoman

My eyes fixated on the final paragraph. Moments later, Maya jumped out from under the bed. The entirely stoic reaction she received nearly shocked her instead.

"You're so boring," she said, crossing her arms. "Why're you just standing there, looking at the note all funny, anyway?"

'Mr. Lazy Bones' . . . could it be that Diane . . . no, what are the odds of that? It has to be a coincidence.

I set the parchment back on my desk. "Just some deja-vu, I guess. Doesn't matter."

Uninvited

A wet tongue lapped at my face, as if trying to erase the annoyed expression from it.

"Aren't these stupid things supposed to be nocturnal?" I barked at Maya, swatting the tongue away. She laughed and petted the bat harassing me lovingly.

"They're fox bats, not microbats, so they're fine in daylight. That's why they're so cute and not a little freaky looking. Fun fact: they actually don't even use echolocation, they see with their eyes like we do!"

"You already told me that. How do I get them to see that I don't enjoy being licked?"

She scoffed, waving a dismissive hand. "Whatever, just deal with it. They'll probably give up eventually if you don't pet them. Honestly, though—you should befriend one. They saved our lives and can help out a lot in the future. Besides, how can you not love those adorable fuzzy faces?" She cooed at the scarred bat, rubbing its head.

A sharp clinking noise rang loudly through the air, sending the two beasts into a state of alarm. It was an unpleasant, hollow sound; one birthed of steel crashing into wood. Maya and I drew swords and slowly advanced into the courtyard.

"Maya, I'll take the armory tower and you man the parapet. If you notice a breach, let's meet up here, okay?"

She nodded in agreement, but another bout of the noise halted us. It was slightly less harsh this time, forming a rhythm: one, one-two-three, one-two. Emanating from the entrance gate, rattling across Lake Augr.

Who could possibly be knocking at our gate? This isn't part of the plan, and there's no one else in this world but us.

I turned to Maya, wanting to ask her thoughts, but the hollow gaze she wore gave me pause. I was looking, for a moment, into the empty eyes of a doll that sits on its shelf, helplessly watching as a busy world whirls past.

As she shook the look off and started forward, I grabbed her arm. "You get closer to the gate—I'll head up into the armory and check our surroundings to make sure it's not some kind of distraction. Don't open the gate until we're both there, okay? Promise me."

"Fine, fine. I promise. Don't take too long, okay?"

We jogged along the lake's edge and I broke off at the tower, bounding up its twisting staircase in groups of four. Cresting the top floor, I grabbed a spyglass and scanned the castle's rear wall and weak points for signs of an invasion. There was nothing but still forest, gently swaying in a nurturing breeze, and a strangely dark cloud to the south.

A storm must be coming. But such a small, isolated one?

I ran downstairs, skipping as many steps as possible. Just shy of reaching the courtyard, the thunderous creak of poorly-oiled iron hinges grated inside of me.

Oh, for God's sake.

Sure enough, as soon as I popped out, enormous wooden doors were splitting outward. I sprinted, hoping to at least get there before anything could swarm through our gate and spread out. As the gap widened, I was expecting to see the Yuurish army waving their swords and laughing at how easy their siege had become—and yet, instead, there was but one man who stood before me. A very, very hairy man. Maya ran back down the barbican's interior staircase to join us, and I didn't take my eyes off him until she did.

"Why didn't you *wait* for me?!" I asked when she arrived.

She merely shrugged, and I let out a sigh that could've blown a tree over before turning my attention to the figure standing at our front gate. Immediately, I whipped Somnior from its sheath, sending streaks of emerald light dancing across the courtyard.

"Maya, look at his armor." Our uninvited guest was clad in black and red metal from head to toe. His left arm was in a makeshift sling, the armor around it twisted and gnarled.

"Yeah, I know. You, Zoxan! I thought all of you committed suicide at the King's command. Why are you still alive? Did he order you not to join in, so you could try and kill us when we'd least expect it?"

I chimed in. "Postmortem assassination. Not a bad idea if he knew there was no chance to win the battle."

The Zoxan bowed its head, using a healthy right arm to pull its helmet off. A face of short, light brown fur surrounded by a mane of darker hair was revealed; bear-like, just as the Zoxan king was. There were also thin lines running from his eyes out to his ears, but they were blue rather than red. Its facial features were mostly humanoid, despite having a bear's ears and subdued snout.

"I am indeed Zoxan," the bear grumbled with a low, grinding voice, like sandpaper on my eardrums. "That much I cannot deny. However, I am not your enemy."

"I'll ask you again: your entire race killed themselves at the snap of a finger, and yet you're knocking on our front gate." Maya's arms were crossed, with one hand fingering Vesper's pommel. "Why?"

"That King of ours, he had a telepathic link

to our entire species, one that was impossible to block. From birth, he would fill our heads with orders, strip us from our mothers and break us into beings without will or character; machines that perform at his whim. We could not say no, for his thoughts ruled our minds—he could control any of us like puppets. The reason our army seemed like a swarm of mindless drones was because the King cannot give specific orders when trying to control everyone at the same time. He was so terrified by your arrival that he chose to entirely remove their fear of death and have them flock to you, overriding their personal traits. I saw many great swordsmen fall before you without even putting up a fight. I saw women and young men do the same.

"I, however, have always had a weaker link with him for some reason. I'd hoped to learn why, to break his hold on our race, but his greed took hold and wiped my people from existence. When the order came through, I was unconscious. I had a horrible nightmare like my mind had turned to ash, and not a soul was left alive when I awoke."

He turned his stony gaze to Maya and continued. "When I heard you speak to the King, and shame him for his actions, I was confused. I'd not seen anyone stand up to him before, and in that moment, I realized that no one can tie my will down. When he died, I understood that no one is invincible —even the almighty King, towering so high above us. I am the only Zoxan left, so I am the free will of my entire people in a way; I would like to live a life that all of them would be proud of. Our last moment in history will not be the day that vile coward ended us."

We looked at him, unsure of whether or not he'd finished.

The Zoxan shifted uncomfortably, turning his gaze to the dirt and bowing again. "I apologize if I've been too outright—I have never interacted in this manner before. We've never been a freely speaking people. Always, he was listening."

Maya's arms relaxed, shifting to her hips, and she cracked a warm smile. "Don't worry about that. I like you, Zoxan. What's your name?"

"Name? I'm afraid I don't understand."

"Oh, you must have another word for it. What are you called? So that you know someone is speaking with you specifically."

"We are not called anything. We recognize—*recognized*—each other mostly through a . . . connection, I suppose would be the way to put it. A unique feeling, though the King could override it at will. What is a 'name'?"

I decided to cut in. "Names are unique words given to every person, something to refer to them. It's our way of telling each other apart and communicating easily. I am Reza, and this is Maya. With these names, we can call to each other specifically. Normally they're given at birth by parents."

"I see. Would it be easier for you if I had a name, then? What should I be called?"

"If you can't think of anything, I have a few

suggestions," Maya offered, a sly look on her face.

Oh, God, please don't let her name you.

"Well, actually, I thought of one. But thank you—Ma-ya, correct? May I be called Zoxan?"

I chuckled, rubbing my face to try and hide the laughter. "Well, you're not really supposed to name yourself after your race or country. A name isn't a description or something."

"Why not?"

"It's just strange. You're not a race, you're a person. An individual."

The bear chewed on my words for a moment. "Well, Ree-za, I would suggest otherwise. I have never been a person. Under the King's regime, I was a slave, and now I am the remnant of all that was Zoxum and its people. I am Zoxan."

I couldn't help but smile at that. "Well spoken. It's a bit odd, but I'll get used to it. Nice to meet you, Zoxan. Now, don't get me wrong here; I like you so far, but we don't know you at all. There's also still the chance that your intentions are malicious. I'm going to ask that you hand over your weapons, at least for the time being. Is that okay?"

Without hesitation, he dropped a belt with two swords and his dagger as well. "I would expect no less. You may restrain me, if you wish."

I tossed his weapons into a crate by the main entrance. "That won't be necessary. You picked a hell of a time to come by, though. We're preparing for a siege that should be hitting any moment."

"Is that so? May I help you fight for your home,

then?"

Maya's face contorted. "Why would you want to help us fight? We killed your whole race and stole your home."

"Such is life, Ma-ya. Despite us being enemies, you still showed compassion for us when you heard the King speak. You didn't eradicate Zoxum—he did. And when you killed him, you set me free. I get to experience something my people never did, and for that, I will fight by your side. I believe I can accomplish some kind of good if I stay with you."

"You can have these to help us during the battle," I said, returning his belongings. "But I'm warning you—one misstep and you're dead. You saw us for yourself."

He accepted them graciously, slinging his belt back on. "I believe you. The skills you two displayed in the Motherland were incredible, to say the least."

"Good. Welcome to our home, Zoxan. Pull your weight and we'll help you find your place in this world."

"Thank you, Ree-za. Tell me, what is your home's name? You said all things have names.

I shrugged at Maya, sharing a laugh.

"I apologize if my questions are strange," he continued.

"No, no—sorry, we weren't laughing at *you*. You bring up a good point, Zoxan. Now that I think about it, we never actually named this place. That's kinda weird, isn't it, Maya? We should have a name for our home."

She stroked her chin. "You're right. How about Castle Lakefront?"

"That's a bit too blunt, isn't it?" I asked. She hissed at me, but I ignored it and kept thinking. "Take a little longer to mull it over. The name should be meaningful."

"I like the sound of *Dawnbringer Castle.* Whether we're waking up or going to sleep, it's dawn."

"That's surprisingly clever. I like that a lot. Anyway, we should probably be in the towers watching for signs of advancing armies, it's almost noon now. I'll close the gate."

"Sure, but I want you to see the new armor I'm working on! Maybe I could make you some too, since yours is . . . old."

I fired a death glare at Maya, who recoiled and ran off to the armory. "Zoxan, you'll stay with me today. Maya will certainly lose you when things get crazy. Honestly, she'd lose you on a tour of the castle."

Gears churned as massive wooden slabs swung shut and the locking bar engaged, creaking in protest at the labor. Zoxan was still waiting right where I'd left him—it didn't even look like his feet had shifted position. I led him up the armory tower, walking behind him, ascending the swirling staircase that wound from floor to roof, peeking at a toiling Maya on the way up. *She looks good swinging that hammer around.*

We crested the tower's crown, and Zoxan

stepped as far forward through an embrasure as he could without plunging to the ground, wind whipping his fur into a frenzy.

"This view is amazing," he said with awe, looking across the vast, expansive ocean of leafy green. "I never knew how much existed outside of my city."

"Well, there sure is a lot of forest. Which is why I need your help to look for signs of enemy advancement. It's impossible to see through the canopy, but if ten thousand men are marching toward us, you'll notice the trees rustle with a violence that doesn't come from a breeze. I still don't see anything, though. They must be having difficulty mobilizing that many men through this terrain."

Zoxan turned in place, scanning the region. "Reza?"

"What is it?"

"Is there some kind of garden to the south of here?"

"It's a forest, I'm sure there are plenty of garden-looking things around."

"Yes, but that is quite a lot of orange."

Following his gaze, there was, as he had said, a garden of orange littered through a thinner part of the forest south of us. Or was it orange?

"Zoxan, do you know what two colors make up orange?"

"Yellow and red, no?"

"Correct. Yellow and red. The Yuurish flag is solid yellow, with no insignia. They believe that

Yuura is a land of light that will fight off the darkness by conquering it. I postulate that they chose yellow because it tends to invoke happiness when seen, helping conquered nations stomach their presence. They're Hadrian's favorite pets, and he usually keeps them close."

"That is very interesting. Are you suggesting that they are the yellow in this equation?"

"Yes."

"Then, the red would be?"

We shared a glance, then sprinted downstairs.

"Quit whatever you're doing, I need help!" I hollered at Maya, clamoring into the forge.

"Ah, come on! I'm almost done with my new armor," she whined, a familiar tone meant to annoy me into submission.

"There'll be time for that later! Something is horribly wrong here." We walked out into the bailey, standing lakeside. "When we were scouting, we saw them in the distance. Not yellow, Maya, but *orange*."

"I don't understand the meaning of this," Zoxan said.

I turned to him. "You bleed black, but most other species are red inside."

His eyes widened. "But what could have done such a thing? There must be thousands in the distance."

"More than that, Zoxan. I think there are nearly twenty thousand dead men rotting in the forest"—I turned to Maya, who was idly staring into the distance—"and I don't have the faintest clue as to what could have done—"

She leapt through the air, knocking Zoxan and I to the ground. Less than a second later, darkness swallowed our piled bodies as something devoured the sky overhead, making it look like the warped gloss of painted glass. It passed quickly, however, and crashed into the lake with a force that sent waves splashing across the courtyard. For several moments, it was raining, without a single cloud overhead. Mist swirled through the air and a rainbow sprouted, trying to connect the tiny droplets of water around us. It would've been a beautiful sight, had we not been preoccupied with the imminent threat of death.

Still lying in the dirt, I tried to analyze what was in the lake. *How did someone get a goddamn trebuchet through the forest without me noticing?*

"I don't know what's happening, but we need to find that trebuchet and destroy it before. What are they firing, anyway? That looks like . . . ice? How did they haul a *glacier* through the forest? No —*why* did they haul a glacier through the forest?" Thoughts ran laps around my mind as I laid in the glinting glare of a slick iceberg, scattering light like a frigid diamond.

I understand that sometimes minor details are out of place, but this....

The three of us regained our composure, and I noticed another oddity about the glistening chunk of ice floating in our lake.

"Maya, am I crazy or is that thing pointed? Like a giant, fat icicle."

She approached it, scanning the abomination. "Yeah, it's cone-shaped."

"Someone found glaciers, then carved, transported, and fired them at us? This is—it's ridiculous. It's *impossible*."

She threw her arms up in defeat. "Clearly not. Wait . . . Reza, what the hell is that?"

I traced the path of Maya's finger, uphill, toward the castle. A figure in a dark purple robe, probably shorter than myself, menacingly loomed over our doorstep roughly fifty feet away.

How did he get in here? The walls are thirty feet high. . . .

I turned to the bear, his face considerably more angular and odd when flattened by water. "Zoxan, you furry asshole! Did you sneak him in somehow?"

He half-bowed at me again. "You were with me the whole time. I would not dishonor my people with such tricks."

"Reza, are you screwing with me? What's going on?" Maya's eyes had glazed over once more, and her words were lacking their usual emphasis.

I stared at the robed man, wondering the same thing. "No, I don't know what's happening either. Besides, this guy is the least of our problems—I'll kill him, you worry about whatever is launching glaciers into our front yard. We'll get to the bottom of this, I promise. Zoxan, with me."

Before we could set off, a maniacal laugh echoed through the castle walls, and the robed man raised his arms into the air. "Tell me, friends," he said, his voice dripping like melting ice. "Have you ever wondered what it's like to be a God?"

We kept a careful eye on him, frozen in the field. None of us could muster a response.

"Let me show you," the man continued, taking off what looked like a rucksack. He untied it, lifted it high, and dumped out an impossible number of golden scrolls that skittered and clanged as they fell down the steps. "They're dead. All of them. Even the man you've been so utterly consumed by."

I took a step forward, my thoughts a mess. "What—what are you talking about? Who are you?"

"Hadrian is dead. His empire is dead. The only ones left in this world are us, here in this courtyard."

"No," I said, shaking my head. "This is impossible."

He laughed again, a chilling, spine-tensing laugh like ice against the back of my neck. A white powder accumulated above him, swirling in a vortex that concentrated at a focal point which grew in size with each second, like a blizzard had conjured at his command. The swelling snowball appeared solid, but its shape was altering as if it were made of putty, slowly clarifying and forming a point. It was probably forty times the size of a grown man. The three of us just stood there, gaping at it, and I felt a deep chill settle in. "Unlock your mind. Be free."

"Reza," Maya said as we slowly locked eyes.

"What the *fu*—"

We barely had time to scatter before it came barreling straight at us, a frosty mist trailing behind it. The three of us managed to escape its path somehow, and it slammed straight into the dirt where we'd been standing, catapulting mud across the yard and into the lake. The point was so sharp that it cut right through the earth, raising the ground around it while burrowing deeper and deeper before finally coming to a stop. It rooted itself deep enough to remain there, upright, like a poorly cut diamond had sprouted from the ground, where we hid behind it.

Maya crawled toward me wildly, her face turning bright red. "Reza! You idiot! What happened to your 'no magic' rule?"

"Oh, but giant bats are fine? That's totally realistic, right? Bear people? I didn't even come up with whatever this is!"

"I like animals, okay?" she fired at me, as if trying to fight ice with ice. "He probably doesn't appreciate being called a 'bear person', by the way. It's insensitive."

"I'm afraid I don't understand what's happening," Zoxan whispered to the dirt.

"Never mind all that—I don't know who the hell this guy is, and we need to handle him quickly before he kills us or destroys the place, or both. Maya, you—"

"I'll attack from the front, you run along the wall and get to a blind spot so you can flank him.

One of us will have an opening!" she shouted at me, already running up the hill.

I scrambled to my left, trying to catch up with Maya's placement. Zoxan rose and began to follow, but I turned and stopped him. "No, stay here, okay? Don't move until we have this handled."

"Understood," he replied, closing his eyes. "I will die here, if it comes to that."

"No, you can—whatever."

I ran forward and crouched low, pressed myself against the mossy stone wall, and treaded lightly as I traced it. Thankfully, I'd left some of the forest's trees intact when the walls went up, and they returned the favor by providing cover as I advanced. The biting cry of steel rang out and I hastened my pace.

Here's hoping that if she presses him constantly, he won't have time to form any of that ice.

I reached a thick patch of brush and cut across to approach him from the rear, quietly rushing forward low with Somnior in hand. I halted, sighing as I stepped out into the open and saw a lump of robes on the ground. His neck was cleaved open, head only half on.

"Did you tell me to flank just so you could kill him yourself?"

All I got in response was a light giggle and a big smile, though it melted away quickly. "Seriously, though—what the hell, man? All of this has been for nothing, and now anything goes? Cause if we're going to have enemies that can do this kind of thing, we need to be able to match it."

"I didn't know, I swear. I didn't do this." She squinted at me, sneering. I cocked my head in response and followed up with, "Oh, so you're telling me *you* didn't do this? It's your kind of stunt, not mine."

She sobered from melodrama and fired me a stare that was both colder and sharper than the strange man's ice. "I play by the rules."

I nodded sternly, shifting my attention to the robed man. The two of us stood over his dead body, blood trickling downhill, like a trail of fire ants marching through the grass. "What do you think he was talking about, besides Hadrian and all of that?"

"The God thing?" she said without looking up from his body. "No idea. Weird shit."

"Yeah." I sighed, rubbing my temples. "This is all sorts of screwed up."

Turning, Maya asked, "Why is Zoxan just standing there looking at the sky, by the way?"

I let a bit of air through my nose and sheathed my sword. He hadn't moved an inch, not even shifted his upper body, as if the ice had frozen him solid where I'd left him. *Channeling the wrong part of your heritage with the whole statue thing, buddy.*

"I'll call him over. He's a bit off, that one," I said, kneeling by the fresh corpse. "Fantastic listener, though. You could learn a thing or two from him."

Blurring Lines

"You know, for a wizard, this guy sure has a small wand." We'd parted the dead mage's robes and, unfortunately, he seemed to value comfort over decency. The only thing he'd bothered to cover up was his face; some kind of mask made of ice too cold to touch—with cherry, taught lips, sharp cheeks, and thick eyebrows—was crowned by a mop of hair black as night.

"Maya, he's a mage, not a wizard. Mages don't use wands . . . whatever. Have you found anything on him besides that? Something useful, maybe? We need to figure out what's going on here."

"I know, I know. I don't see anything on this guy that could indicate where he came from. I mean, if he can even be considered a *he* with that lil' thing." She stifled laughter as I continued to turn out empty pocket after empty pocket. The bag he'd brought the scrolls in had been empty, as well.

He came at us wearing nothing but a robe and

doesn't have a single possession on him. What the hell am I supposed to make of this?

With nothing useful on his front, I flipped him, blood and dirt wedging into my fingernails. To my surprise, at the nape covering, there was white text woven into the velvety purple material that read: 'Tagless for maximum comfort. 75% silk, 25% cotton. Made in Delirium.'

"Where's Delirium?" I asked.

"I do not know of such a place," Zoxan replied, bowing his head. "I apologize I cannot be of more help."

"Is that even a real name? I've never seen it on the map before, and it sounds terrible. *Delirium.* Gross." Maya held her tongue out and scraped at it, as if the word had left a foul taste behind. "Let's go check a map again, there should be one in the armory."

"There's no point, that place doesn't exist. It's not on our maps, and it never has been. There has to be some other clue here, something about who this guy is...."

"Reza, there's nothing left to search. Unless you've got no dignity and a pair of gloves you don't want anymore, let's just go check the map." She started walking back downhill, tracing the lake's edge.

I sighed in defeat, following suit. "Fine. Let's go, Zoxan."

It was a short walk, but we took it casually. There was a sense of urgency to be sure, but nobody ever talks about how draining the aftermath of an adrenaline spike is. Burning thighs, a pounding head; it's a bit like a hangover, where all the discomfort previously avoided finally catches up. On our left, Maya was slipping and sliding around, waving her arms around in wild circles to balance herself on the massive icicle floating in the lake. Since it was conical, the pointed end sank first, leaving a massive, perfectly smooth surface exposed. *Damn, that thing has already risen the water level so much. When the other one melts . . . well, it's a good thing we don't keep anything important on the first floor of the armory, I guess. How did she get on top of that thing, anyway?*

Maya was doing her best to remain upright despite her feet betraying her on the slick, glimmering ice glowing blue in sunlight. After a little struggling, she seemed to gain control of herself, thrusting her arms into the air. The victorious motion threw her body's equilibrium off, sending her reeling to the ice, which bobbed under her weight, tilting over and dumping her into the lake with a loud splash that quickly muffled her shouting.

I laughed, allowing much needed levity to seep through aching muscles. Zoxan met my eyes for a moment, then released what can only be described as a choppy growl. The laughter caught in my diaphragm, choking off with a cough.

"Are you . . . copying me?"

His eyes sunk to the dirt.

"Do you not know what *laughter* is?" I pressed.

His gaze remained downcast. "I think I understand the concept, but we were very heavily re-strained with little interpersonal contact. It seems to be an expression of enjoyment, one that is shared, but it won't come naturally for me. Many social constructs are acquired through group learn-ing, so perhaps I will grasp it with time."

"That's pretty sad, Zox. But yeah, if you hang around with us, I'm sure you'll figure it out. Maya keeps things interesting."

He cocked his furry head at me. "Zox?"

"Yeah, it's a nickname. 'Zoxan' is a little rough to say over and over, but Zox is a pretty cool name. It's shorter."

"You are shortening the value of my people?"

"Wh—no. No, it's just easier to say out loud. It still has the same meaning, but it sounds cooler. It's not literally cutting the meaning in half just be-cause the word is shorter."

"Oh, okay. I accept. I am, henceforth, Zox."

"Okay. Well, we should go help Maya out now. She probably needs a towel." I patted him on the back and walked into the tower, where I'd stashed several linens in a thick, carved chest for situations like this. I grabbed one, hand-dyed deeply with lapis lazuli, and shut the oak's mouth shut. Walking back out to the shore, Maya was shaking the water from her body like a dog, a tornado of wet hair whipping violently around her. Her face was glowing, split from ear to ear with a bright, pearly smile, even though I could see the skin and hair on her forearms tightening and raising with little bumps. A light, mid-day breeze was rolling in on us, and I even felt a chill setting in.

She accepted the towel as though it were merely some sort of decorative hood, tossing it over her hair, completely dismissing the rest of her body. Through the soaked comfortwear sticking to her skin, I could see the musculature of her upper thighs and the outline of her ribs where the chest-piece underneath left a gap. *Ugh, the thought of wet clothing and armor chafing. . . .*

While fidgeting with fitting the towel to her head, she asked, "Did you check the map?"

"Oh, I forgot about that. You kind of distracted me. I'll run and grab one."

I scaled the winding stone staircase, entering the armory and scanning the room. The one we took with us to Zoxum was lost in the midst of battle but, thankfully, I always kept extras. In a corner, tucked under some older, worn-out armor, I found one rolled up.

When I got back downstairs, Maya had fully abandoned drying herself off and had begun playing rock-paper-scissors with Zox, who looked extremely focused on their game.

"Rock, paper, scissors, go!"

Zox held his fist out, and Maya had her palm open and held up like she was going to hit Zox with a karate chop. Upon seeing the result, she gave him a scornful look, like a dissatisfied teacher. "Zox, you gotta mix it up. I'm going to keep beating you if you play rock over and over! This is no fun."

"But stone is strong. Stone would tear through paper. Why do I keep losing with it?"

"Ugh, that's just how the game works. Paper beats rock—that's the rule! It wouldn't make sense if rock beat everything, no one would play anything else."

"That rule doesn't make sense. I don't like this game. How do I pick one?"

I stayed back a moment to let them continue their bit, biting my lip to keep any laughter contained.

"You just pick one, dummy! Paper beats rock, rock beats scissors, and scissors beats paper. Got it?"

"What are 'scissors', again?"

She opened her mouth but held the words in for a moment. "Well, uh, *good question* . . . they're—a part of the game! They cut things, like paper, I guess. So they beat paper."

"What are they made of?"

"Metal? Why are you asking me all these questions? Can we just play the stupid game?"

"So you are telling me that a stone smashes metal, but does not smash paper? This game makes no sense."

Maya wrapped her hand over her face, like one would paper over rock.

"You should automatically lose for bringing paper to a fight," he continued, as if she were listening. "Such poor instincts."

"Sorry to, uh, *cut in*, but I have a map here." I was gesturing my index and middle fingers in a scissor motion, but Maya was still hiding her face and Zox was staring at my hand like it had a disturbing infection. "Right, well, let's see."

They gathered around me as the map unfurled.

"Yeah, this is probably bad." My finger was pressed against the map, a few miles east of our castle, across the Rubicon river. *How the hell?*

"*'Oh, there's nothing on the map, it can't just change.'* Aren't you glad I made you grab one of these and check?" Maya asked rhetorically, each word intending to stab my pride.

"You're definitely screwing with me, then. You knew it'd be on the map, something that's impossible without one of us editing it? Please."

The look of playfulness and warmth evacuated her face quicker than I could keep up with. "I'm getting tired of you accusing me for this. These maps are set to represent the layout of this world, right? Well what if someone else is in here, and they added this place?"

I rolled my eyes. "Am I supposed to take this seriously?"

"Okay, you need to cut the crap. You think you're a genius, right? Well tell me this: why is that idea so impossible? No, actually, answer a different question: am I real?"

I nodded like a child being scolded by his mother.

"Right. So if I'm real, and you're real, what makes you think that someone else couldn't get in?

And if they did, who's to say they couldn't have every bit as much power as us, maybe even more? And if they claimed land, this map would probably change to reflect it. Are you scared, is that why you keep blaming me?"

My eyes lowered, jaw clenched. "I didn't think of it that way."

"Exactly. Please get over yourself already, so we can move forward."

"Sorry," I muttered.

Zox let loose a jagged laugh-growl. It sounded like an obese bear walking down a flight of stairs while roaring at intruders, and quickly cut off with a sharp glance from each of us. "Sorry, inappropriate time? You two seemed to be emotional, so I thought the response was . . . I apologize."

I rubbed my eyes, turning around to take a deep breath and think. "Maya . . . did you mess with the dead body?"

"Ew, what is that supposed to mean?"

"Like, did you do the thing where you hide dead bodies in trees again?"

"That was *one time*—wait, why are you asking me that?"

"Because he's gone, Maya."

She ran up alongside me, squinting, using her hand as a visor. "We're downhill, our view is probably just blocked. Go check if you're worried."

I walked uphill, past the massive glacier slowly turning the earth around it to mud. Tiny streams trickled through gleaming blades of grass, trailing into the lake.

"Maya! Problem!"

Both she and Zox came running toward me, churning mud beneath their feet.

"What's wrong?"

I pointed to the blood pooling in our court-yard, which had become marginally more visible now that there was no corpse resting atop it. "There's a trail, and it ends at the splatter on the wall here. How is this possible?"

"I dunno. Maybe he disappeared after dying?"

"His dead body moved toward the wall before it disappeared?"

She shrugged at me helplessly. "I'm not a sci-entist."

Thunk.

My eyes slowly turned to the ground next to me, where a small needle was lodged in the dirt; it was a transparent light blue and a little puff of smoke was pooling around it. I bent over and reached to pull it out, but recoiled in pain immedi-ately, sending it back to the grass. "Damn, it burns if you touch it. The air around it feels cold, though. It's like—oh, God."

Thunk. Clink.

There were ice needles landing all over the place, arcing from over the castle wall in front of us and landing in the dirt or shattering against stone, and airy wisps of vapor trailed from them. Maya took off toward the front gate, presumably to take him on again. When I tried to stop her, another *thunk* rang out, this time from my left forearm, right near the elbow. I yowled as the needle froze the flesh and blood around it. The pain felt real, far more real than anything else I'd experienced. I tried to remove it myself, but it was far too sensitive to the touch; my muscle was freezing to it, visibly tugging with every pull of the ice. Zox and I stumbled aside, pressing ourselves to the outer wall for cover.

"Zox, yank it out. This thing's going to freeze my veins shut and it hurts too much for me to do it myself."

"As you say."

Without skipping a heartbeat, he grabbed the icicle and ripped it from my arm, bits of frozen blood and meat still attached to it. I screamed as it parted my flesh, which visibly upset Zox.

"I'm sorry, I didn't mean to harm you. I'm sorry, I can put it back." His head was bowed to me.

"Why the hell would you put it back? It's fine, just . . . please, *God,* warn me next time so I can brace myself. We need to go after Maya."

"Your wound needs tending, shouldn't we let Maya handle things herself?"

"Don't worry, it's still mostly frozen shut so I'm not going to bleed out. It wasn't very big, either. Maya can't handle this by herself, let's go." *God, this hurts though. This hurts way more than it should.*

We ducked down, hugging the wall to avoid the incoming barrage of ice that spanned almost the entire length of our courtyard, and made it to the front gate right after Maya had finished opening it. All three of us ducked down and ran along the forward wall, then peeked around the corner. Sure enough, the mage was standing at the forest's edge, arms raised above his head where I could faintly see mist condensing into small needles through a haze drifting up into the sky. He noticed us peeking around the corner and redirected his volley, forcing us to remain pressed against the wall until the barrage ceased.

By the time we could safely step back out into the open, he was already slipping into the thick, twisting forest. Maya tried to chase him down, but I grabbed the back of her breastplate and held her in place.

"Don't. That's an ambush waiting to happen, with so much for him to hide behind. He's gone for now, and we should collect ourselves inside."

She swatted my hand away and scoffed, storming toward the forest with Vesper drawn. Zox looked at me, to which I responded with a shake of the head before following her.

Luckily, the mage was leaving a trail of blood behind him as he ran through the woods. We had difficulty catching up to Maya, who was charging forward without trying to maintain any cover, but we didn't lose her.

"Maya, he's going to target you if you won't try to use the trees to protect yourself. You're giving him an opening!"

I got nothing in response, but as if taking it upon himself to answer the question, an icicle flew straight at Maya. It was the size of a carrot from my judgement, but it was enough to kill anything it hit. She leapt up and turned sideways to thin her profile, barely dodging the projectile, which blasted through a tree, scattering splinters into the air like terrified toothpicks.

For about a mile and a half, we tailed Maya as she ducked and dodged through the trees. At last, we'd reached the forest's edge and the treeline began to thin—which was both a blessing and a curse.

It was a blessing because our visibility increased, and we were able to see the mage seemingly standing on the flowing river as if that were totally normal. We were also able to see him amassing a flurry of needles above his head again, a swarm of crystal gnats in the distance. Therein lay the curse's nature—we had much less cover, and he was not relenting. There had to have been at least a thousand needles collecting in the air, swirling in mist and haze, if not more.

We ran back into the forest, each ducking behind a tree, waiting for the impending volley.

"We can't let him get away!" She was hesitating for once, but I could see the razor-sharp focus in her eyes hadn't dulled a bit.

Sure enough, a faint whistling sound cut through the air as thousands of needles *thunked* around us, covering the trees and ground in glistening spikes. Dense fog released into the air as they underwent sublimation, billowing all around us. *So it's dry ice, then—that's why it burns. The needles are*

different from the glaciers, so he can control tempera-
ture and composition?

Once the hail ended, Maya ran out to the shore. When Zox and I caught up with her, she'd stopped at the rocky shore, balancing on the point of a jutted rock. Something odd was standing straight up in the middle of the river—almost like a sign of sorts. There was a thick mist over the opposite bank, completely obscuring our vision of what lay beyond, swallowing trees and any secrets they hid from us. From behind it, something between the wind and a whisper seeped through. It sounded like the word 'free'.

"What is that thing?" I asked, squinting at whatever was standing atop the river. Ice formed a tall post rooted at the bottom of the river, water rushing around it, but a box of some kind was at the top.

"I think that's Hadrian's head."

My heart sank. Walking closer to where Maya was, the distortion was less prominent, and I could tell it was in fact Hadrian's head encased in a block of ice; I'd have recognized that braggadocious crown anywhere. I sighed, then said, "Let's go back home for now. There's nothing more we can do." My entire left arm throbbed with each heartbeat.

She turned around and stormed back towards the treeline.

Upon returning to the keep, the three of us were greeted by two black blurs erratically flapping down from the reddening sky. They landed, licking

Maya's face in hopes of getting some fruit. Zox fled at the sight of them, which earned a stiff laugh from both of us.

"Oh, I get it. Come by for food and attention, but not when we're being attacked!" I scolded them upon my approach. The scarred bat flapped his wings in disapproval of my quip.

Maya hadn't said a word since we'd arrived; she'd just been staring forward, eyes glossed over, a slow hand petting the two bats.

Without breaking her hollow, statuesque gaze, she spoke up. "What do you think he wants?"

I shrugged. "Our scrolls, maybe?"

Continuing forward into the hall, she clicked her tongue. "No, something's wrong. He's already got so many, and he wouldn't have brought his here if he cared about them. It's deeper than that. We should take a break for a couple days and sort things out."

I wasn't going to argue with a somber Maya. "That's not a bad idea. I could use a night of actual sleep to let this wound heal." I slowly twisted my forearm, flexing my fingers slowly, hissing at the pain. "Hey, have you ever been hurt here before?"

She looked at my wound, recoiling a little. "No, not really."

"Me neither. What—what do you think happens? I mean, I've never really thought about it before. I mean, what if we die here? We couldn't possibly die in real life, could we?"

"I don't know. That seems impossible."

"Then what if we can't come back here if we die? How would we ever see each other again? I don't know who you are."

"You know I don't like talking about that," she said, sighing. "We agreed not to talk about it, Reza."

I rubbed at my temples. "Right. Yeah, sorry. I'm just freaked out by all of this. In two nights, we'll meet here at the usual time?"

"Sure. Let's head up to bed."

As we walked back into the castle, I noticed Zox had already curled up beside a tree near where we'd fought the mage.

"Hey, Zox. What're you doing? Come sleep inside the castle."

He looked up at me, and though he was a good distance away, I saw his eyes light up like candles in the dying light. He caught up with us, stopping on his way in to rest a hand on my shoulder.

"Thank you, Reza," he said with something like a smile before shifting his attention to the grand interior of our home. "This place is marvelous. Absolutely stunning."

"Thanks. Someday, I'll take you around and go over some of the history," I told him, noting Maya had gone straight upstairs. "But not today—I should follow her. If you go to the left and follow the hall, there's a guest bedroom before the dining hall. Make yourself at home. We'll be awake in two days."

"Humans sleep a lot."

"So do bears."

"Oh, this is where I should laugh!" He exclaimed with sudden fervor, grunting awkwardly. It wasn't even close, but it sounded better than the previous abominations.

"Your timing is better! Next time, don't announce it beforehand. It won't be long now before you get the technique down. See you later, Zox."

I found Maya sitting on the bed, eyes full of thought. *I've never seen her like this before.*

"You okay?"

She snapped out of her daydream, warmth returning to her face. "Yeah, don't worry about it. I'm sure everything will be fine. Let's get out of here and take a little reverse vacation, huh?"

"Yeah." I climbed into bed, watching sunset through dark, pinkish windows. "By the way, I have a question."

"What's up?"

"Do you think Zox is a real person, like us?"

"Well, I guess I haven't thought about that. I feel like he can't be a real person. He's so weird."

"That's a good point. Well, whatever—let's go to bed." I turned to her.

She's already asleep.

With a kiss on the cheek, I whispered goodnight to her and pulled the yellow crystal, like a lemon geode, out from under my pillow. Once it clicked into the lock above our bed, a low hum washed over the keep grounds as a protective barrier surrounded our castle—the only defense available when we're gone. It blanketed the sky, swallowing us in an aurora like a dome of slick oil.

It's really weird, falling asleep in order to wake up. One minute, the sun's going down, my eyes are closed and I'm thinking, the next—

My eyes opened to darkness, and I stretched across an empty bed. I checked the alarm clock on my nightstand: 4:52 a.m.

The next, I'm sitting in a dark room, waiting for sunset to come again.

I set my left arm down as leverage to push myself out of bed and pain seared through it, my nerves screaming for help.

My . . . my left arm feels like it's being stabbed. Am I still dreaming?

Free Soda

"I'm sorry, Mrs. Henderson, I need to request today off and see a doctor. There's a severe pain in my left arm and I can barely move it," I groggily explained over the phone, still in bed. With every twitch of the muscle fibers in my forearm, searing pain screamed through weary nerves.

Eventually, though, I had to get up and ready myself to go out. Propping up my left tricep, I tried to walk without letting it swing too much or tense up. There was no sign of an injury where it hurt; not a scratch, bump, bruise or rash to be found. *It's probably all in my head—my subconscious is playing games with me, right? One of those things where you think you're sick, but you aren't? I know I've seen something like that on TV before.*

Driving to the nearest ER with one arm was a nuisance, but far easier than it was to get dressed. After a riveting hour of filling out paperwork, and another dodging coughs while waiting for my name to be called, I was finally taken in by a nurse who promptly checked my temperature, weight, and height, then sat me in a room where even the slightest twitch created an echoing crinkling sound. The doctor took a cursory glance at my arm and found nothing, so I went on another hour-long adventure to have x-rays taken, which revealed nothing of concern. The doctor explained that I'd probably pinched a nerve by sleeping on it strangely and gave me a sling to help with discomfort until it cleared up.

The question was, then: how in the world could that have been a coincidence?

Back at home, I relaxed on my couch flipping between shows on my streaming services with an ice pack soothing the persistent throbbing pain. It helped enough to focus on *The Office* for several hours, zoning out and snacking on potato chips. It'd been such a long time since I'd last killed time in the real world, I'd forgotten how entirely boring it is. Nothing but losing hours to TV and games; I forgot to even eat, most of the day. At one point I somehow managed to drop the remote behind the couch and it took far more effort than it should've to move it.

During any lulls where my attention wasn't sucked into something else, I couldn't stop thinking about my arm. Things had hurt sometimes in the dream world, yeah—but never that bad, and certainly never once I woke up. The only thing that had changed was the appearance of the mage.

Does that mean I can be hurt by other real people? Could Maya hurt me, or even kill me, if she wanted to?

The anxiety ate at me throughout the day; I'd never had to worry about anything like that in the past. I had always been more or less invincible. A warrior unlike any other. *But now. . . .*

I did my best to distract myself from it with just about anything else.

The aura of sheer emptiness was broken by a sharp buzzing sound—my phone was vibrating, which wasn't exactly a common occurrence. I tried to ignore it and resume watching, but it buzzed again. I snatched it with a grunt to see if something important had happened. There were two unread messages:

33% 8:19 PM
Mike
7:25 PM
Jax, come on over to the Golden Monkey for a few drinks. You shouldn't just sleep your life away, man. I know you get all those headaches, but it shouldn't stop you from living.
I gotta take a raincheck. Thanks tho
8:17 PM
I heard you took the day off. Time to cash that raincheck. Meet us at the Golden Monkey, around 9.
You better not try to wiggle out of this one.
8:19 PM
Type a text message
SMS

I sighed, knowing I'd never hear the end of it if I tried to come up with some sad excuse to stay home. Besides, there was something uncomfortable creeping up on the back of my mind as I sat in the empty apartment, trying to find ways to pass the time without deep sleep. It was hard to explain, but it gnawed at me; this sort of splaying unease, this worthlessness of sorts.

After a text back confirming I'd be going, I finished my episode. When it came time to head out, I stared into my closet, pursing my lips. *There's no way in hell I'm putting on work clothes, and I probably can't go out in boxers. . . .*

Gazing at my half-empty wardrobe, I realized there was nothing appropriate to wear because I basically never went out. Most decent clothes looked odd on me anyway, with how lanky I was, and there's no way I would have ever taken the time to go shopping and try things on. Looking good was never my strong point, anyway, starting with my face—I couldn't even grow a beard to hide it. Ultimately, I settled on a pair of jeans and an old black t-shirt, desperately struggling to get around the sling.

Not like I'm looking to impress anyone, anyway.

I arrived at the Golden Monkey, which was some mix of a bar and club—whatever the distinction is between them—a few minutes past nine. Unfortunately, because of how little I went out, I'd forgotten how packed those kinds of places could get.

It was an ocean of flesh; people clearly far too

drunk were pressed up against one another, rocking back and forth, stumbling around to the beat of some washed out pop-rap track. I tried to push through them, as Moses parted the red sea, inching slightly closer to the seated areas where Mike told me they'd be. Terrible singers took the opportunity to belt what few words of the chorus they knew as if it were karaoke, murdering my ears. I finally arrived at the booth, nearly sweating just from trying to push my way through the steaming dance floor. Mike was sitting with a woman I'd never met, and opposite them was Diane, who was sitting alone. She looked nice, almost like she'd come straight from work. I suddenly felt self-conscious about my own appearance, even though I typically don't care.

"I'd forgotten how much I hate these places," I joked, taking the open seat. Diane didn't notice me, because she was on her phone. I would be, too, stuck as a third wheel with Mike and some random lady.

"Hey, buddy! You made it! Damn, what happened to your arm, dude?"

"Nothing cool, just a pinched nerve."

"Ow, sounds annoying. I think this is the first time I've seen you outside of work in like, a year or something crazy. It's a Christmas miracle, both you and Diane came out on the same night. She's like you, lately. Always refuses to do anything fun."

Diane looked up thanks to Mike's ruckus, and broke out of the blank trance she was in. "Hey, Jax! I didn't see you there, sneaky sneaky!"

"I'm not sneaky, you just weren't paying attention," I quipped back, immediately uncertain of whether or not my tone was rude.

"Yeah, sorry, had to check my messages. I didn't see you at work today, is this why?" She pointed at my slung arm, looking concerned.

"Yeah, I was riding my motorcycle with no hands on the freeway and crashed."

"Oh my God, are you okay? That's horrible, you idiot!"

"I'm kidding. It's a pinched nerve. You seriously think I'd do something that interesting?"

"We literally just discussed this, Diane," Mike added with a chuckle as he quickly polished off the remainder of his IPA.

Diane rolled her eyes, dismissing us both with a waving hand. "Well, I'm gonna get a beer. You drinking tonight, Jax?"

"Eh, why not? I might as well get something myself." *Maybe it'll take the edge off.*

We walked up to the bar, and I ordered her an IPA as well as a local stout for myself. She tried to interject, but I was having none of it.

"I get paid to work and spend it on basically nothing. I can pay for your drink, don't worry about it." I could barely hear the words coming out of my own mouth. I had to shout so she could make out what I was saying.

She gave me a stubborn look. "Fine, I'll allow it this one time."

"Hey, did he introduce that woman to you? I literally don't even know her name."

"Nope. He always forgets that we aren't also dating his girlfriends."

I laughed, though it was drowned in the sound of a hundred heartbeats and hollers. "It's super awkward, though. I never know what to say around them."

"Yeah, I know."

Something seemed off about the way she was acting overall. Her mouth may have been forming smiles, but I could see that her eyes were staring through me, and she kept shooting serious looks at her phone. "You okay? How's your brother holding up?"

The smile she was wearing tugged back a little. "Not that great. We're always positive, but Caleb hasn't been responding well to this round of chemo. Hope's not entirely lost, though."

"Of course not. I'm sure he'll pull through, he's a fighter."

Her face lit up a little bit. "Thanks. You know, you're the only one of my friends from high school that still cares enough to ask about him, even though you were never close with him. You're a sweet guy."

I chuckled nervously. "Well, he was always really nice to me. I remember, you'd invite me to parties sometimes and I knew, like, nobody—so I'd be sitting alone with a beer and everyone would go by like I didn't exist . . . except Caleb. He'd stop by, say hi and ask me how I was doing even though everyone else wanted to talk to him. Never knew why, but it always stood out to me. People aren't really like that, you know? I wish they were."

Her jaw clenched a little, and she took a deep breath, but the smile never faded. "Yeah, he's a sweet guy, too. Definitely not many people like him, unfortunately. Oh, our drinks."

We grabbed them and returned to our seats, where Mike was face-down on the table. The girl he was with tugged at his shirt and called his name to no avail.

"Is he dying?" she asked me, fear in her eyes. "He only had two beers. Does he have a condition or something?"

I was wracked with raucous laughter, bending over as my diaphragm cramped. "Probably. We've been friends since elementary school, and ever since the first time he drank, he's always passed out before his third beer. I've never seen him make it to three in my life. I used to carry him home." Slowly I grew somber once more. "He's fine, I'll help him. Have you two been dating a while?"

"I just met him on Tinder earlier today. He should warn girls about this in his bio." She looked annoyed, scoffing and climbing over him to get out, then disappeared into the sea of bodies pulsating beneath strobe lights and terrible music.

"She didn't give a crap about him," Diane hissed, trying to sit Mike up. "Mike, you alive?" He groaned a little, giving her a stupid grin and chortling before passing back out. Diane rolled her eyes and checked her phone again.

"Oh. Sorry, I have to go." She climbed past Mike, grabbing her belongings.

"Is everything okay?"

"I . . . need to go. Sorry to leave you with Mike like this." She too disappeared into the undulating waves of sweaty, rhythmic meat.

I sighed deeply, staring at Mike passed out in front of two empty beer cans, then slammed my beer and walked up to the bar.

"What can I get you?" the bartender asked.

"Did Mike Fonsetti close out his tab?"

"I'm not really supposed to talk about other people's info," he said, looking apologetic.

"He's out of commission. Can you just check so I can pay if he left it open?"

After a confused look and fiddling with a monitor, he returned. "It's closed. Looks like only ordered two beers, though. Is he okay?"

"He'll be fine, he's just an embarrassment to himself. Is there a way out besides the front? I need to drag him home, but there's no way I can make it through that crowd."

He looked behind him, pointing to a hallway. "I'm not supposed to do this, but there's an employee exit in the back for taking trash out and stuff. You can get out that way."

"Perfect. Fitting, too," I said, pointing at him. "Thank you."

I paid my tab with a generous tip, then threw Mike's arm around my shoulder and assisted him to the car. Getting him seated and buckled up was a struggle with one arm, but I somehow managed, albeit with a little roughness.

The drive home was quiet and quick, since most people are either asleep or still out at 11pm. I got to Mike's place, somehow dragged him up the front stairs, into an elevator, then used his keys and dragged him into his apartment. I accidentally dropped him on the floor, my arm was so tired. As I sat there, waiting to regain my strength and taking labored breaths, I gave the front door a longing look.

Can I just leave him here? Hmm....

My left arm was throbbing, and my right was exhausted from carrying him so much—Mike's always been skinny, but the same goes for me.

Ah, screw it.

I grabbed a pillow and blanket from his bedroom, tucking the former under his head and the latter over his body. A can of orange soda from his fridge served as payment, and I returned home, slumping into my own bed with a sigh of exhaustion. I was tired, but falling asleep was difficult without the pills I usually took—of course, I couldn't take them, fearing I'd end up in the dream world if I weren't careful with the timing and depth of my sleep.

Okay, stop thinking. If I don't think about anything, I should fall asleep.

. . .

. . .

. . .

Damn it, I have to concentrate to think about

nothing! How am I supposed to fall asleep like this? Ugh, now I'm getting hungry. Why wasn't I hungry earlier? . . . I wonder if lemurs get sad when they see their friends jump off a cliff, and that's why they follow them. Wait, stop thinking about random things!

I rubbed my eyes, groaning with exasperation; lying at the mercy of my racing mind.

Subtle Cues

I awoke in a room filled with sunlight, achy and stiff; my pillow was damp, and my mouth bone-dry. After a sip of water, I squinted at my phone, slow thumbs plinking at its screen:

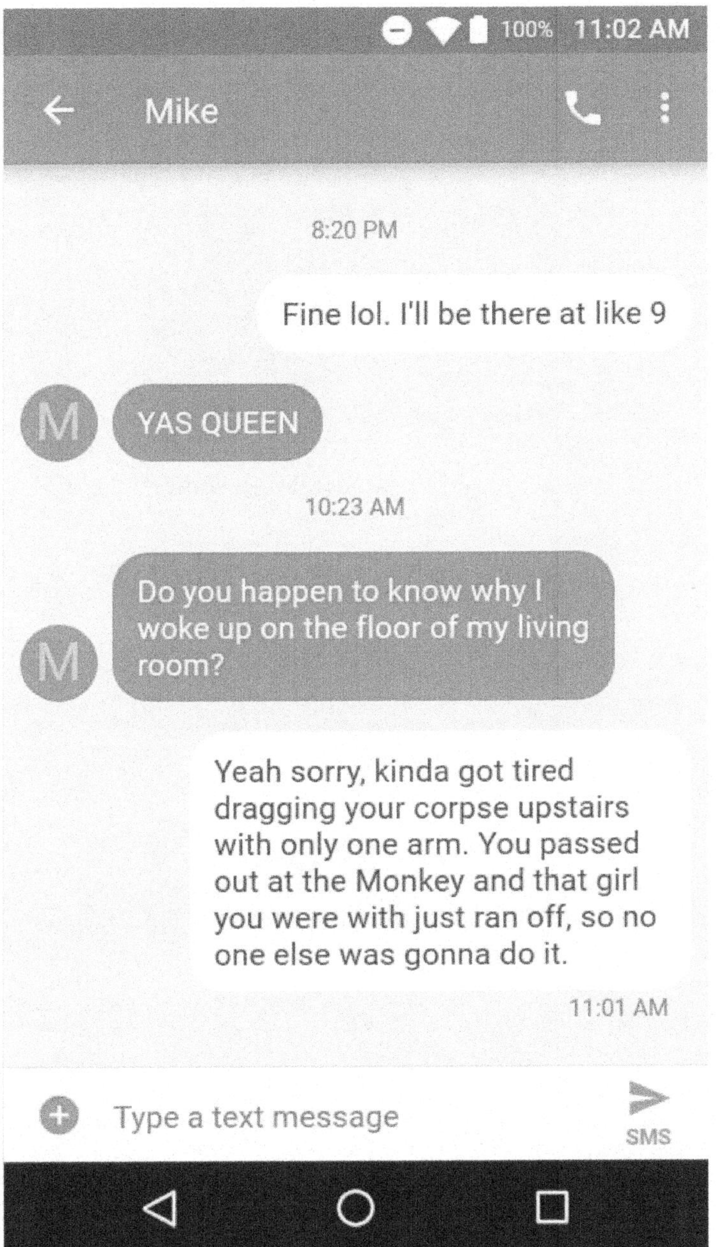
Mike
8:20 PM
Fine lol. I'll be there at like 9
YAS QUEEN
10:23 AM
Do you happen to know why I woke up on the floor of my living room?
Yeah sorry, kinda got tired dragging your corpse upstairs with only one arm. You passed out at the Monkey and that girl you were with just ran off, so no one else was gonna do it.
11:01 AM
Type a text message
SMS

99% 11:11 AM
Mike
11:02 AM
Oh. Thanks? Sorry I passed out so fast though. Damn it, I even got Diane to come out on the same night as you. . .you're both so antisocial. Did you guys hit it off at all?
Not really, just talked some. Nothing special.
Well that's lame as shit. Also did you steal a Fanta??
Wtf do you keep an inventory of your soda?
Thief. Anyway, let me make up for last night. Lunch, maybe? Pizziori at 4?
Ah fuck it, I love pizza
11:11 AM
Type a text message
SMS

I tossed my phone aside and sank back into bed, performing my best imitation of sleep. After several hours of tossing and turning, I couldn't delay getting ready any longer and struggled into the same pair of jeans from my bar adventure, tripping as I fumbled with tennis shoes.

Walking to Pizziori rather than driving, I decided, would make up for any missed workouts due to my arm. *A whole ten minutes of brisk walking should be grueling enough to justify eating an entire pizza, right?*

On my way out the door, I decided to google the weather. It was—of course—cold, and there was no way in hell I would get a sweater on.

A frigid gust of air cut right through me immediately. Oddly enough, despite the wind chill, a faint warmth kissed my skin; the sun wasn't slacking despite its distance from Earth, and the sky was a perfect light blue without even a cloud in sight. It was enough to make the walk enjoyable aside from occasional icy gusts.

Pizziori sat at the end of Brook Avenue, which I was turning onto from Broad Street—the road I lived on. As I rounded the corner, my eyes shifted down to my phone to check the time.

Papers fluttered in the air and ice cubes rained down on me as I slammed into the concrete. Regaining my senses, I started to pick the papers up and apologize profusely for my lack of attentiveness.

"Don't worry about it, Jax."

I looked up and, to my surprise, Diane was the

one I'd slammed into.

"Oh, I'm so sorry, Diane! I didn't see you, it's like you snuck up on me," I said with a light chuckle, gathering a few flyers and pictures into a manila folder—which I, unfortunately, didn't think to look at closely.

"*It's not sneakiness, you just weren't paying attention.* Sound familiar?"

I ruffled the back of my head. "You got me there. It was even because of my phone...."

My voice trailed off as our gazes met and I saw dark circles under her eyes, which were reddened and slightly swollen. It looked like she'd put some makeup on in an attempt to conceal it.

"Diane, are you okay?"

"Yeah. I didn't sleep well last night, but it's no big deal. Are *you* okay? You bumped that injured arm into me."

I looked down at my slung arm and finally noticed the dull throb. "It's fine, just stings a little bit. Don't worry, it was my fault for running into you anyway."

She took the papers from me and gathered up several more from the ground. "What'd you say happened to your arm again?"

"Well, the doctor said it's a pinched nerve. I woke up with it yesterday, nothing happened."

"Like, your elbow? A nerve pinched near the joint?"

"Not exactly, it's right here. Kind of my upper forearm."

She squinted at me as I pointed to the pain's epicenter. "That's a really weird place to pinch a nerve. You sure something else didn't happen?"

"Sorry, I forgot to mention the knife fight."

"No, seriously. Aren't pinched nerves exactly what they sound like? Nerves that get pinched. There's no joint pinching in your forearm."

My eyes shifted to the side. "I guess I have pinch-y forearms? Don't ask me, I'm not a doctor.

A single eyebrow raised on her forehead. "Right . . . well, whatever. I should get going, Mike is waiting for me at Pizziori."

"Oh, I'm actually headed there too! Why were you walking in the opposite direction?"

She held up her smartphone. "I thought I left it at the printing shop but it's literally in my hand. Guess that's what I get for not sleeping at all."

I stood up and held my useful arm out. "Let's get going before Mike starts blowing up our phones."

She slapped it aside and returned to her feet. "A cripple isn't going to help me stand up."

"Well that's rude. I'm not *crippled,* unless crippling debt counts. Man, I wish I could've filed for disability after my student loans first came in."

She rolled her eyes as we started walking toward the restaurant. I tried to peek at the papers she was holding but couldn't get a good look. *Damn, I should've taken the opportunity to snoop when I was picking them up.*

"What's all this stuff you printed?" I asked

sheepishly, admitting failure to myself.

"Oh, it's just some stuff for work. You know, charts and graphs, traffic analysis." She hugged the documents closer to her.

"I don't mean to sound creepy, but I thought I saw some pictures."

"Oh, yeah there are a few, like, advertisement templates I'm working on."

"Can I see?"

"No. Sorry, I don't mean to sound rude, it's just a work in progress, you know? Temporary stuff and I don't want anyone to see it before I finish up." She tucked them into her bag.

"Oh, okay, yeah. Well, I'm sure you'll do a great job."

I held the door to Pizziori open for her, and we found Mike alone in a booth. Pizziori wasn't *fancy*, but it was a sleek, modern restaurant with clean tile, crisp lighting and a nice, simple color scheme: deep, polished black contrasting luminous white.

"Took you guys long enough." Mike sneered as we sat down.

Diane held her hand out in his face. "Calm yourself, we're only five minutes late. You'll live."

"Jeez, Diane. You look like crap, are you okay? I'm too delicate to be around germs."

"Excuse me? Wow. Can you still taste food with that silver tongue?"

"Yes."

She scoffed. "I'm starting to understand why you've got a new girlfriend every week."

I picked up a menu and browsed the options even though I already knew what was good. "I'm actually kinda surprised you didn't bring another girl with you."

He stared at his menu, using it to shield his face. "Well, I did...."

I raised an eyebrow at the pasta selection. "And?"

"She bailed."

Diane laughed for the first time since I'd bumped into her, and Mike threw his menu down. "Why's that *funny*? It's a travesty!"

A server interrupted us, and we each placed an order. I got a thin crust pizza with Daiya, Portobello mushrooms, basil and garlic aioli.

"What the hell is Daiya?" Mike asked, making a disgusted face.

"It's a cheese alternative."

Diane cocked her head at me. "Why not get real cheese?"

"Oh, I'm lactose intolerant. Can't eat dairy. Well, I mean, I could but it would destroy me."

"Why didn't you ever tell me that?" Mike asked. "I could've accidentally given you something with milk in it."

"It's not fatal or anything. Anyway, you can thank Diane for waking up on the floor. She ran away and I had to carry you by myself."

Mike frowned at her, but her gaze was lost in the depths of a saltshaker. After a few moments, she snapped back to reality. "Oh, sorry. Did I miss something?"

Mike blew a raspberry at her and turned to the kitchen. "I'm so hungry, it's not even funny."

Thankfully, the food came out quickly—that's probably my favorite thing about Pizziori. The smell of freshly baked dough and garlic crept over to our table and I began to salivate before the pizza even came out.

Amidst devouring our food, Mike decided to try and talk through mouthfuls of pasta. "Hey, Jax. You never told me why the boss called you into her office a few weeks ago."

I dropped my slice of pizza onto the table and leaned back, groaning. "You're so persistent. I thought you'd forgotten by now."

"Well?"

"Can't we talk some other time when our mouths *don't* have food in them?"

"Stop trying to avoid the question."

I sighed, poking a mushroom that had fallen onto the table. "She had a few things to nitpick about my performance. Said that I wasn't keeping up with quota every week and my desk needs to be tidier. She's not wrong, I do get a little lazy here and there with how boring and pointless the work is. It's just so hard to motivate yourself when what you're doing is meaningless, you know? Like, all I do is cold call people that hate me and try to trick them into buying actual garbage."

"Amen to that. I think we all slack off here and there, too—sucks that she singled you out on it though, you need to be careful from now on," Diane chimed in while twirling another bite of her spaghetti.

"I've tightened up. Haven't let myself fall behind on quota since then, and I keep the cubicle clean. Can't really afford to lose this job, no idea what else I could do."

We finished the rest of our meal in silence, much to my relief. Changing the subject became much easier.

"You guys want to go anywhere else?" I asked, faking enthusiasm. I hear people like that.

"I'd be down to play some pool," Diane suggested. "Sharktop has good bar snacks, too."

"Sounds good to me. Mike, you in?"

He took a deep breath, leaning back and turning away from us. "Oh, you know . . . I have some, uh, plans to do . . . stuff and shit. Can't make it, looks like you two have to go alone."

I closed my eyes and hung my head down. *Mike, that was the worst attempt at being discrete I've ever seen.*

We paid our bills and Mike split off from us, waving and giving us a stupid grin.

"Does he think I'm an idiot?" Diane asked, still smiling and waving back.

I sighed. "No. It's him."

We walked into Sharktop, which was in an adjacent building complex, and claimed a table for ourselves. Diane dropped her bag by a leg and we walked over to the bar.

"Jax, you want a pretzel? I'm gonna get a plain one, but they have flavors and stuff."

I motioned to the bartender. "Excuse me. Two plain pretzels, please. Leave the tab open."

She glared at me. "You *are* sneaky."

I gave her a goofy smile and waited for the pretzels while she prepped our table for play. I got back just as she finished racking the billiard balls, handing her a piping hot twist.

"Thanks. You can go first—I know you'll need a head-start," she said with a wink.

I sneered at her and grabbed a pool stick from the racks behind me. Diane had one hand over her mouth and several other bystanders watched as I lined up my first shot, whispering amongst themselves. Right before I could take it, Diane ran up and stopped me, laughing so hard I saw tears glistening in her eyes.

"Oh my God, Jax . . . you're holding it backwards, sweetie." The rest of the people nearby joined in with her laughter once she corrected me.

"This end has a rubber bumper on it! I thought that was what you hit the ball with!"

My protests only earned more laughter from the crowd, and Diane was laughing so hard that she had to bend over and rest on the table to keep from falling over. Amidst the fit, she accidentally kicked her bag over and several papers fell out. This time, I saw them.

Diane saw that I saw, immediately scrambling to push them into her bag. The laughter and light in her eyes faded.

"I should go, I don't know why I'm out so late on a work night. Sorry for bailing on you."

She stormed out the door before I could even say anything in response. Her pretzel was sitting on the table's edge, no longer steaming, and I sat there blinking at it for a few moments.

"Struggling tonight, huh?" the bartender asked, sliding my card and receipt over. I silently scribbled a signature on the check and ran out of Sharktop holding both of our pretzels, feeling eyes on my back.

I didn't have to go far to find her; she was sitting on a bench not even a block up the road, face buried in her palms. As I approached, I heard sniffling, and she tried to wipe her eyes clean. She didn't move when I sat down beside her, staring forward blankly; a statue as hollow as the night.

"Is this why your eyes have been red all day?" I asked, breath fogging against the light of a sole streetlamp that hummed steadily.

She didn't say anything but nodded ever so slightly.

"I saw one of the pages you printed out. Well, I didn't see it very clearly, but got the gist of it."

"I shouldn't have gone out tonight. I thought it might help me forget for a little while," she said, closing her eyes. A thin trail glistened down her cheek, depressing a ravine of peach fuzz backlit by the buzzing streetlamp. "He wants to help plan what the memorial service will be like."

"Memorial? Oh, God. . . ."

"We thought it was in remission, but nothing's worked. No experimental treatments, no ungodly amount of chemo.

I drew a deep breath and sank my face into hands I didn't even realize were trembling.

"I convinced myself that he'd make it, you know? I don't think I ever convinced *him*, but I convinced myself. I—I'm not ready to lose him yet. I know that's selfish, with all his suffering, but. . . ."

"It's not selfish to care about someone."

"It can be."

"Diane, you're not hurting him in any way. It would be selfish to blame him or be angry at him for it. You care, and because you care so much, you're afraid to let him go. That's what he needs right now, to see how much love there is for him. I wish someone cared about me like that. He's lucky to have you, so don't doubt yourself.

She turned to me, her lips hinting at a smile, then looked back down.

"I'm sorry, Diane. I can't even imagine what you're going through right now. Life is so cruel, sometimes. I wish we could all live in a dream, where things like this don't happen."

"That sounds nice. Somewhere where we have the power, instead of being powerless."

Watching her in the wan light, old suspicions surfaced. The note Maya left on my desk. Conspiracies I suddenly wanted to be true. I sighed, sinking back down into the bench and blowing another foggy breath into the night. "You want to know a secret?"

"No."

"Too bad. I know how to hold a pool stick."

She scoffed at me. "Yeah, because I showed you."

"No, I'm serious! I thought it'd be funny if I did something stupid, and I could tell you needed a laugh. I'm not a *total* moron, it's pretty clear how you're meant to hold the stick. It was so hard to jam the fat end between my fingers."

She was smiling a little more visibly, now. "You've always cared more than other people do, picking up on little things."

"Speaking of which, you left this at Sharktop." I handed her a pretzel, though it was pretty cold by then.

She looked at it and giggled, reaching out to accept. Her fingers brushed mine and wrapped around them. I stared at the pretzel for several seconds, unsure of what I'd find if I searched out her gaze. Our eyes locked for what felt like an eternity, and I could see all the pain, the hopeless sorrow in hers. She leaned forward and I froze, so she pushed in further, until our lips touched. She kissed just like Maya did. *They're so soft and warm. Is that mint? My God, this is incredible. It feels like I'm in a dream.*

Jerking back, she shook her head. "I'm sorry. I'm so sorry. I'm broken and I used you to feel better . . . I shouldn't have done that." She stood up and stormed off, squeezing her bag to prevent the papers from flying out. I sat there, frozen, staring at the ground.

She was already gone by the time I found it in myself to speak up.

"Please stay," I whispered to concrete and fog. Only the streetlight bothered to respond.

Jade and Gold

Thoughts swirled through my mind like the frozen dinner spinning around and around before me. *Does she hate me now? I hope she doesn't regret that. Should I? Did I just cheat on Maya, or did I find her? Why did I bring these pretzels all the way back home?*

The microwave's timer buzzed, snapping me out of a trance; it might have run all night if not for it. *It doesn't matter right now, I have bigger things to worry about.*

After eating the TV dinner, I gulped a sleeping pill down with some water, tossed the cup into the trash, then shuffled upstairs and collapsed into bed. *Oh, I didn't even brush my teeth. Whatever....*

When next I opened my eyes, soft sunlight washed over me, gently drifting in through fluttering draperies. I sat up, stretching and cracking my back with a groan of relief. Light cast shadows across my rippling muscle, making it stand out even more, and I flexed my arms. *Huh. The pain is gone. No damage either, only a scar where the wound was.*

A small scrap of parchment lay on my desk, which I read while stretching.

Out for a walk.
Look for bats.

I crumpled and tossed it, completely missing a wastebasket. *Boy, don't get too endearing.*

Flowers on our balcony danced to the tune of a lovely summer gale that hugged me with coolness as I scanned the courtyard for Maya. Two black masses were bouncing around erratically near the main gate. *I hope she's not trying to leave right now.*

Glancing toward the bed, I confirmed that the barrier was still set in place before gearing up and walking over to the main gate. Both glaciers were shrunk and sweating under the sun, and a thin stream trickled downhill from the one closest to the castle, fattening it. *That's going to fall over soon and make one hell of a mess.*

"Maya! You going somewhere?" I called out

once I'd passed Lake Augr.

She stuck a hand out at me and flicked at the air. "I'm just out for a walk. It's a nice day. Oh, your arm! It's healed!"

I held it out, letting her run up to ooh and ahh over the shiny, pinkish patch of skin. "Yep, it seems wounds clear up quickly here. Be careful, though. In real life, I—"

Her face hardened like stone, and she turned away from me.

"Right, sorry. I thought . . . never mind." I took a deep breath and looked around for something to change the subject with.

The two bats were flapping overhead, occasionally bumping into the barrier and screeching. Even from thirty feet in the air, I could feel the wind of wingbeats blowing down on me.

"Looks like they're struggling a little," I joked, watching them bump against what nearly looked like nothing.

Maya was also looking to the sky but didn't seem to be following the bats. "It *is* invisible. They're probably freaking out."

"Yeah. Where's Zox?"

"Sleeping, I think. Bears really do sleep a lot."

"Makes sense, I guess. You okay?"

She shook her head like a dog fresh out of

water. "Yeah. Yeah, sorry. Anyway, I gave our little wizard issue some thought, and there's really only one way we can deal with him."

I bit back a comment on her choice of descriptor. "Lay it on me."

"Hear me out: we need magic. That guy's on a completely different level than us, and we can't fight him with swords alone. We need range and firepower."

My brows knitted together. "I thought we agreed not to do any of that."

"Yeah, well, whoever is out there doesn't give a crap about your feelings, does he? This is the only way to move forward," she snapped back.

I held my hands up in surrender. "Okay, okay. Yeah, that's a good idea. Sounds kinda fun, too, honestly. If he's an ice mage, I should be a fire mage and melt his ice! Checkmate."

She rolled her eyes at me. "It doesn't matter what it is, as long as it's strong. I'm still deciding what I'd like to have as a power. If you want fire, try making fire."

I widened my stance and held my hand out, facing upward, fingers curled slightly. Staring at it intently, I imagined searing, crackling fire swirling around it, raging hot flames licking at the air. A fire hotter than the sun that could melt any ice in milliseconds.

Nothing happened.

"I have no idea what I'm doing. I've never really gotten anything in here without sketching or planning it first."

She sighed, looking to the sky again. "Yeah, we've been doing this for a while now without any kind of magic, so there's a chance we can't. It feels natural to forge a sword, but I don't know how to go about poofing things out of thin air."

I kept staring at my hand, squatting a little and groaning like a cartoon character trying to charge up power. Not even a spark strayed from my pathetic palm.

"Well this is going swimmingly, isn't it?" I flexed my fingers several times before clenching a fist. "You said you've been thinking. Have you tried at all?"

"Yeah. Out of curiosity, I tried making ice, but I couldn't get it. I don't really know what the trick is."

"Maybe it's something we have to plan out better before we can use it here?"

"I doubt that matters at this point. Damn, we shouldn't have made that stupid rule, anyway. Magic is cool."

"Yeah, but a lot more complicated if it isn't

completely overpowered." I looked around, hoping for some sort of inspiration, taking a deep breath to clear my mind, and found a distraction instead; Zox was licking the glacier lodged in the ground.

"Uh, I don't know if that's a great idea, buddy. We have water you can drink, if you're thirsty. . . ." I was trying not to laugh at him.

"It's so cold and fresh, though. The purest water I've ever tasted." His tongue continued to flicker across its light blue surface, though his eyes were avoiding mine in shame.

"Okay, but if that stuff makes you sick, I don't want to hear about it. God knows what that guy makes it out of."

Zox peeled his head away from the ice for a moment, turning to me. "I was thinking about that, actually. I think it's safe to drink this water because it's the same water that rains down from the sky."

"I mean, all water is the same, Zox." Maya giggled a little.

"No, I'm saying that it's the same as rain. It tastes like the air in a storm. I suspect he pulls water from the air, and that's what the mist around him is. He could probably use a lake or river too, if one was nearby, and become even stronger."

I stroked at my chin. "That would explain why he seemed so strong when we chased him. He had the whole river to fuel him. I think you may be right, Zox. Clever thinking."

"Sorry."

I gave him a blank look. "Sorry? For what?"

"You praised me."

"Why would you apologize for praise?"

"Oh, I meant 'thank you'. I get them mixed up sometimes. Sorry."

Maya ignored him and picked up a jagged rock, staring intently at it for what felt like an hour. "Oh! Look, look, look!"

To my surprise, and hers, it finally bobbled a little. She lightened her stance and took a deep breath before resuming. Slowly, it began to stretch out and smooth until it was a perfect sphere.

"That was incredible!" I said. "Can you shoot it or something? Maybe reshape it into a weapon?"

She held it out, furrowed her brow, and slowly turned the rock into a perfect arrowhead. In the blink of an eye, it was gone, and I heard a cracking sound behind me. A tree had splintered, the arrow passing right through it.

"As if you weren't scary enough. . . ." I muttered under my breath.

"What was that?" She had another stone arrow pointing at me.

I screamed and threw my arms into the air.

"No! Don't shoot!"

Her face relaxed and she giggled, lowering the arrow. "You try, now. This is really fun. I wonder what else I can control."

Zox came running up to us in a panic. "Are we under siege? Someone shot at a tree by the castle!" He was looking around wildly, crouched. "Do I need to stand still again?"

"No, don't do that—it was Maya. We're trying to work on new ways to fight back against the ice mage, and she's controlling stone now. It's my turn!"

I picked up a rock, centering it in my palm. Concentrating with all my might, vision narrowing to nothing but the stone, I envisioned it shifting and turning into a shuriken sharper than steel.

Yet again, nothing happened.

"You can always just throw the rocks," Maya quipped at me with a wink.

I growled at her, attempting to morph it once more and failing. "Why can't I change it? This is ridiculous. How do you make it work?"

She lifted a rock into the air without even bending over to pick it up, freely transforming it as it approached her hand. "I guess I'm a natural. I don't really think about it at all. Don't worry, baby Reza, I'll protect you in battle."

Casting the stone aside, I stormed off toward

the armory. Maya's laughter rang through the castle grounds, fading as I walked, but Zox followed me. I sat down on the tower's front steps, staring at the tree with a hole blown through it, scoffing. *I don't need magic to be a strong fighter. I'll use swordplay—real skill—to take the mage down! Damn, it looks so cool, though.*

Zox sat beside me, still clad in the same worn-out, twisted armor he'd shown up at the main gate wearing. "Do not give in, Reza. I believe you will find strength, even if it seems impossible right now."

I let out a sarcastic chuckle. "Yeah, maybe. Thanks. Pretty sad that you're more encouraging than she is."

"She believes it too, I think, despite her words. Perhaps in some way, it's how she motivates you."

"Doesn't suck any less. She's seemed . . . off, lately. Distant, like she's not really here." *Like she has something weighing on her mind.*

"You can always ask her."

I peeked at her, a flurry of sharpened stones spinning around her body. "Yeah, right. Before she'd just brush me off, but now she'd turn me into Swiss cheese."

"Swiss cheese?"

"Yeah, like—nevermind. Inside joke. Anyway,

can you do anything like that?"

"I don't know, I haven't tried." He picked up a small stone, giving it an odd look before enclosing it in his fist. When he unfurled his fingers, a little, grey bear cub figurine greeted me. "It appears I can. I don't think I could weaponize the stone, personally. I wouldn't want to."

I squinted at it, sighing deeply with defeat. "This place is supposed to be where I'm feared, not the weakest around. Whatever."

"I'm sorry, should I not have changed the rock?"

"That's kinda condescending, Zox."

"Oh. I apologize." He forced out a laugh-growl again.

"I guess that could've been a nervous laugh. You're getting closer, at least. I think." I stood up and walked into the fire-lit dimness of the armory's interior, figuring that, if nothing else, I'd practice my swordsmanship—we had a room tucked behind the forge for testing out new weapons.

Twirling, dancing, I hacked at the straw target, ducking and weaving through imaginary counterattacks. As time went on, my grace abandoned me, and I hacked at the post with all my strength, splinters and bits of hay flying through the air as I reduced it to nothing but a distant memory of itself. Somnior looked strange in the light of a torch, the orange flames clashing with its gold and jade.

Attacking the post with brutish, sluggish swings wasn't good enough for me, and I paused, dropping Somnior to my side, turning to the next dummy. *I can hit the damn thing as hard as I want, but I'll still get killed if I fight that mage one on one. What would I do if we were fighting, and I couldn't close in? Throw my damn sword at him? There has to be something I can do.*

I tried to imagine fire, ice, and rock, anything at all really, but nothing in the room stirred. I imagined the post exploding, but still, only the air from my lungs sprung forth, sharp and heavy. *If that were the Mage, I'd be dead right now unless Maya saved me. This is supposed to be my world. My escape.*

I sat on the stone floor, crossed my legs, closed my eyes, and breathed deep. In, and out. In . . . and out. Inhale the fresh and new, exhale the bitterness and anger. The negativity washed away, but something else took its place.

Memories of the 2001 Chinese New Year festival flashed through my mind. I was a child then, clinging to Mom's hand as we shoved through packed crowds to get a better view of the dragon kites sailing through the night sky, glowing, whipping in the wind. Lanterns were like little stars overhead, shrinking away towards the heavens to go home.

Why am I remembering this? No, stop. Stop.

The food was incredible, the dresses were vibrant and beautiful, and everyone was having a wonderful time. Mom was white, and even though you probably couldn't have guessed it by looking at her, she loved the culture. Ironically, Dad was born in China, and far too busy to bother with such frivolities as festivals. He was probably working on something, at home or in the office. It was the first year she'd brought me with her, since I was old enough to stay nearby. I remember having fun; feeling genuine, unadulterated excitement and awe for everything around me. Entranced by the world. When was the last time I'd felt like that?

Please stop.

She was wearing these beautiful gold and jade dragon-head earrings, passed down to her from my grandmother. Passed down through five generations, she'd told me—or was it ten? I couldn't remember. They were so beautiful in the quiet lantern-light; I could still picture them as if they were in front of me . . . they were clearer in my mind than her face.

"Stop!" The word was meant to be a thought,

but my voice echoed hard through the tower's stone walls.

I opened my eyes, glancing toward the stairway. No one came. With a deep breath, I turned back to the post and found two jade and gold dragons dangling in front of me.

Mom?

One of them lunged out and nipped me. As my eyes wandered, it became clear that they were certainly not earrings. Somnior's sculpted crossguards were three times their normal length, bobbing and wriggling in midair, stretching forward from the handle. They looked like gold snakes with dragon heads being charmed by a flute; despite their increasing length, the rest of my sword was not shrinking or off-balance.

Of course, it's not her.

My eyes fixated on the dancing gold before me. Out of sheer curiosity, despite my complete shock, I looked up at the post once more. Without imagining anything or trying to picture an end result, the two dragons lurched at an incredible speed, slamming into the post and biting down with their gold teeth. They had enough strength to lift the target straight off the floor, dangling it in midair like an infant.

Huh. Would you look at that? Not really what I

had in mind—not even remotely what I had in mind, honestly—but I can work with it.

I practiced a little more, and slowly, the new sword felt like an extension of my arm. The dragons could serve as a whip, cracking a metal head against the post, or constrict the target for me to finish off. Controlling both at once was a little jarring at first, but getting the hang of it only took several hours.

Once satisfied with my progress, I decided to go out and join Maya in her training. Zox was still sitting on the steps where I'd left him, watching Maya practicing manipulation on wood now. I stopped next to him, and he looked up at me with a fuzzy smile.

"It seems you've figured it out, Reza."

"I have. By the way, if you heard me a yell little a while ago—"

"I heard nothing."

We shared a glance as I passed him, both of us nodding slightly.

Maya giggled as I drew closer to her, a miniature, wooden bat suspended over her head. "Why did you ever say 'no magic' again? This is *so much* fun! Wood is easier to control, though it's way weaker. Aww, don't look sad, Reza. I'm just a natural! You'll grow up big and strong, one day."

Without even unsheathing Somnior, I flung a

dragon to snatch her bat out of the air. She didn't even have time to comprehend the situation by the time the little wooden creature was nothing but splinters; toothpicks in the teeth of my beasts. I heard Zox shudder, not far behind me.

"What the hell was that?" she shouted, ducking a little. "My poor bat! What'd you do to my bat, you monster?"

A smug grin smeared itself across my face, and I let both dragons stretch upward from Somnior and hang in the air above me. "The sword you made clicked with me, I guess. I think I was trying too hard before, rather than feeling for something natural."

She was gawking at them, enraptured by their slight sway. "Looks like you learned a neat trick while I was training. This place is somehow even more awesome than it used to be, now. Sorry if I sounded . . . I dunno, condescending, before. I haven't been in the best mood."

"Yeah, I can tell."

She glared at me, sneering before setting her stones back into the ground and mending the wooden bat.

"Sun's gonna set in an hour or so," I said, looking to the sky. "We should call it a day. So much has changed in so little time, and it feels overwhelming."

"Yeah, you're probably right." She was still focusing almost entirely on the toy bat, dancing it around in front of her. I wanted to make fun of it, but her face was relaxed and she was smiling. *That's what I wanted to see.*

"Let's call it a day," I said, and she agreed.

Zox broke off to his guest bedroom with a wave, and Maya sprinted up the steps to our chambers, leaving me behind. By the time I caught up with her, clothes and armor were already strewn across the room, and she was sitting at the bed's edge.

"Hey, you okay?" I asked after hanging up my chainmail and weapons, sitting beside her. I ran my fingers through her hair, then down her back, and massaged the tense muscles that lined it. She rolled her head down and I moved up to her neck, trying to loosen the knots.

She sighed, closing her eyes. "I just have a lot on my mind. Everything's completely different now. I mean, even us, you know. Who are you, if not Kinghunter?"

"I'm still the man you've known all this time." With a gentle hand, I turned her face toward mine, looking deep into her eyes. There was a familiar pain woven into their blue and gold streaks, softening them. I leaned in and she met me halfway, slowly working her hands around me, kissing with the passion we'd share after a long-awaited victory before our world turned upside-down.

Robes scattered across the room. Her hands in mine, woven like our bodies in the dying glow of sunset, we were one again. I could feel her heart drumming to the beat of pleasure, fixing to burst from her chest. The sound of it drove me mad.

"I love you," I whispered as she lifted her back away from the silk sheets; an arch fit for the most regal landings. She didn't respond, but I didn't care.

From my balcony, I watched the sun melt into a pinkish red on the horizon, like sorbet left out too long. The breeze felt nice on my damp skin.

The note, the sadness in her eyes recently, the way she seems lost in thought so often . . . am I crazy, or could it be true? Could Maya really be Diane? Should I try and force the conversation, or would that ruin what we have?

Or worse, what if I find out I'm wrong?

I sighed, rubbing my face as though I were rinsing it. When I went back inside to kiss Maya goodnight, she was already gone.

Faded Past

I sat up in bed as a glow crept into the bottom few slats of my blinds and was greeted by a rolled blob of fat where my six-pack had just been—a little slap and it bounced. *I hate this place.*

With a scoot and push, I slid out of bed and initiated my morning ritual. After a moment, I paused and looked down at my slung arm—the subtle, dull ache was no longer there, even if I tensed the muscles a bit by curling my fingers, so I unwrapped the sling and let my arm free. It felt a little stiff, but the pain was almost entirely gone. *I can finally put pants on in less than five minutes again! This is good news, though—no lasting damage.*

The parking lot at work was noticeably duller without Diane's bright blue pickup truck in it. With a shrug, I climbed out of the car and sprinted upstairs to avoid being late; that turned out to be a wise decision, because Henderson was near my cubicle, walking forward at a snail's pace.

As I approached, I saw that she was staring intently at her thin silver watch—I could practically see her pupils shift ever so slightly with each second that ticked by, following the second hand like a cat with a laser pointer.

I approached slowly, but she kept her eyes glued to the watch. I could see bags beneath the makeup. "Excuse me."

After a sharp inhale, she finally lowered her wrist, then looked around like she'd woken up in that moment. "Barely on time, Jackson."

"I've been on time every day since you mentioned it to me, ma'am."

"Good. Well, get to work."

"I will, as soon as I can sit down in my cubicle."

"Oh." She glanced down and realized her body was blocking its small entrance. Awkwardly, as if it were her own prerogative, she straightened and slunk forward to the kitchen, checking her watch again.

My squinted eyes followed her until she was out of sight. Mike poked his head up from across the river, beckoning to me.

"What the hell was that all about?"

I shrugged with my hands, then sat down and got to work in case she was monitoring my phone or computer.

After several hours, I decided to take my packed lunch and relax in the break room—normally I'd go to Harry's, but the cost of eating out so much was adding up and choking my wallet. Thoughts churned as I took a bite of a peanut butter sandwich, wondering how I'd approach Diane after last night had turned sour.

Food still in my mouth, I stopped chewing and stared at the peanuts poking out between the slices of wheat bread in my hand. Each chunk was a galaxy in the creamy peanut butter universe, quintillions of atoms in every star, planet and peanut. I took another bite. *I am the almighty Devourer of Worlds.*

I finished the half, slipped the other into a plastic bag, inhaled deeply, and walked over to Diane's cubicle. Crouched a little to not give my presence away immediately, I steadied my breathing, then forced a smile.

"Hey, Diane."

I'd poked out from a surrounding wall, saying the words with a nervous chuckle. All that greeted me was an empty chair and dark monitor.

"Oh." I didn't mean to say anything, but the noise slipped out.

A snicker came from the next cubicle, and Mike stood up, resting his elbows on the divider.

"Aww, you miss her?"

"Would you shut up?" I walked over to his cubicle. "Did she go out for lunch or something?"

He shrugged. "Haven't seen her today."

"Really? She must've called in sick, I guess." *I hope she's not avoiding me.*

"So...."

"What?"

He tilted his head, eyelids fluttering. "How did last night go?"

I averted my gaze from him for a moment. "Alright, I guess. Played some pool, then she went home."

Mike reverted to being uninterested, sighing at me. "You're hopeless."

"Probably."

Mrs. Henderson interrupted our conversation, stepping right up to us. Her curls were hanging a few inches lower than usual, eyes red.

"Is there a party we all missed the invitation for?"

"I'm on my lunch break, Mrs. Henderson. I was going to ask Diane a question but apparently she's out sick."

"Oh. I see." She started and lost a staring contest with Mike's trash can.

I blinked a few times at her. "Are you okay?"

Mrs. Henderson shook her head, inhaling sharply. "Yes. Fine. Just . . . be the best you can be, Jackson. For yourself, if not for the company."

With that, she left the scene brisk as a bee. My eyes were practically popping out of my head at that point, staring into the matte cubicle wall as if it contained an explanation. I found nothing, obviously, and slinked back to my own.

Once Henderson disappeared into her office once more, my phone buzzed:

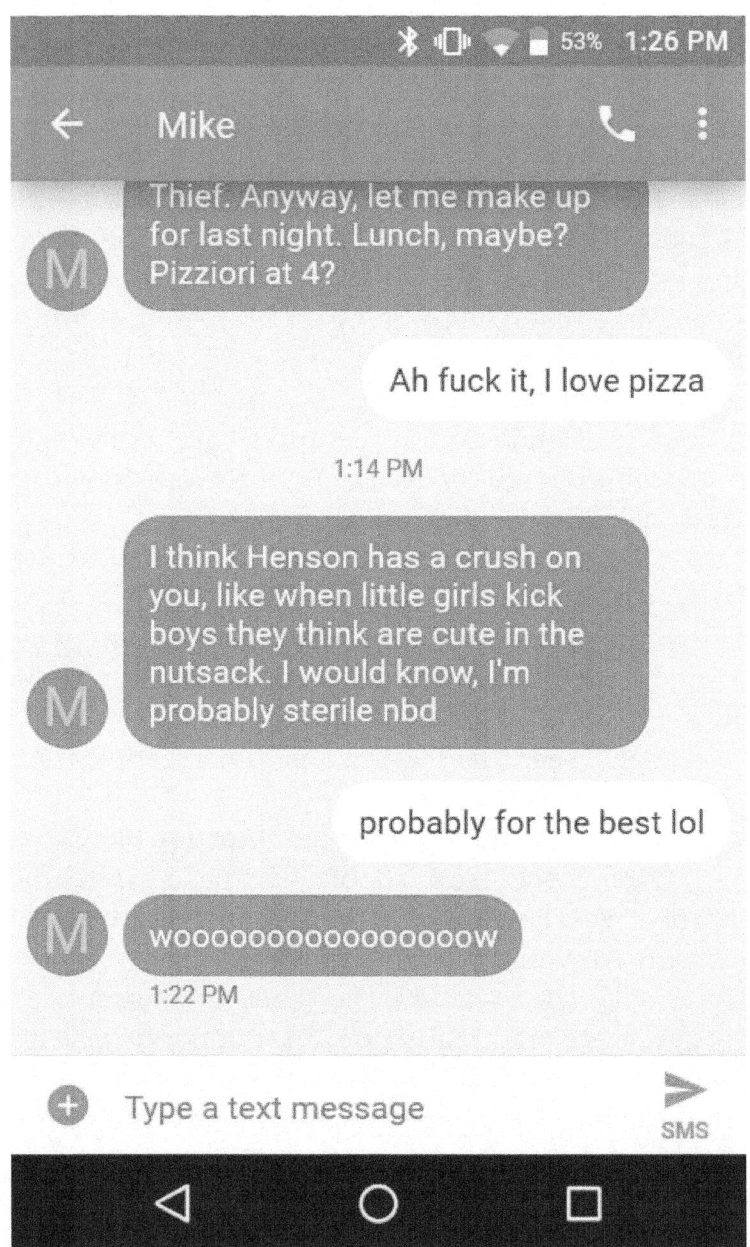
Mike
Thief. Anyway, let me make up for last night. Lunch, maybe? Pizziori at 4?
Ah fuck it, I love pizza
1:14 PM
I think Henson has a crush on you, like when little girls kick boys they think are cute in the nutsack. I would know, I'm probably sterile nbd
probably for the best lol
wooooooooooooooooooow
1:22 PM
Type a text message
SMS

I rolled my eyes and tossed the cell phone aside, swapping it for my work phone; with the enthusiasm of a corpse, I lifted it to my head and punched a number in.

I wish I could become a cat and sleep all day.

"Hey Jax, want to get something to eat?" Mike asked me from several parking spaces over.

I threw my hand up and waved. "Sorry, I need to run to the store, and my head's killing me. Fun day."

Mike raised his eyebrows and shrugged a little. "Well, I can't really argue with that. I think I have one too. You know, I bet if you poured water on her, she'd melt. Ding-dong. . . ."

I exhaled with gusto as Mike fired a finger-gun at his temple. "I don't know how to deal with someone like that, you know? Like, she's being unreasonable and kinda weird, but if I were to point it out, she'd probably fire me. I literally can't do anything. I'm sick of this place."

"You can always look for another job."

That's not going to solve the problem. Who would hire me, anyway? I shook my head lightly and regained focus. "Yeah, maybe I'll do that. Anyway, I should go. See you tomorrow."

"Yep. Hey—if she follows you home, you can call me and I'll bring the artillery." He peeled a sleeve back and flexed. If any muscle in his arm danced, it had the silent grace of a graveyard.

I realized I was hungry on the way home and decided to swing by a grocery store, which is always a dangerous idea, but living life on the edge was my forte. Nature's Mart was a small, friendly store focused on locally sourced foods and interesting alternatives to normal produce. I typically grabbed easy, quick items that taste good, like frozen dinners and dumplings, or chips and other snacks.

In the starch aisle, however, and there was a sale on fresh wide rice noodles. My stomach growled, and a vibrant image of my favorite food as a kid filled my mind: chow fun, a type of stir-fried Chinese street food. I hadn't had it in years, but I also hadn't craved it, and for a little while I stood in the aisle and pondered why it was hitting me so suddenly. I closed my eyes and saw the dragons of my dreams, dripping with jade, and sighed. Call it nostalgia, or longing; whatever it was, I wanted to eat some, and Mom had spoiled me into being unable to settle for frozen or instant variants.

The noodles went into my basket, and I backtracked to the grocery section for some scallions, a tube of ginger paste, firm tofu and bean sprouts. I bounced from aisle to aisle grabbing what I needed from memory, even the sauces: dark soy sauce, sesame oil, and Shaoxing wine.

A solid line-up of frozen dinners and snacks topped off my hand-cart beyond its limits. I found myself carefully balancing the basket, a tightrope act to maintain equilibrium or else suffer the shame of spilling its contents in the middle of a crowded store. My arm seared, and eventually I had to focus more on not letting go of it. *I can't even hold my groceries without getting winded and sore. Oof.*

A bright orange bouquet of single-serving chocolate bars greeted me as I approached the cashier, marked with a hand-drawn sign that read: 'Sale —75% off assorted dark chocolates'. After checking the nutritional labels, I decided to clean the table off. *There's only ten or fifteen bars left. I can't pass up on a deal like this! Besides. . . .*

Carefully slotting the candy into every nook and cranny in my pile of groceries, I checked out in decent time and burst through my front door carrying three large paper bags filled with food, one of which had begun to rip and sag—close call, but there's no way in hell I'd have made two trips. *Who needs a gym membership? That was enough exercise for today. And this week.*

Once my groceries were stuffed into cabinets and the freezer, I began the process; cubing and marinating tofu in soy sauce and sesame oil, with a little bit of sugar, then set it in the fridge while I diced green onions and heated sesame oil in an old, worn-out wok that had been gifted to me by my mom way back when I first moved out. It had been beaten down over the years and it showed, but it still worked like new—if only relationships were as durable. Once the smell of searing hot oil was in the air, I threw in the marinated tofu and tossed them until caramelized and the kitchen smelled of salt and soy, then set them aside and reheated the wok with a little more oil. In a separate pan, I briefly boiled the wide noodles until softened, then threw scallions into the hot wok. They immediately steamed and sizzled, and a pungent, bright green aroma embraced me. Once I added the ginger, I was almost salivating with how fragrant and fresh it smelled. It'd been so long since I'd cooked anything fresh that I'd forgotten how wonderful it can be, even if you're a terrible chef.

The pan was so hot that sweat was accumulating on my brow, but I remembered that if nothing else: the wok has to be blazing hot for a proper stir fry. The noodles went in, then a splash of rice wine, soy sauce and dark soy sauce, sputtering and spitting and furiously bubbling. I swept the pan forward and up, pulling back a bit, watching the food tumble through the air and land back in the pan with a hiss. The tofu went back in, and after a few seconds, it was ready. I turned the stove off and pulled out a paper bowl; subconsciously, I began to sing under my breath.

"Ding-dong, the witch is dead, the witch is dead."

Ding-dong.

"Ding—wait, what?" I dropped my chopsticks and carefully tip-toed to the door, peering into the peephole at an angle as if the person outside would be able to see me through it if I looked straight-on.

Oh. Why . . . ?

"Are you going to let me in, Jax? I could smell whatever you're cooking from the elevator."

I unlocked the door, desperately trying to make my face look like whatever it normally looks like. *What does it normally look like?*

"Hey, Diane. How are—I . . . wasn't really expecting any visitors, you know? Sorry it's a mess, and for the smell. . . ." I glanced toward the trash piling over and unwashed dishes in the sink, some clothes tossed around the room, dust gathering on countertops tables, suddenly hyper-conscious of them though I usually don't even notice. Thankfully, the sizzling aromatics masked any musk that might've scared her away.

"I get it, my place is like this sometimes. Still not as bad as my dorm, nothing will ever be worse than that." She closed her eyes, lifting her nose a little and taking a deep whiff. "It smells delicious. What're you making?"

"Oh, well, I was just making myself a dumb little dinner."

"Damn, you can cook?"

"Uh, not really, I mean I'm not very good at it. Once in a while I make something easy, usually it's easy, instant stuff."

"Well it smells amazing. Look at you, masterchef."

I laughed a little, rubbing at the back of my head. "Well, thank you. By the way, I don't mean to sound awkward, or anything, but . . . how do you know where I live?"

She gave me a blank look for a second before breaking out into laughter. "Oh, God. Sorry, I asked Mike and I sent you a text but you didn't respond, probably because you were cooking. I didn't really even plan on it, I was just in the area and ended up here, I guess."

All I could see in my mind was Mike leaning his elbows on a cubicle wall, eyelashes fluttering madly with puckered lips. *I'm never going to hear the end of this.*

She looked up and made eye contact with me for the first time that night. They were pink thanks to the creeping hands of whatever red-fingered monster lives in the corners of our eyes. "Hey, are you okay? It looks like you didn't sleep much, and I didn't see you at work today."

She took a second to respond. "I'm fine, yeah. Maybe a little sick, and pretty exhausted."

I ran back into the kitchen and grabbed another bowl, transferring the chow fun from the still-hot pan before it overcooked. Diane was still standing where I'd left her, staring at a wall like it held the solutions to all her problems.

"Hey, why don't you sit down?" I called to her, wok still in my hand. "I'll make you some. It's got ginger and other spices in it, so it might make you feel better. Come on, sit."

"Oh, I don't want to bother you. Sorry, I should—"

I motioned her inside, thankful the cooking

offered an excuse for my face to be flush. "Sit down, and I'll make you some food. Do you like tofu?"

She scrunched her nose up. "Isn't tofu mushy and gross?"

I laughed. "Yeah, if it's raw. It soaks up whatever marinade you set it in like a sponge. Then, I fry it heavily on all edges, caramelizing the sugar in the marinade. It's crispy outside and a little soft inside, but not mushy when done well."

Her lips twitched for a moment, and she crept in, falling onto my worn-out couch. "Alrighty, master-chef. Let's see what you can do with squares of bean mush."

I set a can of breadcrumbs on my head, doing a poor job of balancing it. "Zis is my chef hat, I will cook now. Yes."

Diane giggled a little, dismissing me with a wave, and I began to prepare a bowl for her. First, I filled it with steaming stir-fry, then topped it with a sprinkle of sesame seeds, thinly sliced scallion and a little bit of black pepper. I could feel my face getting hot and her eyes on my back, and suddenly I cared intensely about the presentation of it, arranging the scallions to look pretty.

"Dinner is served," I said, placing the bowl in front of her with chopsticks. She took a deep whiff of it.

"This smells incredible. Do I just kinda. . . ." She waved the chopsticks around.

"Yep. You know how to use chopsticks, right?"

She gave me a troubled smile that said, *"A lit-*

tle." I laughed and beckoned her to dig in.

We ate in silence for a time, aside from her occasional "mmm"s and sighs, until finally she broke it about halfway through her bowl. "I'm majorly impressed. And the tofu is, like, not *nearly* as terrible as I expected it to be."

I bowed sarcastically and ran back into the kitchen to clean up. Once everything was put away, I came out with a bowl of my own.

"Is that gonna be enough?" I asked.

"Oh God, yes—it's so much food . . . but so yummy. Who would've thought you could cook so well?"

I glanced down. "Ah, I'm not great at it. This stuff is easy, and I didn't even get it quite right."

She furrowed her brow and leaned forward. "Dude, this was delicious. I definitely couldn't make something this tasty. Stop being so hard on yourself."

I shrugged, unsure of what else to say.

"Where did you learn to cook?" she continued through a mouthful of noodles.

My eyes turned down. "My mom used to make me help her out in the kitchen all the time, and I guess I picked up on some stuff."

"She's Chinese, right?"

"Nah, that was good ol' dad. My mom was born in the US."

"But she taught you to cook Chinese food?" she asked with a light laugh.

"I know, it's backwards. My parents separated

when I was young, and my dad wasn't really in the picture, but my mom was obsessed with Chinese culture and tried to get me to embrace more of it. Didn't really stick with me, I guess, growing up in American schools. Most of my friends were white."

"That is weird. I always forget you're half Chinese."

"Me too," I said with a sigh. "That part of my life has always been kind of distant. It's strange growing up in America, having a cultural background but being removed from it. Like, I've had a few people say racist shit to me, and it's really weird, because I don't feel Asian. I just feel like a white dude, but I don't *quite* look like one."

"I never thought about what that kind of situation might be like. Do you talk to your dad anymore?"

I shook my head, taking my time chewing a piece of tofu. "Nah, not since I was a kid. I always remember him being kind of an asshole, you know. He wasn't fun like all my friend's dads were."

She sighed. "Sorry, that's rough. What about your mom, then? I bet you two are close, right?"

The mostly-empty bowl of noodles held my gaze for a time, until I finally whispered a response. "I fucked that up a while ago."

Like I always do.

When I looked up, I could tell she wanted to ask another question, but refrained from it and returned to her meal. We ate in a brief silence.

"What would you do if you only had six

months left to live?" she asked after a noodly smile.

"Well that's a morbid question."

"Ugh, come one. What would you do with the time?"

"Well, for starters," I said, then took a bite and savored it. "I wouldn't sit around answering hypothetical questions."

She shot me a fiery glare—one I knew far too well. It made me light up inside, and that didn't feel like a coincidence. *Am I crazy?*

"Okay, okay," I continued, hands up in surrender. "Well, I guess I'd quit my job first. Obviously."

"Obviously."

"Then, after that, I guess it'd be a free-for-all. The things I have to worry about here wouldn't matter anymore, so I'd throw it all away. Savings? More like *spendings*. Don't need a retirement fund in the grave, so I'd buy a bunch of stupid stuff."

She giggled. "What kind of stupid stuff?"

"I dunno. A bounce castle. Or a ball pit. And I'd get real drunk and go wild in them, have the stupid fun I used to have as a kid."

Another snicker from her. Our eyes met, and she quickly broke contact to continue laughing.

"What's so funny?" I asked.

"Nothing, nothing. It's just—I don't know, most people say 'travel the world' or have a bucket list or something. They want to go visit the Taj Mahal or the little hobbit houses in New Zealand. And you...."

"Want to get drunk in a bouncy house. Yes."

Her laughter was contagious, and I caught a case of it. After a minute, she took a series of deep breaths. "Okay, but why? Like, I mean that sounds amazing and all, but why that and not something crazy like jumping out of planes or visiting other countries?"

I shrugged. "Traveling the world would be amazing, yeah. But the funds would dry up fast, and there'd be so much time spent doing the actual traveling, sitting in planes and trains and all that. And to be honest, for me, traveling is more about the experience. The change in worldview that comes with seeing part of the world you haven't before, and how it affects the way you think or live. But with no time left to grow, it'd lose that, and I'd just be hopping around looking at pretty places."

"What's wrong with that? Some of those places are *really* pretty."

"Yeah, I mean, you're right. I guess—remember when you were a kid, and you thought growing up would be . . . I dunno, fun? It's not like I thought I'd be sitting at a desk answering phones or sleeping through meetings. But remember how simple feeling happy used to be? I thought growing up would mean that I'd get to do all of the fun things I wanted to, the stuff mom and dad wouldn't let me because it seemed ridiculous."

She cocked her head, but didn't interject.

"That's what I'd want my last days to be like," I continued. "Full of the simple, stupid things little me dreamed about doing once I'd have the freedom.

The things I genuinely believed adulthood would be like instead of . . . this. No bills, no planning, no worries about health or the meaning of life, or meeting quotas, or politics. A whole pizza? Breakfast. A water gun fight between two warring pillow pits. I might not have known how to file taxes or make any money, but I sure knew how to love being alive even if I didn't know it."

"And you don't anymore?" she asked, voice soft.

"It's just not the same now, is all." I took a deep breath, then stacked her empty bowl in mine and threw them out. The nearby plastic bag overflowing with candy bars caught my eye. "Hey, want a piece of dark chocolate?"

She perked up from her food coma. "Yes, sir. I stopped by Nature's Mart on my way here and they had this crazy sale—sixty percent off, or something like that—and it was all gone. Some asshole must've taken it all."

I pursed my lips, darting my eyes around the room. "Sorry, I'm that asshole. I took like, twenty, or something."

She threw her arms into the air. "What kind of person buys all the chocolate at a grocery store?"

"Sorry! I got them mainly for you, though. I know you like dark chocolate. Take as many as you'd like!" I ran to the kitchen and brought the entire bag over to her.

She flushed rose as I handed her an almond coconut bar. "You didn't have to get anything for me."

"I know, I . . . whoa, hey, are you okay?"

"What? I'm fine."

I knelt down beside her. "Diane . . . you're cry-ing."

Two little rivers trailed down her cheeks, and she touched one. "Oh. I guess I am."

"What's wrong?"

"This is Caleb's favorite candy." She danced the candy bar in front of a hollowed gaze, then shook her head, squeezing her eyes. "Was."

My breath caught.

The wrapper crinkled in her trembling hands as she placed her head against mine.

The Hunt

"How did it happen?" I was trying not to be morbid or invasive, but thinking of the right words was hard. It's incredible how eloquence escapes in such tender moments.

Diane blew her nose into the fifth of what would be many tissues. "Peacefully. He was surrounded by dozens of people that loved him dearly, friends and family. He chose his time to go, so he could see everyone one last time before the memorial service."

My eyes widened much more than I'd meant them to. "You mean . . . he—"

She held up a hand, trying to wave away my worried thoughts. "No, he was on life support at the end. His condition degraded so quickly. We weren't prepared for the decline. Or maybe we were, and I was lying to myself. It was his way of getting to spend his last moments with everyone he loved, before it got so bad he wouldn't be able to."

A sigh fled me, and I rubbed my temples. "I—I don't really know what to say. I'm so sorry, Diane. He was an amazing person. I guess I'm glad he got to spend the end with so many people, you know? That sounds like the best possible way."

"Yeah. It's just so surreal, you know? I don't think it's really sunk in yet," she said, sniffling a few times, groaning. "I keep thinking I'll go home and he'll be there to crack a joke and make me feel better with that smile of his . . . even at the end, he tried to make *me* feel better. *It's okay, Diane. I'm moving on to a better place, and I'll always watch over you. Be happy —for you, and for me.* That's what he told me. How can someone be so incredible, even when they're sick and frail and dying slowly? I should have been the one to comfort him, but instead I just cried and cried. . . ."

Sobs overtook her once more, and I squeezed my eyes shut, putting a hesitant arm around her. "That's who he was. There aren't many people like that."

Diane sat up, blowing her nose again. "I'm sorry, here I am wallowing in pity and littering your house with gross tissues. I should go."

My mouth tried to tell her no, but no sound came out. She stood up, collecting the tissues.

"Don't worry about all that, I'll get it for you. It's okay."

"Oh, no, I can't have you clean it up, that's so nasty. Please let me at least get those."

I nodded. "Yeah, sure."

Once the tissues were all disposed, Diane slipped into her jacket and boots, but stopped on her way out. A hand drifted out to the dream journal I'd left at the edge of the kitchen counter without even realizing it; it had stupid doodles all over the front and throughout the pages, along with notes and names and all kinds of ridiculous looking things that no one else was meant to see.

"Wow, Jax," she said, flipping it open, sniffling. Her voice was ragged and stuffy. "I had no idea you could draw so well. These are really cool."

I felt sick; something hot brewed in my belly, and my thoughts bounced all around my head. "Oh, I . . . no, that's all a bunch of garbage. It's a—an old notebook from high school, you know. Lame stuff from when I was bored in class and had nothing else to do." I started forward to take it from her.

She pulled back a bit, flipping through more. "Why didn't you ever tell me about this? You always say you're not good at anything. I bet you could sell these—"

I grabbed it from her, and she started a bit. "You don't have to be nice about it; like I said, it's an old notebook from high school. Just silly, quick stuff."

Her brow furrowed, and she scoffed. "Sorry, I didn't mean to pry."

"Sorry, it—it's not—" I fumbled to find another way to back out of the conversation.

"No, I get it. It's probably a personal outlet for you. But seriously, you should consider pursuing it further, maybe start an IG account or something because you're really good." She walked back over to the door, then turned around. "Anyway, thanks for having me over. Getting out of the house for a little while really helped, and the food was great. Sorry I'm such a mess." Her bloodshot eyes bounced between mine and the ground.

"No, please don't be sorry. Oh, and take some of the chocolate with you, too. I don't need it all."

She held a hand up. "Oh, you've already done enough—" I shoved a bag with six bars into her hand, and a weak smile crept onto her face. "Thanks. You're sweet."

"Compared to dark chocolate, most things are."

She rolled her eyes and scoffed at me but couldn't hide the light laughter my joke earned. The smile she wore quickly faded.

"Will you come to the service? It's tomorrow at ten, since everyone is still in town."

I looked down and blew air out of my mouth. "Uh, well . . . I wouldn't really know anyone—"

"A lot of people from high school will be going. Katie Brecker, Danny Haurbaugh, lots of people from our grade. And I'll be there. Please?"

My eyes shifted up and met hers, a deep collage of light brown and gold flecked with green sunken into dark and worn sockets. All sense fled me; my mind paralyzed and though I wanted to say no, something else slipped out.

"Sure, yeah."

Another weak smile tightened her lips. "Thanks. Meet me at my place tomorrow morning, around nine."

"Yeah, of course. I'll call out of work, I haven't taken a sick day yet. I swear, if she tries to raise hell about it...."

"Henderson? She still all over you?"

"Yeah, I was on lunch break and stopped by your cubicle to—uh, on the way to Mike's, to see how he was doing." She nudged an eyebrow at me but didn't question anything. "Anyway, yeah, she wandered over to me and said something about me slacking off. I told her I was on break and she acted real weird, kinda drifting off and stuff. I cut the break early and got back to work."

Her face contorted. "Something's up with her. Why does she single you out, anyway? Plenty of people in the office are just as lazy as you."

"Wow, thanks," I said, flattening my lips. "Mike joked that she has a crush on me."

Diane giggled softly. "Definitely a Mike joke. Though I wouldn't blame her if she did."

I flushed, and with no stove to grant me cover I let a nervous chuckle out toward my feet. My gaze crept upwards and she was staring right at me with tired eyes, searching for something. Thoughts began to form, thoughts of touching her face and loving her body, but memories of how she'd run off the other night and knowing how much she was hurting crashed into them in a mangled mix of confusion and pity. Memories of Maya's smile, and how it might fade if I hurt her—if I was wrong. After a few moments, I couldn't keep a single thought in place for long.

"Well, you should get going. It's late. I'll see you tomorrow morning, yeah?" I asked, avoiding her eyes.

She straightened, opening the door and turning back to me for a moment. "Yeah, I'll see you tomorrow. Thanks again, Jax."

A kiss on my cheek sealed her farewell, the door closing in my face. I stood there for a little while, staring at the flecks of imperfection in its paint, thoughts swirling like a whirlpool of dirt.

Was I supposed to do something differently there? Did she want a kiss? No, she's just in pain and I'm the closest thing to her right now. Stupid. Why would she ever seriously want me of all people?

I downed a sleeping pill with some water, falling into bed with such little care I heard something crack beneath the mattress. My mind, as if trying to reject the sleeping aid, refused to stay quiet.

She shouldn't be sending all these mixed signals. How am I supposed to figure this out? Is she Maya or not?

No, dumbass, don't think like that, as if there's some shred of hope to debate about. She's confused right now. Besides, it's so wrong to kiss someone that's grieving. It was the same situation as the other night, where she ran away after we kissed. She would've just run away again . . . yeah, she would've. Anyone would've. Even if she is Maya, she's better off not knowing who the real me is.

I'm nothing in this life.

I'm no one.

⚭ ⚭ ⚭

My eyes snapped open to sunlight and a beautiful woman getting dressed not ten feet away. Her proportions were even more pleasant from a comfortable view on the bed, the sun kissing her skin like a long-lost lover.

"Morning, sunshine," she said, slipping into a pair of deep, sea-blue armored pants.

"It's good to see you again. I missed you." I rose, closing the distance between us.

She half-smiled and offered the slightest nod, grabbing her top. "Come on, we have important things to do."

"There's no rush," I said, a deviant smile on my face, but she only responded with a dry laugh before leaving the room.

Why does it seem like she's pulling away from me? Without our old backstories, we're free to be whoever we want . . . do whatever we want.

I sighed and followed suit, strapping Somnior to my waist once dressed. The cross-guards were glimmering gold, smirking like puppies that had played fetch with the morning sun.

That was supposed to be a metaphor, but one of the dragonheads cocked at me and, in a golden blur, offered me a pen that had been sitting on my desk. I accepted and threw it out into the hallway, right next to Maya's feet. She looked up from it slowly, unamused.

Her foot was tapping, arms crossed. "Are you ready? Why am I bothering to wait for you if you're just standing around throwing things at—"

A dragon launched forward, thin red streaks following the path of its eyes. Maya jumped back, lifting a foot up like a spider was scurrying beneath her—though, ironically, she'd have been far more comfortable around a spider—and the dragon snatched it up. I patted it on the head, and it dropped the pen back on my desk.

Maya was eyeing Somnior, still recoiled. "What, they're dogs, now? Sheesh, leash them or something. It almost took my foot off."

I started down the stairs and looked back with a grin. "Now you know how I feel with the damn bats flapping over my head."

"Oh come on, they don't bother you!"

I shot her a sarcastic look of disbelief from the side, tilting my head. She rolled her eyes and followed me into the courtyard, where I was immediately swarmed by two massive, furry, shrieking beasts.

"Oh, *they don't bother me*?"

"Whatever, they're sweet. They love everyone! They know you're a grumpy meanie and want to give you hugs."

"Well tell them to stop hugging me!" I ducked

with my arms up as they coated me in saliva. Maya walked past me and called them back.

"Yes, he's a big grumpster, isn't he? But I love you, yes I do!" She was petting one with each hand, the bats crooning.

I stood alone as she ignored me in favor of the animals. "Anyway, I think we should practice together, today. Now that we each have a skill to hone, it'd probably be useful if we could work on them together."

Maya kept her focus on the bats. "Maybe later, right now I'm a little preoccupied."

I raised an eyebrow, still standing there like a moron while she showed two beasts more love than she had me in the past week. "Well, I'm going to go practice. Whenever you feel like you're ready enough to take me on, you can come join me." I turned and walked toward the lake, but before I'd taken even five steps, there were blurs of rock whizzing beside me.

"Aww, you think I'm scared of you?" she said in the voice one uses to speak with a toddler.

Easy.

"Let's go, then. Bring it." I unsheathed Somnior, raising it in front of me and letting the dragons roam free. They were itching for battle, bobbing and waving through the air like snakes ready to strike.

Maya spread her arms wide and a stream of pebbles flowed from the ground, swirling above her head. I could see them morphing, lengthening and shifting from dull to scarily sharp. *I might have pissed her off a little too much....*

"I wonder who's scared now, Reza. How serious can I get before you can no longer handle me?" The stones stopped, and pointed themselves at me with a snap like they were needles and I was a magnet. One cut through the air at full force, heading straight for my shoulder. I could see it, but my body couldn't react quickly enough to move out of the way.

A loud *clank* rang out and dust scattered across my face, dusting my cheeks. A dragon was smiling at me with crumbling dirt trailing from its jaw.

"You almost killed me! What was that about?" I yelled, flailing my arms.

"What, you can't handle one projectile? What happens when I fire them all, Reza?"

"You know, that thing I said earlier was just—"

A shadow overtook me as every single rock she'd shaped hovered higher. *She's not going to shoot them all at me. No. She—*

Yep. She is.

For a fleeting moment, I felt sick to my stomach. With what had happened to my arm, concern bled into panic and I froze in front of her. The instant where she began firing felt like it stretched an eternity; all I could think about was what might happen if I died. What I might lose.

A clanking, whirring sound filled my ears, as if I were surrounded by a legion of broken fans. My hair gently flapped in the turbulent breeze of what felt like a sandstorm, filling my eyes and ears and nose with debris. When I could finally open my eyes without dirt raking them, I couldn't make much out; everything was a dim, swirling haze of particulate, and I could barely hear anything over the sound of grinding and cracking.

As it finally faded, there were no rocks to be seen, and I stood on a sandlot amidst a meadow. The two fans in front of me, spinning and whirling circles of green and gold, slowed to a halt. My dragons turned to me. They seemed smug again, satisfied with their work, and I patted each of them on the head. There wasn't a speck of dust sullying their sheen.

Maya was staring at me, mouth frowning but eyes impressed. "That's one hell of a defense you have there. I knew you'd been working on something, but damn is that strong."

I gasped, realizing I'd been holding my breath the entire time. "Why would you do that?"

"You were *fine*."

"Yeah, I didn't die, but what if I had? I told you what happened to my arm already, and you seriously risked killing me? What if I actually died?" The words came out hot and fast.

She paused, flushing red. "I didn't think about that. Sorry, I'm not used to worrying about that kind of thing."

"God, I—" I took a deep breath, wiping dust and sweat from my brow. "It's okay. I'm okay. Just try and be more careful from now on, please. I don't want to lose you or this place."

She nodded, then started toward the lake. "I got carried away—I don't want to lose you, either."

I smiled, though she didn't see it. "Okay. Can we try this again, but a little more careful, maybe?"

She kept her back to me. "No, I think I'm done practicing for today."

"What are we going to do all day, then? Sorry for snapping at you, but I still want to practice more."

She turned, firing at me the same devious look I'd given her earlier. "We're gonna find the bastard that tried to kill us."

⚅⚅

Sea of Stone

It took several moments to register what few words Maya had said to me, and in the meantime, I stood there like a moron, gawking at the grass.

"You—you can't possibly be serious," I called after her. She was heading toward the main gate, where Zox was standing guard. "We've barely learned how to use our skills, Maya. This is insane! What did we *just* talk about?"

She shot a burning glare. "If you want to stay alive and protect this place—protect *us*—then we can't sit here and wait for him to try again. That guy out there attacked us in our own home, and I'm going to put an end to this."

"Give it a few more days, let's practice our skills and come up with combos—"

"I'm *not* going to wait until it's too late."

I shook my head, arms flailing in front of me. "We have a shield if we're in here, one that, by the way, we can't have up if we leave. So if we go out there, the castle is at a greater risk. It's safe if we're here."

"Yeah, and what if that's not true?"

"What are you ta—"

"We declared no magic, and no one could use magic. Then, he came along and now we have glaciers in our courtyard and a new river. We said, 'this is the map of our world', and set it in stone. Then, he came along and added an entire region without us even knowing it. What if he can get past the shield? We'd be in here, comfortable and off-guard, waiting to be slaughtered."

Zox peeked at us from atop the main wall, near the gate controls. "Hey, Zox! Tell her she's crazy. Please tell me you have my back."

"Why would I have your back? Are your backs detachable?" he called down in response.

I placed my face into my hands, sighing deeply. "Will you tell her it's too dangerous?"

"It's too dangerous. Like that?"

"You could at least *try* to act like you mean it."

Maya broke into our exchange. "Look, I don't care if he thinks it's dangerous any more than I care that you do. I'm going, and you can either help me or run back into the castle and put the shield back up if you feel like hiding."

"What are you going to do, then?" I asked, unable to disguise the frustration in my voice. "Knock on his front door and ask him, politely, to die?"

"No, asshole. I'm going to go where the map

says he is, sneak into his castle, and kill him while his guard is down. He's probably just like you, sitting up in his tower, thinking nothing could ever bring him down." She walked past the gate and picked a few apples out of an apple tree near some spare trunks. One by one, Maya tossed the apples toward the middle of our courtyard, and within a few moments, there was a flurry of jagged flapping sounds overhead. Her bats landed in the mud, attacking the pile of apples voraciously, devouring each one in a single bite.

"Zox, run upstairs and lock the shield in place," she called out to the bear. "There's a crystal in the right-hand nightstand—push it into the slot above our bed. Hurry and get there as fast as you can, while these two loveboats are occupied with food."

Zox jumped down and scurried over to the castle, leaving Maya and I alone. I expected some kind of annoyed lecture or ceremonial begging, but instead she simply climbed up the gate's inner staircase and jumped off the wall without so much as looking back.

"Oh, for. . . ." I trailed off into a sharp sigh before I traced her path, over the wall and into the forest. As I gained on her, she suddenly rose into the air, a wafer of stone beneath her feet. It floated her along while another plate of rock in front acted as a windshield of sorts.

"Wait, Maya, don't—"

She continued to rise, up through the canopy,

where she'd presumably catch a better glimpse of our enemy. *If she won't listen to reason....*

I sent both dragons out, each one wrapping itself around her torso and lifting her off the disc, which continued through the air like nothing had happened until out of sight. Maya was thrashing about grunting and yelling.

"Let go of me!"

As I went to place her down, a boulder came hurling at me with terrifying speed. My dragons operated on their own, dropping Maya into the mud and latching onto a nearby tree, pulling me out of the rock's trajectory.

"What the hell did you go and do that for?" I huffed, out of breath from the terror. "I was trying to put you down gently and instead you tried to kill me again. Now look at you." She was covered in mud, spitting out what was in her mouth.

"Why did you pull me out of the air? Did you follow me just to get in my way? Here I'd thought maybe you'd help me, but no, you're still trying to lecture me and hold me back. Go *home*."

I lifted my hands, palms up, giving her a wild look of disbelief. "I pulled you out of the air so you wouldn't be a massive beacon giving away our location and plan. Yeah, let's just go up into the sky and let him see us coming from five miles away! Why don't we bake him a cake and set off some fireworks from the shore, too? He might have seen your little surfing attempt already, and if he did, we're in for a one-way battle. We need to catch him off-guard so he can't have time to build up his ice defense. Do you ever think, Maya?"

She nodded slowly, followed by a short scoff. "Yeah, I'm so stupid, aren't I? You always need to protect poor little me, who's too stupid for her own good."

"I didn't mean it like that."

"Sure, whatever. Thanks for saving me from my own stupid self!" She shaped a conglomerate of stones into a seat levitating several inches up. "Well, I'm going to go by ground, then. If you still want to follow me and yell about how much smarter you are from time to time, I can't stop you." Her seat hovered forward.

I sighed, pinching the bridge of my nose. *What the hell am I supposed to do? Just let you go up and get us both killed?*

After standing in place like an idiot for several minutes, I took a deep breath and ran after her. The better part of an hour passed as I trudged beneath a salad sky, keeping Maya in my sight yet far enough to contain the awkwardness. The leaves above were rustling, a comforting sound that soothed the painful silence hanging over both of us. *Must be nice outside of the forest with a breeze like that.*

Maya was getting faster and faster in her stone-mobile, with two sawblades in front clearing a path. It got to a point where I couldn't properly keep up on foot, and she went from doll-sized to a speck within minutes. Soon enough, I couldn't see her at all. *At least she's clearing a path for me, I guess.*

I looked down at the sword bobbing on my hip. "Why can't you guys fly me places like that?" Two dragons cocked their heads at me, golden teeth clacking with disdain.

Another breeze ruffled the canopy overhead, this time much louder. Leaves rained down as I pressed forward, caressing me on their journey to the dirt. Sticks and splintered wood soon joined their leafy companions, followed by a massive branch taller than me. My dragons anchored ahead, lurching me several yards forward and out of harm's way. The log sent mud splattering across trees and bushes when it landed, some of it getting on my boots. I approached it out of curiosity, noting the severely splintered end and a deep crack nearly splitting it in two. As I peered at it, the foliage above me shifted, dancing to a tune much more sinister and violent than a gale might offer. The canopy was stained a matte, sticky white that almost made it look like a sack had been placed over my head.

That's no breeze.

"Maya!" I whisper-shouted, though I knew there was no way she'd hear me. I wanted to warn her, but there was no way without completely giving my position away. "Farax! Run!"

Rays of light stabbing the earth around me disappeared as darkness rolled in like fog. I leapt off my right foot, turning about and dashing away —I knew speed alone wouldn't be enough, though, to outrun the shadow overhead. She always found a way to catch up with her prey.

Something crashed behind me.

I spun, drawing Somnior, dragons at the ready. My heart beat like a war drum, my hands tight on the pommel. Sweat accumulated at my brow.

Of all the dangers in the forest, nothing could've been a worse fit for me than a giant spider, but that was not what I found at the sound's epicenter. There was only a log-shaped mass bigger than myself lodged into the soft earth, covered in webs that stretched to a patchwork sky. I inched closer to it. There was an acrid smell in the air, and it stung my nose. No shadow lurked overhead. Something rustled behind me.

I nearly realized it too late.

Without even turning, I buried my dragons into the dirt, thrusting myself forward hard without care. I nearly hit a tree, just barely dampening the impact in time, and caught a glimpse of the monster from my seat on the ground. Taller than me, each leg segment a branch off a great winter pine, the sight made my heart skip and stomach sink. Eight beady black eyes watched me, filled with the anger of a failed trap, as it dangled with queer calmness from a thick white line connected to the canopy. There was only a split second where we studied each other before it disconnected, abandoning all trickery, and rushed at me. I buried golden teeth into the tree near me, swinging around it and perpendicular to its trajectory, which it did not expect. A moment of hesitation let me put a few seconds worth of distance between us, I used the dragons to dig a trench big enough for me to lay in, then had them rip shrubs out of the ground to cover the hole with.

As I began counting out a dreadful wait of five minutes, shivering as sweat dripped down my spine, I felt the cold of gold wrap around my wrists and ankles, gentle yet with the sureness of steel; without any permission from me, the dragons had hatched a plan of their own. They rotated around my body like a spiral jump rope, moving at quite literally blinding speed, and we sank several feet farther into the ground as the soil was churned away. It was too dark to see anything clearly; I'd been encased in a spinning sarcophagus and lowered.

"What are you doing? How is this help—"

The skin of my face stretched, all my blood and several organs rushing to my head. It's hard to say, but we must've been going hundreds of miles an hour.

Twenty seconds later, my colon finally fell back into its rightful place from my mouth as I flew straight out of the ground, the landing blunted by a mound of freshly aerated soil. I was on my back, still reeling from the G-force I'd experienced, when Maya floated up to me.

"Where did you come from? How do you get *ahead* of me?" she asked incredulously.

"Pain," I groaned, still on my back. Tilting my head up, I could see a path of raised, aerated soil leading up to my corpse. "Lots of pain."

She gave me an odd look as I raised myself

from the dead. "Well, we're almost to Stonepoint Shore. Hope you don't lose a boot this time, or things are going to get real ugly."

"Maybe just hold the door open for me, then."

She rolled her eyes and hovered forward, stone-blades resuming their work. Thankfully, this time her pace was much more manageable, and I followed along with ease.

"We're lucky Farax didn't show up today," Maya said as we approached the forest's edge. "Would've been a terrible time to get ambushed."

I let out an empty chuckle that turned into a groan, brushing dust off myself. "Yeah...."

We crested the treeline, immediately greeted by the rocky expanse of Stonepoint Shore—which had been very aptly named, given that a barefoot man would make it all of two steps before needing amputation. As Maya started to press ahead, I placed a hand on her shoulder, pulling her back gently behind the cover of a massive tree.

"Well, at least you didn't lasso me out of the sky this time," she said with a stone-point tongue. "What do you want now?"

I pointed out to the riverbank, where a man was rinsing his hands off. Despite the distance, I recognized his robes. He was on our side of the river.

"I *told* you," Maya hissed at me. "Look, he's probably been stalking us this whole time. Maybe he's even seen us using our new skills, plotting how to handle them. We have to deal with him."

"Okay, I agree, but this guy is strong and we

should come up with a plan—"

Maya slid off her stone chair, breaking it down into a thin, long needle with sharp branches poking out, like the vein network of a leaf.

I continued as I tried to keep up with her. "Look, he's got the home advantage here, remember? Remember last time, with the murderous needle hail?"

She shot me a burning glance, beaming with confidence. "He's not the only one."

She lifted her arms up and the shore itself followed, a swarm of pre-sharpened stones rising like a crocheted blanket of death against the sky. I wanted to tell her that we needed to capture him, not just kill him aimlessly again—especially since he survived death once already. I wanted to tell her that we'd have better luck using a coordinated attack, with me flanking. I wanted to help, but I was made a statue in the hollow forest, smothered by a harrowing sky of shadow—but it wasn't the looming death above that scared me.

It was the look on her face, the fire dancing in her eyes. A brew of determination, confidence, and hate, with the strength to drink it and stay upright. I felt a little like the sun in the moment, overshadowed by her aerial sea of swirling stone.

What happened next was a total blur. She rained a funnel of rock upon the man, like a tornado touching down from a thick, brown cloud that then expanded and swallowed everything. The noise was deafening, even from my distance to the shore, and for a brief moment, water and earth replaced air. It took about a minute for her barrage to finish, and another for the river's tumultuous scene to quell enough that visibility returned.

He was gone, and so was the shore.

Planting Seeds

"**W**ell, at least there's no shore to rename, now," I said dryly, the words like a cough. I looked down at a trembling hand and scoffed at my own inadequacy.

Maya's eyes remained fixed on where the mage once stood, her brow trying to dig into the depths of her mind. There was a pillar of ice the height of a man, stuck with a hundred stone needles and crying in the sunlight. Without a word, Maya leapt up onto a stone disc and whizzed off. My mouth opened to protest, but no sound came out. Any calls would fall on deaf ears, that much I knew, and so I sank both dragon heads into a tree on either side of me; the simplicity of Maya's skill allowed her to constantly adapt with little forethought, but I needed a good dose of creativity.

I took a deep breath and closed my eyes after taking ten steps back, turning into a human slingshot. In an instant, my eyelids were pulled open by the force of wind and I was forced to watch the Earth blur beneath me. Before I could even scream, one dragon wrapped itself around a tree and I spun around it violently ten or twenty times, descending slightly with each revolution until I plopped onto the ground. Maya pulled up behind me as I crawled out of the dirt, face straight ahead but eyes pointed at me.

"That looked a little fun," she grumbled, passing me.

"Maybe if you hate your organs," I replied, the words more like vomit. Regaining my composure, I found that nothing hurt much, aside from an overall queasiness. *If I can survive something that violent, then the danger is clearly limited to damage done by real people.*

"Well if you're gonna be whiny about it, just use them as a helicopter instead of a slingshot, next time."

I stopped walking and looked at the two jewel-laden beasts before me. *Why don't you come up with ideas like that?*

They chattered their teeth at me.

I let them go on autopilot, raising me into the air like a two-legged spider hobbling forward. "Where are we going, Maya?"

Her head turned halfway toward me, then faced forward again. "Inland, I guess. He's gonna be around here somewhere, and I'm going to smash whatever shack he's holed up in. I'm going to kill him for good."

"Look, maybe we can work out some kind of peace agreement, right? This whole thing is probably a misunderstanding. If he actually is real, we should try and talk to him."

"You can talk to him all you want, but I'm not going to have a conversation with a man that's tried to kill us multiple times." She sped up, putting enough distance between us that I couldn't respond. *This is going well.*

Overhead, bright blue streaked against thick plumes of dark grey no more than a mile ahead. The clouds were so dark that, at points, they were black. I sped up to try and close a little of the distance between us.

"Hey, there's a nasty storm up ahead. We should be careful moving forward," I yelled.

She lifted stone over her head, shaping it into a wide dome that covered her from anything above three times over, equipped with clearing saws at the edges. I shrugged and leaned back once more to watch darkness engulf the sky. *Well, at least she's listening, I guess.*

Soon, visibility was nothing more than a memory trailing behind me and Maya faded into a blur. Branches I could no longer dodge swiped at my face, taunting me with each stroke. If I hadn't known better, I'd have thought it was midnight rather than midday, and a deep chill settled in that left me shivering. Light, ice cold flakes landed on my face and melted, short-lived thieves stealing warmth from my skin before fading into nothing.

My eyes adjusted to the new lighting enough that Maya became visible again, and I pushed forward at full speed to catch up to her.

"Hey, I don't know about you, but I can't really see anything and it's freezing cold out here. We should wait until tomorrow.

She didn't respond, but I could hear her teeth chattering. Both of us had dressed to the warm weather of our castle.

"See? You're cold, too."

"I'm not cold," she retorted as though the weather had chilled even her words.

"Come on, make a little room for me on this rock thing, at least. I keep getting hit in the face with branches and it's snowing hard as hell."

She uncrossed one arm slightly, expanding the stone seat enough for me to sit beside her. I grabbed the end, swinging myself onto the floating stone bench, and retracted my dragons. *You guys could use some rest, anyway. Or, actually, do you?*

I scooted up to Maya and wrapped my arms around her, feeling the trembling of her body, the hairs on end all over her arms. She was probably colder than me, judging by how violent the shivers were. Warmth pooled between the two of us and her body stilled a little more with each shuddering breath.

"Thanks," she mumbled defeatedly.

I wrapped myself around her tighter. "We're supposed to be in this together, remember?" Her left hand crawled up to my arm and squeezed. As we held one another, a faint glow birthed in the cracks between the forest of dying trees and slowly grew brighter, breaking into numerous, smaller lights. Our bodies separated, both of us drawing our weapons in preparation. Maya still carried Vesper with her for some reason.

Soon the sea of empty wood was behind us, and only a faint haze of yellow marred the pure white ahead, like a lone cloud raining light in the distance. It grew larger and clearer until a blinding brightness swept over; clouds parted in a perfect circle, like God was shining a flashlight onto the land. With the return of our vision, breath and courage had vacated to make room for it.

Can death look beautiful?

Despite the pervasive chill, we were in a meadow full of thriving tulips and daisies and petunias, ferns and blue bonnets, pushing against the surrounding haze. They were almost neon in the holy glow, impossibly vibrant, and birds flitted through the rustling leaves of great oak trees. It was spring hidden inside of winter, utopia tucked into desolation, and at the very center of it all a hand, bluer than oceans deep and big enough to hold our castle in its grasp, reached for the heavens. Each fingernail was hollowed out, likely great chambers, with smaller lit openings dotting the hand like pores. It held something. Thick, scaly ice tubing, nearly the thickness of a spire, wrapped and weaved about them. It was unlike anything I'd ever seen. It was. . . .

Breathtaking.

Terrifying.

The frozen hand of something terrible reaching out from the Earth's depths, as if to crush God in its fist.

"Maya, we need to go back," I pleaded, eyes still set on the monstrosity before us. "We're outclassed here. Severely."

Her face said she wanted to protest, but only the fog of ragged exhales sprang forth into the cold, a whirlpool of awe and hatred swirling in her eyes. Something stirred ahead, a low cracking sound resonating through the hazy air heavy with our lingering breath. The tubing shifted, slow but enormous, and a pattern of blood red diamonds formed along the top of it.

No, that's not decoration. That's. . . .

A triangular, spined serpent head poked out from between the thumb and index finger, bearing upon us with two eyes greener than spring. It flickered a muted blue tongue, then slithered downward like an avalanche, ice and grass crashing beneath it. It stopped well short of us, thought it clearly could have closed the gap with quick ease.

"So nice of you to visit me," a deep voice boomed from within it. "Jackson."

How can he know my name?

I froze, but that didn't help me hide in plain sight. Maya looked at me, concern scrawled across her face, but only for a moment before the bass of his voice plowed through our chests once more, rumbling everything inside.

"I've been waiting for you to show up for some time now; this moment, this inevitability, is so delightful for me. You feel it, don't you? The beauty of this power. Give up that which does not matter and become one with this world; live in eternal paradise, or be erased from it forever."

Become one with this world? As in, let go of my real life? Is that . . . possible?

"Your heart yearns for it, I know," he continued. "A chance to trade pain and meaninglessness for a taste of the impossible. Now, go home, and think about what it is that matters most to you—what you desire. I will come to you tomorrow."

Maya started forward, kicking at the snow and wriggling as I hauled her back. " We're not ready to handle this, not right now. We need to leave!"

She fought less and less as the sun was swallowed by a pool of black and grey, cursing under her breath as we fled on her stone vehicle. Receding into the dying treeline brought a false feeling of safety, though the sky overhead darkened. I couldn't stop thinking about the mage's words and what they meant; what was possible.

After a time spent in silence, I spoke up. "That guy seems crazy."

She nodded angrily. "Gonna kill him, no question."

I danced around the words a bit. "Yeah . . . but it does sound kinda nice, doesn't it? Staying here forever, I mean. Not with him, but, you know . . . in general."

Our carriage stopped abruptly, nearly tossing me into the snow. "You can't possibly be saying what I think you're saying."

"Don't get all worked up," I said, throwing my hands up in surrender. "I just mean that it sounds nice, you know."

"It doesn't sound nice, it sounds like hiding."

I tensed and leaned forward. "Was just a thought."

"Think less thoughts like that," she muttered, and continued driving.

"Okay. Well, there's something else concerning."

Her jaw clenched, but she did not reply.

"He knows my name, Maya."

She shut her eyes, inhaling deep. "Please stop."

"Why?" I asked, my voice raising. "Why are you so afraid of talking about it? It was one thing before that guy showed up, but Hadrian's dead, along with every other part of the world we've been living in all this time. Are you sure I'm the one that's hiding?"

Icy eyes shot towards me, but I did not falter. She said, "This place is supposed to be an escape— but if anything, it's becoming a nightmare instead. I always wanted to keep things separate for a reason, so this world could be a little slice of Heaven, free of any other bullshit. You understand that, right?"

"Yes," I replied, nodding. "But like you said,

things have changed—so should we. Who are you, Maya? Really."

She hesitated, drawing a long, cold breath that came out like smoke. It was hard to tell where it ended and the sky began. "You know who I am. Can we finish this ride in peace, now?"

My heart skipped a beat, but I bit my tongue rather than push my luck.

I knew it.

We floated at full speed through the dead forest, across the stoned points of both shores hugging Rubicon River and back to the safety of our home. Moments after our arrival, the air grew heavy with a new cold, and light snow followed.

"Damn, we forgot to tell Zox that he needs to let us in," I muttered as we stood by the gate. "Maybe shape a few rocks into words and drop them on top of the shield?"

Maya silently followed my suggestion, shaping the word "GATE" and dropping it over the center courtyard. However, the plan fell through rather quickly—not unlike the stones, which made a distinct *splash* in Lake Augr and muffled a distant, guttural scream.

I told him to put the damn shield up, what is he doing?

Zox popped up over the top of the wall, fur slicked to his skin. *"We're under attack!"*

I groaned at the pitiful display. "That was us,

Zox. We thought you put the shield up and wanted to get your attention. I take it you couldn't find the key?"

He shook himself off, a small rainbow forming in the mist around him. "No, I found it and locked it, but when I saw you two coming back, I unlocked it and ran to open the gate. That's when something fell from the sky!"

"Wow, it's lucky you saw us. I thought you'd be sleeping."

"I was standing by the lock, looking out the window the whole time."

My jaw dropped. "You stood there the *whole time*?"

"Well, yes. I had to keep watch while you were away."

"Okay, well, that wasn't entirely necessary—but thank you for your devotion. Can you open the gate, please?"

"Oh, right." He scurried over to the gate wheel, but Maya airlifted herself over, and I followed suit with less grace and more damage to the outer wall. Wood creaked and gears crunched beneath us at first, but it stopped, and Zox was looking up at us in awe. When we landed, he promptly shut the gate and ran down after us. I stopped to wait for Zox, but Maya trudged ahead without so much as looking back.

"Is she okay?" he asked, approaching me.

I watched her heave into the entrance, ignoring the yearning bats. "Sort of. These are trying times for us all; she's just overwhelmed."

"What happened?"

I took my time inhaling. "Long story short, we're going to have a visitor tomorrow."

"Oh, good, guests! Shall we roast a hen?"

I rubbed my eyes, hand dragging down my face. "No, I don't think he wants to have dinner."

"Lunch, then?"

"No, w—" I exhaled with defeat. "The ice mage. He's coming here tomorrow. Says he has a proposition for us, to live in an eternal utopia or something. Maya wants to smash his brains out with a rock, so I'm sure it's going to be a great time."

"Ah, I see. I rescind my offer of a roasted hen, I don't like that man."

"Yeah, you're not the only one." I walked toward the castle, every step heavy with dread. The lake was now two feet higher than it was a week prior, dangerously approaching the armory's entrance. *I'm going to need Maya to help me get these damn glaciers out of here before our castle turns into an aquarium. Thank God all those needles sublimated or we'd have drowned already.*

When I finally shuffled upstairs to speak with her, an empty bed was all that greeted me. The sun was still a good distance above the horizon, and I sat on the edge of my bed, contemplating the next move. With a wistful glance out the window, I locked the barrier and got comfortable under the thick bed linens. Thoughts whipped like wind through my mind as I tried to think of ways to further unlock Maya, and create a bridge between her and the real world—but I decided to put that off for the time being, at least until the mage was handled and things calmed down again. The last thing I thought of were the strange man's parting words, and what they could mean. Whether they were true.

Stay here . . . forever?

A Home for Regret

Sometimes, when I'd first wake up from a long, tiresome night, it felt as though I was dreaming. I never questioned the validity of the world I entered in my sleep, ironically—it always felt like I was anchored in reality there. And yet, when I was lying in the dark of my bedroom, staring at the ceiling, sometimes it just seemed like a mediocre dream.

I often asked myself whether or not that was a bad thing.

The feeling passed after a few moments, of course, when I'd feel the heaviness of my body and a dull throb in my head, firmly reminding me that I was definitely *not* dreaming. Though, honestly, I wished I were.

With a groan, I pushed my comfort and comforter aside, glancing toward the nightstand. 6:03 AM. *What am I supposed to do for the next three hours?*

Nature called and I pushed the thought aside to answer, grabbing a set of socks and boxer-briefs to knock my shower out as well. I took it quickly, with only one light on to ease my photosensitivity, and emerged from the bathroom feeling a little refreshed.

"Huh," I mumbled, the clock once again catching my eye. "It's seven. I thought that was a quick one...."

With a shrug, I tossed the towel, the kitchen my next destination. I rifled through the fridge, each item within disappointing me more than the last, until I settled for a strawberry oatmeal bar. Washing it down with a glass of orange juice was a necessity to prevent choking on the damn thing. As I ate, I couldn't help but think about all the things I'd want to ask Diane—things about Maya, and the dreamworld, to finally set us straight—but I knew it was not the day for it. I would have to stifle them, bottle them, and let her grieve.

I walked back into my room and rifled through the shirts hanging in my closet. I'd never really dressed up for much outside of work, since there was really nowhere for me to go. The last funeral I'd been to was my mother's, when I was around nineteen. Nobody else has passed since then —there aren't many people left in my life to die.

I settled on one of my five gingham work dress shirts, with an old pair of black dress pants instead of khakis. *You're supposed to wear black, right? Or is that only a thing in movies? Black is probably safer. I guess it would look bad if I showed up in my exact work uniform, anyway. . . .*

Sunlight crept through cracks between the curtains, stinging my eyes with the searing brightness it always has at dawn. I stiffly squeezed into my jacket, squinting at the clock on my way to the restroom. *Seven-thirty.* Next was my tie, which I fumbled with at first since my hands felt clunky and tired. Normally I'd leave it that way, but. . . .

I patted a bit of cologne an aunt gave me nearly a decade ago onto my wrists and flailed my arms around in an attempt to spread the scent. *Ears, right? Chest, I think. Legs? Maybe if I just get it all over. . . .*

I walked out of the bathroom, more put-together than I'd been in recent memory—disregarding how low that bar may have been—and for what? Why was I putting so much effort into my appearance? To look nice while sending off a dead man I barely knew, surrounded by strangers who couldn't care less if I died right there, right in front of them? And yet, when eight came around, I was driving to Diane's house, fidgeting with my hair and sleeves. It would have made more sense to stay home, change into something comfortable, eat, relax, and kill time until it got dark enough; it would have made so much more sense. So why was I in that car, desperately trying to hide the sun with one hand so I could read street signs? Why was I subjecting myself to additional nuisance and discomfort just to attend a gathering of miserable people in mourning?

Thoughts pulsed through my mind with every heartbeat, like it was the only thing keeping me going, as if my body acted on its own, pulling me the way an ox pulls a cart that has no say in the matter.

Only one spot left in the cul de sac—I was lucky, as the only other parking options were half a mile away. *But I have to parallel park. I hate parallel parking so much.*

The weather was perfect for what I was wearing, cool with a kiss of warmth from a sun trying its hardest to blind me. *Why can't we put a big UV shield in space? Damn sun is so bright.*

Stupid breeze is messing up my hair.

Why do we have to designate 'nice clothes'? Is it a crime to be comfortable? These shoes are killing my feet.

I knocked on the door, afraid the doorbell would be a bit too much, first thing in the morning. I heard the bolt slide and lock click.

This is so awkward. What am I going to do when I get in there? Sit in a corner and wait? Why am I even h—

People say silence is golden, but silence is more like a shooting star to me; rare enough in my own head that it could be nothing more than myth, a thing of impossibility...but as I stood there, looking into those shimmering galaxies of golden brown and green as they caught the sunlight that had burned my own eyes all morning long, my mind was totally quiet. The heartbeat of thought had stilled, flatlining all complaint and annoyance, all commentary and aggravation. It was just me, and her, in a moment that hung for hours. There was something so incredibly enchanting about them, something different than I saw in Maya's eyes—though they seemed equally pained—and I wasted far too much time trying to figure out what it was.

"Are—are you okay?" she asked, leaning slightly to catch a different angle of me. A redness plagued the white of her eyes, like blood-stained ceramic, padded by bluish bags underneath that make-up couldn't fully hide. She was a mess, and still, I. . . .

"Jax?" She rapped her knuckles on the door frame beside me. "Anyone home?"

She was so beautiful, in a different way than Maya was. Even when her heart was decimated, and her body exhausted. When it felt as though waking up was more like dying than coming alive, and every breath reminded her that this life is a path which will always lead to pain. Even in that moment, at the crack of a sorrowful dawn, there was something deep in her eyes that felt more real than anything else.

"I'm sorry—I didn't sleep that well last night," I replied, shaking off the thought. "I space out real easily this early."

"Yeah, no kidding." She let out a chuckle that died halfway through, then stepped aside. "Come on, come in. Unless you want to stand there a little longer."

I do.

I followed her inside, bracing myself for the

crowd of sorrowful strangers. The first was an older woman, somewhere in her late sixties. She wore a loose, black dress hemmed with crimson roses, but it retained an air of elegance without being tacky.

"Oh, you must be Jackson, is that right? Come here, darling." She approached me with outstretched arms and embraced me with a power I was not expecting from a woman her age. Some of the air was sucked out of my lungs as she retained her grip while rocking sideways ever so slightly. "I'm Diane's mother, if you haven't realized."

"Oh, of course. It's nice to meet you, Mrs—"

"Please, call me Merry. I don't much like formalities, especially in my own home." The more I listened, the more I picked up on a faint English accent that refined her image further.

"Merry?" I hadn't meant to ask so bluntly, but the question slipped. "Sorry, I don't mean to sound rude, I just—"

"You haven't met someone with my name, I take it. Well, unless you've read a bit of Tolkien."

"That's the first thing that came to mind, actually. Is that your real name?"

She waved a hand at me. "Oh, no. My name is Meredith, of course, but what a dreary name that is. It makes me feel so old, like someone is approaching me in a nursing home. *'Say, Meredith, would you fancy a game of bridge? We'll be swapping dentures at five, I hear that Bridgette's are massive'*. Don't you think?"

My eyebrows did most of the talking, mildly arched despite my best efforts to tame them. I glanced over at Diane for a moment, whose eyes were closed. "I—I think Meredith is a fine name."

I was met with a wry chuckle. "You're a sweet boy. Be a sweet boy and call me Merry, then, will you? Now, I'll stop bothering your . . . friend, D. We'll be leaving in about twenty minutes for the funeral home, since everyone is here. Would you mind carpooling, Jackson? Parking will be awfully cramped at the church."

"No, carpooling is fine with me."

"Wonderful. Why don't you show him around, dear?"

"Sure, Mom." Diane's lips were taut, and her eyes pointed toward the floor.

"Oh, don't be like that. If a boy can't handle a bit of *my* quirk, what's he to do with yours?" She scurried off, Diane's frightening gaze catching her back.

"Sorry, Jax, she's—"

"She's pretty damn awesome." We shared a glance before she started off down a hallway, beckoning me to follow.

Her house carried itself like one built a century prior; high ceilings, natural light spilling in through large windows, and a dark oak lining the floors, creaking now and again underfoot. There was artwork in most every hallway, all seemingly from before the 18th century. It was like being in a museum, at times.

We passed through most rooms on the first floor without pause, be it the dining room and its rack of imported china, the living room fitted with a 60-inch 4k television, or the kitchen and its surprisingly sleek, modern furnishing. Diane was carelessly tossing her hand around, trying to put effort into showing me around, and I didn't mind. I wasn't looking at the furniture or flooring, anyway.

"Okay, now that the fun part's over," she said, rolling her eyes, "I have something else to show you. Come on."

I followed her up a set of even creakier wooden stairs, to the second of two stories. She led me past what I assume were bedrooms—I wasn't going to ask—and into a library.

"This is the only part of the house we should show people. It's just downhill from here." She was looking up to the ceiling, which had two sunroofs installed. Something about how the sunlight struck walls of books and leather seats, foreign rugs and wooden furnishings; it was magnificent in every way. Strangely enough, though, there were black and white photographs in place of the usual paintings that marked virtually every other inch of the house. They were portraits of American presidents, like Lincoln, Roosevelt, and Reagan.

"It's beautiful," I said, scanning the shelves. Many of the books were fraying, and quite dusty as well. Everything I saw looked like non-fiction, biographies and the like. "Did you add this into the house?"

Diane was in the room's center, looking toward the desk. "No, actually. In case you were wondering why we live in such an old house . . . *this* is why. My dad paid more than he should have to keep the books, too. He added his own, of course, but a lot of these are where they were thirty years ago."

"You'd think someone with a library like this wouldn't give it up."

"I don't remember the buying process too well, since I was, like, fifteen. I was too busy being angsty to have cared about this old house. I knew the creaky floorboards meant sneaking around would be impossible, and I was convinced that was why my dad wanted this place so badly.

"All I really remember is that they were old— the people that lived here before. They were probably happy knowing it'd end up in good hands. I'm sure seeing my dad turn into a little boy when he found this place helped convince them. It's something else, seeing someone so quiet and somber and kind of regal turn giddy and childish."

I walked past the desk, spotting a smaller bookcase behind it. Shelved were series by Rowling, Snicket, Dashner, Sanderson, Paolini and the like.

"I see you had a few books to add here," I said, brushing my finger across their bindings. Many of those books I had read as a kid, and I like to believe they served as a foundation for my world. That hunger to live a life other than your own, one of adventure and importance . . . once I'd tasted it, nothing else was sufficient.

"Yeah. As you can tell, I'm also a master of literature."

"A good book is a good book. Better worlds than ours."

"My dad used to say, 'I choose to get lost in what was; you choose to lose yourself in what could be. What matters is not where we are, but that we must find our way back, and, hopefully, ourselves along the way'—or something like that."

"That's beautiful. Your dad sounds like a hell of a guy." I walked back toward her, still standing at the library's heart. Her eyes had shifted to the sky-lights, sucking in the sun like hungry plants yearning to grow. I unconsciously moved closer to get a better look at the nebulae in her eyes, searching the stars for secrets long hidden. Perhaps, for a moment, I understood Galileo and his passions.

Her lips twitched the slightest bit, and she paid no mind to my approach, nor did her gaze waver.

"He was."

I wanted to say something, then. Something powerful and comforting, something to move her. Something to pull her eyes from the sky and over to mine. Something . . . anything. An indistinct voice beat me to it, muffled by layers of wood and drywall.

She snapped back to reality, blinking thoughts away. "That's Mom. It's time to go, I guess."

"Yeah," I replied, trying to exhale away my apprehension—it didn't work. "Let's go."

I followed her to the door, reaching to shut it behind us. Lingering, I offered one final moment to honor that regretful mausoleum, shelved with history bound in leather and memory.

Too much history.

Too much memory.

Too much regret.

And despite that, I had added some of my own.

Weeping Sky

I was thankful to crawl out of the minivan we'd ridden to church in after an hour of being awkwardly squished amongst six strangers and Diane. Some were cousins, I think an uncle, possibly a niece; meeting an entire family in thirty minutes is overwhelming, and I didn't want to be that guy who asks everyone's name a second or third time. We unpacked from the van into a strangely cold day, far too cold for early March—even in Virginia—and made our way around to the entrance.

The Episcopal Church of St. James was a beautiful building, and surprisingly modern for a religious institute with such archaic architectural influences. They'd clearly found inspiration in classics such as St. Peter's Basilica, but with a sleeker, modern edge—and a slight reduction in size, of course. A magnificent archivolt, stained glass windows, incredibly high, complex vaults fitted with bosses, a façade with stone sculptures of Christ on the Crucifix, and polished, white marble flooring;

it felt more like a billionaire's personal art project than a church. I suppose it may have been.

An older man greeted us in the reception area, his wrinkles not unlike vaults sweeping the ceiling above us. "Hello, brothers and sisters—so good to see you well on this blessed day. May I help direct you?"

Merry firmly grasped his outstretched hand with two of her own. "So good to see you again."

"I'm so sorry that it is under such terrible circumstances. May the Lord lend you all strength in these trying times. Caleb is in Procession B." He pulled his hand away and pointed to the western wing; we followed.

There were a fair number of people moving through the lobby, and an unfortunate percentage of them were drifting into the western wing with us, riding the current down a squally and sorrowful stream. It flowed mainly straight and true, driven by sullen men preserving their concept of masculinity as they shuffled with stony visages aimed low. Occasional tumultuous waves crashed against the current as someone lost control, swept up by a fit of sobbing and whimpering whilst embracing a loved one. What was strange to me, though, were the occasional eddies of people gathered in circles, greeting each other with warm faces donning smiles long missed and soft laughter. Children played with one another, sparking mixes of adoration from bystanders with anger from their parents. The western wing was a turbulent mingling of pain and love, of tears and smiles; loss morphing to reconnection and emulsifying into a confusing concoction of emotions that ultimately tightened the bonds between everyone present.

Near the hall's end we reached a large set of doors, swung open and stopped, with the words "Procession B" inscribed on a gold plate above them. There were clumps of stray visitors lingering near the doorway and in the hall, some of which Merry stopped to greet for a moment. It was only 10:26am, by my very old watch, and yet there were already more people in attendance than there are members in my family—on both sides.

Our group trickled into the procession room, taking a seat in the front row, with me near the center. It figures that my first VIP experience would be sitting in the front row at a funeral. I was sandwiched between Diane and one of her cousins—Jimmy, I think?—in a row of the people closest to him. Out of all the people in attendance, I felt like wasted space in the front row. People in the back were crying, I could hear it. Why shouldn't they have taken my place? It felt undeserved and strange, like I was out of place even though his own sister was the one that asked me to do it.

There was a sense of apprehension for me that I couldn't explain as the procession grew nearer, like a tension building in the crowd's hum, everyone mingling in their own way while I waited for someone to come on stage and announce that a man I'd last seen happy and healthy had officially died.

He was dead before, yes, but the moment a priest says, "We gather here today to remember. . . ." is the moment a person has truly died. You become nothing but fading memories after one final gathering to cast your body into the dirt.

Diane sat like a statue in her seat, eyes glazed, staring through the procession halls like they were windows into some unknown void. She hardly blinked, let alone said a word, and I dared not break her out of whatever her mind had wandered into.

After what felt like forever, an older man in white robes and a hat bigger than his head walked to the podium, a trail of cloth behind him. He smiled, then waved, cleared his throat, and ended a life amiably.

"Good morning, everyone. I am Father Armos. We gather here today," he said, adjusting his glasses, glancing down at his cards. "To remember the life of Caleb Teton."

Rest in peace.

It's an odd thing, to deal with the realization that someone you remember so clearly is just . . . gone. It's different than losing someone who was really close to you, where there's a giant void gaped into your heart, like your soul has been hole-punched, but it's also different than hearing that a stranger has died. It's a confusing sensation, like seeing the moon casually sitting in the blue sky of a summer day, or losing something you could've sworn was just in your hand.

The priest continued on, reading a summary

that was supposed to encapsulate the life of a man; a person, full of pain and dreams and so many things nobody else will ever know stuffed into a few hundred words cut apart by Bible passages. He paused his sermon, craning his head, brow knitted into a quilt. There were some murmurs behind, and I turned, seeing the cause.

It was snowing. In March.

Global warming, Virginian weather—it was my life, all I knew. But snow in March? That was something I'd never seen before.

"God sends his love to Caleb on this day," the priest said, his arms outstretched. "Now, if you'll turn to Peter 4:12...."

My mind wandered again, ambling through endless corridors of thought. There was a song that swallowed me, led by a volunteer choir member I didn't hear the name of, joined by the crowd. The lyrics may have been in the pamphlet somewhere; I didn't care to look. The words didn't matter to me. But there was something haunting in those few minutes, listening to hundreds of broken people joining as one voice, and I swayed a little to it despite myself. A connection between loved ones and strangers alike, mingling in a beauty unseen, but one that settled in like fog over me. It was everywhere. It was everyone. As we sat beneath vast ceilings and floating voices, I began to understand the architecture's elaborate, expensive design a little more. It was a final send-off; a grand finale, and why shouldn't it be as magnificent as possible? A strange and ritualistic yet beautiful goodbye that makes it feel like life really does matter.

Then it was over, and everybody sat once more, and the priest continued on with his verses and life lessons. There was a small, old pamphlet and a stub of a pencil tucked into the back of the seat ahead of me. Something compelled me to pull them out and write:

I sat in my seat, hundreds around me.
Ghosts of friends, classmates and teachers.
I wonder, how many would leave home for me?

A thousand teary eyes, my own two among
them, gazing with love and admiration.
Longing, wishful, and proud; silently coveting.
I wonder, how many would shed tears for me?

Snow fell from the heavens; soft, flittery
flakes reaching for Earth.
Delicate and graceful, frozen tears dancing
on wind's gale.
I wonder, would the sky open its heart up for me?

I do not believe in God, yet I see something
akin to Him in all those around me.
Soul and heart bound by beautiful
hymn, connecting all as One.
I wonder, would lungs burst with song for me?

Yes, it is selfish—incredibly so. Yet, nature takes

> *hold of us when confronted with such things.*
> *Is my existence meaningful, or momentary? I suppose,*

My pencil hung limp over that final comma, urging me to continue, but I simply couldn't. I had no words to follow, to close the poem, to make sense of the longing I felt. It was as though a feeling was on the tip of my heart, right where I knew I should feel it, but the emotion refused to manifest, hiding away and burning like an itch that can't be reached. Father Armos droned on about God and love, and many other things that were dulled against the walls of the thought bubble I'd trapped myself in. He talked for centuries, eons even, and still I couldn't think of a closing line; millions of lives raised and fell, cities burned and grew, children turned to dust, and still the priest and I refused to yield our stances.

Until finally, he did.

"If anyone would like to say a few words, please come up and do so," the priest said, a smile lost in his wrinkles, and Diane stood up. He stepped aside with an arm outstretched to beckon her in, then shuffled aside, his off-white robes catching light cast by stained glass as he passed it by. I tossed the pencil back in the little cubby I pulled it from, folding the note in half and wedging it into my wallet where cash would have been, if I'd had any.

She dropped a disheveled stack of cards on the podium, the slightest waver of her lip betraying an otherwise statuesque face, and breathed deep.

The audience fell silent as the snow that fell outside.

"My brother wasn't like most of the people you meet in this area. He had the brains to be a lawyer, or a doctor, or anything he wanted, really. He was raised with no needs going unmet, and was a handsome man. He had all the things that I find usually end up breeding arrogance, yet was the kindest soul I'll ever meet. None of his success or talent went to his head or inflated his ego. Instead, he did things that should have been beneath him.

"Caleb was one of the most popular kids in our high school, but always tried to be nice to the kids who didn't have friends. The ones some of our other friends might call 'losers'. I asked him why, once.

Diane met my gaze, turbulent with deep pain that lurked and snarled, fighting to break loose.

"He told me something like this: Diane, why wouldn't I? All of our friends are doing fine, they have great lives, they're happy. I love them, but why wouldn't I take a little time to say hi to someone that's clearly alone? Honestly, they're usually the most genuine, and always have interesting things to talk about that I don't hear from people who live lives like ours. Troubled, sometimes, but why is it that loneliness should pile up on people who need a friend the most?"

The breath sucked from my chest like something had punched me hard, and I looked away. The crowd was nodding, murmuring, sniffling, hugging each other, and though the muscles of Merry's face remained locked, the thin valleys of her leathery olive skin glistened.

"I always hear," she continued, her voice cracking the slightest bit, "that people with illnesses tend to be the most positive because they've experienced some of the worst life has to offer, and that changes them. But Caleb was *always* good. He saw something beyond his years that I wondered at from a young age, trying to understand. I'm worried I might never, but I think I'm closer than I used to be. He has—had—a way of doing that to people, changing the way they think just by being himself. Most of you probably know what I mean.

"From the time we were little kids digging around in the mud to the day he passed away, Caleb was teaching me things, whether he meant to or not. It's not right that he was taken so soon, but even in his suffering, he taught me the most valuable lesson of all: he taught me how powerful life is. We live short, fleeting lives, but I saw him fight so hard while smiling that it was almost hard to believe he was a human. Even with everything in his life going wrong, even when—"

The layer of ice cracked, and the avalanche came down, shaking her so hard that I don't think a single person in the crowd, even me, could stop from joining her in tears.

"—Even when his hair had fallen out for the third time, and he was so, so skinny I was scared to hug him, he didn't go quietly into the night. He smiled, with I don't even know what energy, and told me everything would be okay. And suddenly all the things in my life that I thought I couldn't do became so petty and simple. Seeing him beat cancer, then beat it again, and still smile when it came back after that, I realized that we have the power to do anything. *Anything.* This world is ours, and these lives are a chance for us to burn brighter than any star.

"That's the most important lesson of all the ones he taught me, and I'll never forget it until the day that I join him. I, ah—" She put a hand over her mouth, squeezed her eyes, then regained composure. "I wrote a poem for him. I'm not much of a poet, but he inspired me. It's based on our time together, and our final moments."

She pulled out a card from the pile, dropped it, and picked it up again. The crowd murmured briefly, but settled before she began. What followed was the most haunting minute of my entire life as she read a poem that made mine feel like pointless scribbling.

> *I have you now, O' sun-burnt star,*
> *A memory once man.*
> *You dangle down a ledge so far,*
> *I'll hold you if I can.*
>
> *I have no strength to lift you high,*
> *No way to save you, no.*
> *We're falling down a summer sky,*
> *I will not let you go.*

Leaves turn ochre, bloody red,
Your grip is weak, I know.
The world grows dim, but still I scream,
I will not let you go.

It's winter now, our darkened dawn,
The land all dressed in snow.
Sun's embrace is long, long gone,
But please don't let me go.

Falling for years has been so hard,
What life's spent holding on?
Our hands are splitting, cracked and scarred,
Our fingers halfway gone.

"I'm sorry," I say. You start to slip.
"I wish I could've saved you."
But with a smile and not a skip,

You say to me: "You did."

She descended from the podium like a soul entering purgatory, speech cards a mess, burying her face into her hands when she sat. I drifted a hand to her shoulder, offering some semblance of consolation that I knew could do nothing against such cascading sorrow, and the crowd had been destroyed. How could someone else follow that?

Merry sensed it, too, and rose to the podium. She gave a solemn, loving speech that acted as a bridge for the rest; his best friend from university, an uncle—I think—it all blurred together after a while. A conglomerate of stories that were the final remnants of a man who touched so many lives that it was almost as if they took the shape of him, like he was there with us, smiling, even though his body lay unmoving.

I'd often wondered what the afterlife might be like, or if there even is one, but maybe it's just us. Maybe Heaven is the smile a mother has thinking about how beautiful her son was before he passed, or friends sitting around, sharing a beer, thinking of the good times they used to have even if not all of them are there anymore.

A strange, sinking feeling crept up on me.

When the service ended, the crowd scattered, breaking off again into groups that drifted in and away from the immediate family to offer condolences and hugs and tears of their own, and compliment Diane on her speech. A few people I recognized from high school would wave or nod to me, maybe attempt small talk, but it always died out within a minute. I had nothing to offer.

"What have you been up to?" a guy who started a rumor that I killed turtles for fun in high school would ask, and what was there to say? I didn't do anything. There were no exciting adventures or accomplishments to recount, and I hated talking about myself anyway. Something told me they wouldn't want to hear about the world I actually mattered in, the world I'd focused so much on lately.

So, "Oh, not much, just work." is all they'd get in return, like everyone always got from me. The past seven years of my real life summed up in five words.

By the time we were heading back to Diane's house, I knew. I knew there would be no reconstruction of me when I died, through stories or song, because there was nothing to remember.

Couch Lock

I don't quite recall making it back to Diane's house, only that it snowed along the way, because at a certain point upon returning I'd found myself awake and dusted like a fresh donut.

There was a strangeness woven into the air, tangled with laughter and brushing against salty cheeks, to which I found myself most strongly associated with. Not the people and their plethora of feelings, not the soft snowflakes plunging to their deaths on ground far too warm, but the strangeness of two dozen people coping in their own ways with a sudden pockmark on their souls. The man was gone, and so too had his commemoration passed; what, then, was there to grab hold of? To keep it at the forefront would be wallowing, but one does not forget loss so quickly, and because of this it merely sat there, hanging over every conversation, burnt into the back of every mind.

Some did a fine job of ignoring it and going on

to talk about their lives or the state of the world, smiling and laughing.

Some fought through visible pain to interact with loved ones they hadn't seen in years—Diane was the best example of this, distracted from the distraction of conversation.

Some left almost immediately, too weary from travel and tears.

But I had sunk deep into the living room couch, laden with thoughts like lead. In fact, it had been that very couch that I'd sat on some years prior, similarly alone, watching people and conversations wax and wane from above my phone screen —with a single distinct difference, one that was heavier than any rare metal by volume.

Caleb was not there to say hello when others would not.

My wandering eyes found Diane, too often, in some pained juxtaposition between her grief and crowd management. *How does she do so well to fight what's inside and handle being around so many people? I can barely do that on a good day.*

She's so strong.

After about half an hour had passed, Diane plopped beside me with a sigh, her once wide eyes now drooped.

"Sorry," she said, the words low. "Had to make the rounds, you know. You didn't need to stay if you're not feeling up to it."

I shrugged. "Oh, I don't mind. Not my first rodeo on this couch."

A single eyebrow arched. "What does *that* mean?"

"Oh, God. Uh...."

She chuckled, lazily whacking my arm. "I know, I know."

A brief blanket of silence fell over us, which she broke. "Well, whatever the reason, I appreciate that you stuck around. It's nice to take a breather and just chill here with you."

"Yeah, of course." *God, what do I even say? Acknowledge or distract?*

As if the Lord were answering my prayer, a faint, bounding jingle came from the outside hallway, growing louder, and in the least dramatic way possible, a little white dog skidded across the slick hardwood floor into a sprawl near my feet. Rather than correct itself, the pup chose to roll a bit and splay its belly, tongue cascading down the side of its open mouth. Diane giggled, scooping the dog up, and it draped over her hand like a rag, panting.

"Oh, you sweet, silly thing. Did you break out of jail? Yes, you just want some love." Diane had it in her lap, scratching its stomach, but the dog was still upside down and flopped across her leg, looking at me with beady little brown eyes that said 'the world could be ending and I wouldn't really mind as long as someone keeps petting me'.

"You have a dog?" I asked, locking gazes with it.

"Yeah, Alice. We keep her crated when company comes over 'cause she'll roll right into the middle of whatever you're doing and try to eat it. One time, while I was at work, she got onto the counter somehow and managed to slurp an entire pack of tortillas out of the bag it came in without tearing any big holes into it."

"Well that's impressive. Alice is kind of a weird dog name, though, isn't it?"

"Look her in the eyes and tell me she's not so far down the rabbit hole that the rabbits have accepted her as one of them."

The dog recaptured my gaze, panting, a waterfall tongue dripping slobber onto the leather couch cushion. I scratched an incredibly soft, floppy ear, getting *just* the right spot, and Alice thumped her leg into the air.

A smile finally broke across my face. "Okay, I think I get it now."

Merry broke around the corner, her hustled shuffle a mediocre performance at seeming hurried. "Oh, you little devil. She didn't eat any shoes, did she?"

I leaned forward to try and get a line of sight with the front door.

"Nah, she came right around the corner and slid into the perfect belly-rub position. She smells all these people and wants some love, isn't that right?" Diane airlifted the dog to her mother like a pile of freshly dried laundry.

Merry cradled her, turning. "Come on, now.

Off to the slammer you go."

Diane groaned, but I laughed, the dog eyeing me until it disappeared behind the corner. *I wonder, does Alice think I'm gone now? Disappeared forever? How does a dog deal with the world around it constantly changing in ways it doesn't understand?*

But I guess we deal with the same thing, don't we?

"Earth to Jax." The softest of smiles flickered on Diane's face, then faded just as quickly. "Hey, come with me to the library."

I didn't bother questioning it, following her down the hall, conversations fading into muddled blurs, and found myself gazing through the glowing midday skylight when the door shut and snapped me back to reality.

Diane drifted toward the center of the room, where I was standing, her eyes scanning the stretching bookshelves. "You know, when things get pretty rough, I like to come here—I shut the door and hide from everything else. Does that sound crazy?"

I shook my head. "No, of course not. That makes total sense. It's really relaxing in here."

"Yeah. I could stay here forever, never run out of books to read, never have to deal with any of life's bullshit."

"That sounds amazing. This would be an awesome place to spend forever in." *Though, I know of a better one. God, I want to ask her about it . . . but how could I right now?*

She let a finger drift across several ancient book spines, then lifted it, lingering, turning to me.

"But I can't actually do that; it would be nothing more than hiding. How can it be forever if you aren't even really living? Isn't that just a single moment stretched way too thin?"

"I—" The words fumbled, and my brows knitted. "Well, I don't know, I mean it sounds nice to me. Finding somewhere close to perfect. I bet things are always nice in here; it's like a safe place."

A step forward, then two, she took toward me. "Is it safe though? If I hide in here, that means I'll have no idea what to do when I have to leave, and I'd have to leave eventually. Right?"

Wordless motions of the mouth were all I offered.

"Jax, I've seen it for a while now. I saw it in high school, too. You always say you aren't feeling great, or that you're busy, when people invite you places. Don't get me wrong—I hate crowds. Being in that bar with Mike and his . . . whatever she was, that was terrible. Claustrophobic. But you hide from people that care about you, even when you're right next to them."

A step forward from her, then one back from me. "Why are you saying all of this?"

"Life's too hard to face alone. It's too hard, but with some help, it's worth the struggle. Caleb taught me that. Equal and opposite reactions; the best things in life take equal work. Nothing just falls into place."

My eyes turned down. "I don't know what you're talking about. I appreciate your worries but

I'm fine, really. It's you I'm worried about."

"Why don't you try, Jax? Just try to open up a little. Tell me something you feel, something that hurts or feels amazing. Something you love or something you hate."

Is she testing me? Pushing me? I can't tell. I shrugged in response.

"What about your mom, then? Tell me about what happened between you guys."

Something that had been welling in me burst, something dizzying and hurting and confusing that made it hard to think straight anymore. "What does that have to do with anything?"

"Sorry if I'm overreaching, but I feel like you're hiding from things. Our time here is so short, who knows when it might end? You have to make the most of what little we get. Otherwise, what's it even for?"

I rubbed at my throbbing temples. "It's not always that simple."

"Why not?"

Because sometimes you make mistakes that can't be taken back. Sometimes you hurt someone in ways they'll never forget, even if they've done nothing wrong. Have you ever made a good person cry? Hurt someone who was trying their best to deal with a shitty hand?

I sighed, drowning in the middle of a dry room. Why did any of it matter to her? Why did she have to ask so many questions, when I'd worked so hard to bury the answers?

Why was it so hard to let someone care about

me?

"Say something. Talk about something else, if that's easier." She'd somehow gotten within arm's length of me, burning, weary eyes like spotlights on my very soul, words delicate as a fog of breath in cold air. "There's nothing you want to tell me? Nothing at all?"

I. . . .

"I—" Truth be told, I don't know what exactly overcame me in that moment, but it was something far out of my control and it swallowed me whole. "I'm Reza."

She scowled. "You're what? What is that?"

I froze like a deer in headlights, breath caught. *Oh, fuck, no. No, no, no.*

"I don't understand what you said," she pressed, face dressed in confusion. "But I'm trying to have a serious conversation with you, Jax." I could tell by the way she looked at me that it wasn't some kind of ruse or a prank Maya might pull; Diane's reaction was honest.

There was a brief moment between us that lingered longer than it needed to, where I realized how naïve and insane I must have been to truly believe that somehow Maya happened to be a woman that I went to high school with. It crushed my insides and made it hard to breath. "Sorry, nothing. I'm fine."

"Jax. . . ."

Without even the spine to look her in the eyes, I turned, slinking toward the door. "I should go. Thanks for asking, it was nice of you. You're a really good person to ask about me when you're in such a difficult situation."

The doorknob cold in my hands, her voice like a spring gale whispering through the still-dead trees of winter, she said, "You don't have to be able to run. You can stumble, even. But if you don't chase things, Jax, you'll never catch them. You'll just be stuck watching as the world moves on without you."

I rushed out of the library past odd looks, doing my best to politely say goodbye to Merry on my way out. I broke out of the house and into the open chilled air like cresting from beneath water to finally breathe once more, snow kissing my skin, the world white and hazed. The thin layer on my car was opaque enough to act as a shield.

A safe place.

And within it, I shattered.

Cocoon

I think I almost crashed on the way home.

The world was like the inside of a snow globe, and so was my mind; thoughts swirled, whipping in and out of sight at high speeds, nothing lingering for long except the chaos itself. I remember someone blaring their horn, but not much besides that.

At some point I ended up in my living room, shivering and damp, staring at the static of an unlit ceiling from my couch. Diane's words were titans in my head, crushing my brain to paste, pounding against the inside of my skull so hard it felt like it was going to shatter. I kept seeing the face she made when I confessed, the image seared into my skull, taunting me.

I can't believe I said that to her. How can I ever look her in the eyes again? I feel sick.

Who is Maya?

"If you don't chase things, you'll never catch

them."

She's right, obviously. I'm lost, and helpless, and useless . . . what is it even for? I have no idea. But that's only in this world.

It doesn't have to be this way.

She's wrong.

I have control, it's just different. What does this life matter, anyway? It's full of pain and misery, searching for meaning that isn't there, working jobs that are pointless until I die like an ant scurrying around, waiting to be crushed by an unknowing boot.

Some people aren't made for this place. I'm not a genius. I don't have motivation, I hated every second of college, and I can't smile through it all. I'm not Caleb, or Diane, or even Mike. I don't understand people like them.

I wish I did.

I want to be happy. Why is it so hard?

. . .

. . .

It's not here.

Maya's not here.

There's nothing here.

I gripped my hair, hunched over in the loudest room anyone has ever been alone in, trapped with thoughts that screamed into the darkness trapped with myself.

It was too much.

I just want to be happy.

My eyes had adjusted to the darkness, and so had my mind. It settled into a numbness that's difficult to describe, one that nobody should know;

the internal quiet of a graveyard with no visitors, or an unused cradle gathering dust in the garage. I was hollow and drifted through a dim hallway to the kitchen. On the counter was a notebook—one of my planners, with sketches and other blueprints for dreams. I held it limp in my hand, staring at the cover for a while as if it had something to say.

It didn't.

Tossing it aside, I wandered to the cabinet and grabbed the bottle of sleeping pills, taking one, or three, or something—I don't remember.

It didn't matter.

Nothing mattered.

Nothing but the sweet comfort of drifting off into the unconscious.

It came for me with quick vengeance, numbing the rest of my body to match my mind, and I laid to sleep somewhere. It was comfortable, I think. Soft. My body felt heavy, so heavy, like I'd been turned to stone. Like I'd sink through my apartment floor, and the floor below it, all the way through the Earth and out into space somewhere.

That would've been fine.

As I slipped deeper into the void, I heard a faint echoing whisper, like the dying breath of an angel—or, perhaps, the sigh of a disappointed God.

Decisions

Morning embraced me like a long-lost lover in an empty bed. Sunlight oozed from every window and showered me with intense warmth as I sat up, clenching my fist, feeling the strength I'd so dearly missed.

I was whole again. I was right. I had purpose.

My armor went on with ease, and a chilling breeze drifted in through rippling curtains as I looked over the terraformed courtyard; I realized that the sun felt so warm because, by contrast, the air was oddly cold. Lake Augr had grown even wider, its edges lapping at the steps leading into the armory, and shrunken icicles glimmered like diamonds in dawn's fresh light. Rather than enjoy the decor of the great hall, I leapt out the window, reigning in my dragons so they couldn't assist. For a moment, the fertile soil felt like stone beneath my feet, and I savored the impact with a smile.

Yes, this is where I belong.

My dragons chittered, as if to agree with me. "You're here."

Maya was to my right, a swarm of pebbles buzzing over her like bees. She looked lovely in the wan light, skin radiant and ocean eyes ablaze; a warrior, fierce and unyielding, perfect in every single way. I walked up to kiss her, but her hard gaze gave me pause, and she turned back to her task of boring perfectly round holes into courtyard trees.

"I didn't expect to see you so early," I said, still a couple yards behind her. Those rocks were a menace.

"I'm making damn sure I'm ready for that smug bastard when he works up the nerve to show his creepy mask around here." There was a hole in every tree within sight, and she wove her swarm through them with perfect precision, not so much as a splinter protesting their looping dance.

"Ah, I suppose I should've expected that. Your dedication and strength . . . it's why I love you."

Her stones halted, not a single one falling out of line, but she did not turn to me. "You don't love me."

I started, contorting my face. "What?"

"You don't love me."

"Why would you say that?"

Maya finally turned to me, eyes bright and cold like the melting icicles nearby. "You always kept me at arm's length, ever since we met. Now, all of a sudden, you love me?"

"That was different. We had backstories, you

know? But none of that was real anyway."

She stepped forward slowly, one foot at a time. "If none of that was real, then who are we? Just two strangers, lost in a dream."

"Stop," I said, my voice weak. "Stop saying things like that. You don't mean it."

"You know it's true. Our stories, our history—none of it means anything now. What are we even still doing here, Reza?"

I paused. "Call me by my real name."

"No."

I shuddered, burying my face in my hands, rubbing deep into my eyes. When I looked up, she was looking back at me with eyes that looked far less familiar than they once had. "Who are you?"

"It doesn't matter," she said, shaking her head. "Enough about this for now—the mage will be here soon. When he shows his face, are you going to fight with me, or just run away?"

"I'm going to hear him out," I muttered. "Maybe we can all share this place, and why shouldn't we? It's a paradise. It doesn't have to be this hell you so desperately want to make it."

She nodded glacially, then turned back to her training. "He's insane, and so are you, if you believe him. You'd better pick a side when he shows up. Be the hero you've been telling yourself you are."

I scoffed, heading for the armory to spend some time practicing myself, when I ran into Zox. He'd taken cover behind a boulder in the courtyard, hands around his knees, tail tucked between them.

"You alright?" I asked, sliding into a sitting position beside him.

"Yes, I am alright. This is a safe place; her rocks can't hit me here."

"Well, you realize you're hiding behind a rock, right?"

Zox turned to the boulder, then back to me, and if fur could pale, his would have. "Oh."

We sat in silence for a time, accompanied by a soft breeze and the rhythmic, somehow aggressive whir of stones through trees, before I finally asked, "Zox, am I crazy for wanting to talk more with the guy that attacked us?"

He considered the words for a time, sighing in his own way. "I think you both have merit in your arguments, Reza. Your casual demeanor towards a man that attempted to slaughter us, and even wounded you, seems reckless. At the same time, it's admirable that you have such great forgiveness in your heart."

I sat forward, hugging my knees. "I guess so. I mean, we also killed him once already and he came right back, so why even bother? Better to have an ally than an eternal enemy."

"A fair point, though you'd do well to remember this, Reza: kindness and eagerness are good things, but be careful not to befriend evil out of a fear to inconvenience it."

"Oh, come now," a deep voice replied from everywhere, settling in like a chill. "I'm not evil—quite the opposite, really."

We leapt away from the boulder and Zox growled, hunched somewhere between a human and animal stance. Maya didn't move a muscle, but her stream of stones halted for a moment, then rose from between the trees like steam from hot pavement, each one frozen in space but shaking with excitement. They were ready to taste blood.

The mage was sitting on our wall, legs dangling with childish casualness, and a thin mist crackled over his head. He was alone, mask glistening like a daylight star. Ice crystallized amidst the mist, forming not a weapon, but a....

A heart.

He laughed, cocking his head at Maya and her swarm. "I see you've been working on your parlor tricks. I propose a truce—"

A single stone, small but sharp to be sure, cut through the air at a blistering speed and stopped inches short of the mage's face. He flicked it aside like garbage and chuckled again.

Maya finally moved her body, turning to him, rising into the air with the aid of a flat disc. "No truce."

"I know we got off on the wrong foot, but I wanted to talk with you about something. An offer."

Maya's face was, too, like stone. "There is nothing I could possibly want from you."

"Well, you're not the only one here, now, are you?" He turned to the two of us, arching an eyebrow. "One minute—that's all I need."

I looked to Zox, who shrugged, then Maya,

who fired me the kind of look that can kill a person. "One minute. Everybody stay calm for a single minute, alright?"

Maya must have hated me for it, but made no move to fight. She did not relax her stance in any way, though. The mage smiled, stretching his arms out. "Wonderful! First of all, my name is . . . well, it doesn't matter. What matters is but a single question: what is real?"

His words hung over us a moment in silence. When my eyes met Zox's, he was squinting, and leaned closer to me. "Why does he speak in riddles? I hate riddles. They make my brain itch."

It was my turn to shrug, but our guest took the liberty of continuing without an answer. "I'll tell you: reality is whatever you desire most. It's what you decide your life should be, not what others tell you it is. We have to seize control and dictate our own realities, far away from the polluting grasp of those above us, and what better place for it than one like this?"

Maya rolled her eyes—even thirty seconds was too much for her to sit through. "There's no point in talking out of your ass at us, dude. Get to the point so I can kill you—*again*."

He put on an act, mimicking the motions of a noble being insulted at a royal gala. "How utterly rude of you. Fine. It's quite simple really. I'm here to suggest you form a truce and choose this world as your home. Forever. I can show you how, if you come with me."

Another silence; Maya's disbelief that the man was still—as she would put it—'blowing smoke out of his ass' created an air of annoyed shock as wide as the courtyard. Within that vacuum, Zox and I floated, facing each other. He looked confused, almost painfully so, but could not think of the words needed to try and clarify the situation. Even if he had, it wouldn't have helped. I was lost in my own bubble of thought and couldn't do anything but wonder at such a simple yet genius idea.

Choose this world?

Our little pocket in time imploded with a jarring laugh from Maya. "You're pathetic. I've heard enough of this."

"I don't like this man," Zox added, his nose twitching. "He smells like madness and sounds like it, too."

"Okay, we have an answer from the dog, then." The mage met my gaze, pursing his lips. "What do you have to say? You've been silent this whole time. Surely you think thoughts in that pretty head of yours."

I felt their eyes on me, all judging for different reasons. Maya, with preemptive disappointment. Zox, because Maya was doing it, and he was likely also hoping I would explain what a dog is to him. And the mage, for a reason I couldn't quite understand. It was an uneasy, heavy feeling that betrayed his false visage.

"How would that even be possible?" I finally asked and lightened as the gazes lifted.

It looked almost as if the mage's mask smiled the slightest bit. "Simply stay awake tonight instead of sleeping. Do that, choose *this* world, and you'll be free. Free from all the pain of a world that will never be yours."

"Why are you offering this to us?"

"Have you ever felt like there is no place for you?" he asked, his words suddenly solemn. "Like you are alone in a world full of strangers and ghosts?

My eyes turned downward.

"There is a place for everyone, here, to live a life of meaning—one where you have all the power you could possibly dream of. What say you?"

The rocks orbiting Maya agitated, stirred into a cyclone like an enraged school of fish. "Shut up and die, already. We don't want to hear any more of this."

But before she could launch an attack, I froze her whirlwind and turned her body to stone with a single word:

"Yes."

Within it lied a thousand regrets which no mausoleum could possibly hold, and a numbness matched by no enduring cold. It was my pain, and its long-awaited relief. A key to unlock my mind and be free; or, possibly, nothing more than a prison. Whatever else it may have been, it was certainly absolute. It was something, which is infinitely more than nothing, and I seized it.

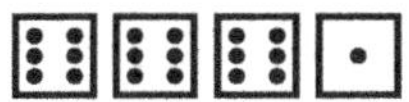

A Quiet Place

It's amazing how many different kinds of quiet there are, and how different they each feel. Confusion, shock, sadness, awkwardness—all discernible from something as simple as a lack of words.

Oh, and anger. That's probably the most palpable one of the lot, a hollowness scooped into the air by rage so tight it could be rolled up like a newspaper and used to beat me in silence. The sound of my answer was long gone, but it had left my mouth and hung over us like fog, woven into wrath and thin mist. Another smile split itself across the mage's face, and he cut the quiet with a curt, almost shrill laugh, slapping his knee.

"Oh, my—I suppose you didn't expect *that* when you told him to pick a side. Even your dog looks confused. Granted, he has looked confused this whole time."

"I am no dog," Zox replied, followed by a deep

growl that betrayed his argument.

"Right." The mage hopped up from his perch on the wall, turned to the forest, and stood over it for a moment. "Well, this has become rather awkward for us all. You should pack a few necessities and come back with me for at least a few days."

I nodded to him, slow, as if minor motions might go unnoticed by the beast beside me. Her breaths were drawn but sharp toward the end, and deep—like she'd been fighting the entire time. Dangerous eyes tracked the mage along our wall.

"The offer extends to you, miss—" He bent backward, throwing his arms out for balance, to dodge a sedimentary missile that exploded a treetop behind him into plumes of splinters and shredded leaves. My dragons shot forward into a defensive position, traumatized by too many of Maya's stones, but the mage simply smiled at her and turned back to the forest. Before leaping down, he called out, "Well, never mind, then."

Once he was gone, the silence in our courtyard condensed, and suddenly it felt as though gravity had increased tenfold, making it harder to breathe. Maya's storm settled for a moment, each stone perfectly still and evenly spaced from one another in the air. It was like a hovering work of abstract art.

With a deep breath, she screamed, and the entire cloud shot into a picturesque sky where it, perhaps, hoped to become a real cloud someday— but, after a moment, it tore through a pleasant puff of wispy white, mangling in the stratosphere. No, it did not aim to be a cloud, it aimed for the heavens, to tear through the ozone and become the smallest meteor field in space.

I stared a while at the white splatter, though the stones had long since become invisible. Perhaps they'd simply disintegrated—but, no matter the fate of the stones, the simple reality left on Earth was that a perfect sky had been slain, and I was left looking at the corpse.

When at last I peeled my gaze away from it, I felt hers hot on my cheek, trying to pierce me like I, too, was nothing more than a wisp of vapor. Avoiding her eyes, I started for the castle entrance, but a boulder slammed into the ground before my feet, splattering mud all over them. The boulder split in half, like a cracked egg, except the yolk was another rock carved into text.

Piss off.

She never was very subtle.

I stared at it a while, sighed, then met her burning gaze. It stung, and I flinched. "Hate me if you want to, but this place is my home."

Silence.

"Why is it such a sin that I'd want to stay here forever with you?"

A deep breath, head tilting upward, but still not a word.

"Fine. Well, I don't need anything from the keep, anyway. I'll just head out."

I turned toward the wall, dragons at the

ready, because scaling it seemed like a much preferable option to awkwardly cranking the gate open. Before I even broke the interior treeline, she finally ended her protest.

"We're not that different, you know. Not in who we are or what we want."

I turned back. "I don't think that's true, based on recent evidence."

She lifted her eyes to the cloud she'd murdered and left them there. "You're wrong—the only difference between you and me is that you're a fucking coward."

My heart sank into my stomach, leaving an acrid taste in my tongue. "What would you know? Quick to judge, as always. It's my choice and I've made it."

All she offered in response was a chuckle so dry it could've kindled under the midday sun. A guttural laugh came from the left.

"Sorry," Zox said, ruffling the streaks running down his fur with a lazy paw. "I was nervous that time, and Maya . . . sorry."

I accepted his excuse with a half-hearted shrug, then clamped one dragon onto the stone wall. It crumbled, looking more brittle than it ever had before. "Will you come with me, Zox?"

Our eyes met, and I felt a familiar fire in them, though dimmer and duller. "I don't think so, Reza. I am the final will of my people, and this doesn't seem like a life to honor them with. We hate the cold, anyway. I never liked the icy man."

"I understand."

"Sorry, Reza. I'm indebted to you both."

"No, I understand. No need to explain it."

Stone cracked and groaned in golden jaws as I vaulted up the wall. Atop it, I paused for a moment to look back across the castle grounds, a place once so full of life and warmth, where only joy awaited me, and sighed. The shattered courtyard scarred and flooded, the woods cracked and smashed from Maya's beatings, and the cold, dead air that hung over it all like graveyard mist—it was hardly the place I once loved; a shadow of greatness cast on hollow ground and hallowed hearts. Maya was retreating to the castle without even a glance back.

I'd always thought that, if no one else, she understood me. She loved me when I thought no one else could, and we took on the world together. Why, then, wouldn't she want the same thing I did? Why wouldn't she jump at the chance to stay in a perfect world with me for eternity? I felt familiar hollowness as Maya shut the main doors behind her, sealing our fate.

I was on my own—maybe I always had been. A pang of sadness tightened my chest knowing full well that we might never see each other again, but I quickly bottled it up. *Apparently, I'm just terrible at reading people all-around. It'll be fine—as long as I'm here, I can make my life into whatever I want it to be.*

The wind was strong as my dragons catapulted me through their currents. Frigid air dense with the scent of pine and mud stung my face, but it was hardly a bother.

As I hit the ground, scattering dirt across nearby trees, I realized it was the first time I'd be traveling through it without her. It was a second type of chill, layered into the cold, and I shivered as I whisked through the forest with golden legs.

The journey was quick, quicker than it had ever been before, thanks to the increasing control I had over the metal beasts at my hip. They worked graciously without much thought on my part, keeping me balanced in the air even over rough terrain and at high speeds, though the process left a trail of churned soil in my wake.

A pastel sky turned white, then grayer still, as I approached. A dusting of snow kissed every dead tree and their crystal limbs, which was jarring given how much life the outer forest still had. When finally I crested the forest's thinned edge, my breath caught again at the magnitude of the hand bursting from the earth, like a buried frost titan grasping for life. Something stirred behind fog in the distance, but further still I pressed, through the snowy field dotted with petals of vibrant flowers refusing burial. The hand grew and grew until it became almost all I could see.

What had once been shifting fog clarified as an ice-blue tongue flickered from behind a colossal thumb, and even colder eyes tracked me. I took a step back, my dragons coming alive and snapping at the monster as it slid closer.

"Forgive her—we don't often have visitors," a deep voice called. The mage strode forward from somewhere, wearing a white, fluffy version of the robe I'd once murdered him in. My dragons clacked their teeth at him. "I see our pets have become acquainted."

"They're not pets, really, I don't think. They're . . . well, it's hard to explain, I guess."

He nodded glacially. "Right. Well, then—shall we?"

I willed the dragons to rest, then followed him toward winter's wrist, where a cave just big enough for us to walk through without crouching was scooped from the ice. The interior was somehow warmer than the outside air—I couldn't even see my breath—and there were no lamps or torches posted on the walls. It was a single room with nothing hidden from sight, lit by the hazy cerulean walls gently filtering sunlight, and was marred only by a single wooden door across from the entrance. I started forward, but he held up a hand, then lowered it and raised his head.

The whole room lifted.

Aside from the feeling of moving upward, the only other clue was a gentle waviness in the wall's glow. We eased to a stop, and he walked for the door, so I followed him. When it opened, a wave of cool-but-not-too-cool air caressed me, inviting me, and for a moment I had to shy my eyes away from a glimmering brightness beyond.

The walls were like half-melted diamonds, with a kiss of teal, that struck against blood red tapestries. Shattered sunlight became murals that stretched across the room and stole my attention. It was breathtaking in every sense of the word, like being inside the gem of a goddess' wedding ring.

"Welcome to my home," he said, leaving me behind, "where the drinks are always cool. Speaking of which—"

A section of the wall near him swirled into a protruding spout, which turned a dark brown as liquid flowed from it and into a crystal cup. He held it toward me, and I accepted it, rich, deep notes of chocolate and coffee wafting in as it approached my lips. It was a bitter stout, sweet at the same time, with a light carbonation and a healthy hint of ethanol to round it all out. Nothing was overwhelming, not even the flush I felt in my head.

"This is delicious," I said, licking a bit of the nitrous foam from my lips. "How is this possible? It tastes—and feels—so real."

He smiled, taking a sip of his own. "It is real; I argue that this place is more real than anything else. A world where everything is what you want and only what you want."

"Now that's something I can drink to." I returned his smile, raised my glass, then took another gulp of the stout. "What's your name?"

"Ah," he said, giving me the sort of odd look one gives a child when withholding secrets beyond their years. "Call me Alduin."

I nodded, twisting my cup in a circular motion. "Flows like good ale. Now ... how do you know my real n—"

"Careful, Reza," he said, wagging a finger at me, his lips thinning. "Some questions you do not want answered, for even a simple question posed at the wrong time can erode the foundations of the tallest constructs. So, the question I have for you is: does it matter?"

The remaining drink in my cup held no answers, despite how hard I searched for one within it. "I suppose it doesn't, Alduin. Not right now, at least."

His signature smile returned, and he raised his glass. "Cheers, then, to the beginning of a new adventure; of new passions and endless wonder."

We drained our cups. I saw no trace of a sink or kitchen, and asked, "Where should I put this?"

The cup he had been holding slipped from his hand, careening toward the ground, and I flinched in preparation of the coming crash—only, it did not come. A part of the floor not covered by tapestry rose up and swallowed it like a snake would an egg, recycling the cup back into its body. I dropped mine, and the building happily gorged upon it.

"That's a neat trick," I said, running my foot over where I'd dropped the cup. The floor was perfectly smooth and glinting, as if nothing had happened.

"I have learned many things in my time here, and honed will into skill."

"I can see that. Where were you hiding before we first encountered you?"

His smile waned. "Oh, here and there. I found places to live, places where no one might find me, where I could make a home without anyone realizing it. That is, before you and that very angry woman slaughtered me."

I ran a hand through my hair. "Yeah, sorry about that. You seem fine, now."

"I am not one to die quietly, not before I feel I have fulfilled my purpose."

"And what might that be?"

Alduin walked across the wide room, thinning a portion of the wall to become a window for him to look through. "I help people who are struggling in life. I believe my calling is to bring joy to those who feel joy is lost to them. Toss a rope into the well of despair."

"That's a very selfless goal—but are you implying that I'm struggling, and need you?"

He turned to me, smiling. "Who am I to say? However, you *are* here, aren't you?"

I drew a deep breath, then shrugged. "Yeah, I guess so. And with ale like that, I can't say I regret the decision."

"Trust me, there's more than plenty where that came from."

A short pause fell upon the conversation until I broke it. "What are you hiding from?"

He eyed me a time, fighting back a smile. "The version of myself I hate the most; the weak, inept, worthless person I burst from, like a butterfly out of its cocoon. And a world far too big for those who are small."

"I understand."

"I know you do." He sighed. "I have a hundred other flavors of ale, but let's save that for another day—follow me to your room. You can set it up however you'd like."

Through swirling, curved hallways with less luminous walls, we walked past impressions of famous art pieces embossed into the ice and toward a large oak door. He beckoned me to enter, and the doorknob was smooth and warm. "Ordinary plebeians like me have to use normal doors, eh?" I asked, turning it.

"Feel free to come up with a better system for yourself," he said after a dry chuckle. "I wouldn't want to risk you being trapped in your room."

His words were logical, and even cautious, but a shiver shot down my spine. *I really am in a coffin, if he wants it to be one. Was this a mistake?*

No. Alduin understands this place, he understands what it means. I have to trust him.

Somnior stirred at my hip, so I subdued it and swung the door open. It protested with a great groan that curved through the halls, as if to scold me for daring to open it. What lay beyond was. . . .

An empty room.

A completely empty room, with ice walls a much darker blue than anywhere else in the building, and notably dimmer. It was something between a dungeon and a place to store vegetables in the winter.

I turned to Alduin, my chest tightening. "This doesn't look quite like a person's chambers."

He looked through me and into the cellar. "It is, once you're inside. It's a room that molds itself to you and your desires, where you can have everything you need. Just go in, close your eyes, and when you open them, everything will be perfect."

There was a conflict brewing inside me, one foot trying to take the step forward, the other planted firmly, unsure of something so strange. The room had an ominous air to it, dim and cold and so utterly plain, as if loneliness itself had taken the shape of a dome. My better half lost, and I stepped into it, a bead of sweat tickling my brow.

"Now close your eyes. . . ." a fading, thin voice whispered. "Close your eyes and see."

I obeyed but saw nothing. My thoughts refused to settle, nor would the uneasy feeling stay down in my chest. I know I must've opened my eyes after a time, because I felt it, but what I saw betrayed that feeling. Surrounding me was a void that swallowed every bit of light; a pure, inescapable blackness. It was as if my body had been melted into it, and my thoughts scattered into an abyss neither here nor there. Somnior was unresponsive, and when I reached for it, felt only air.

"What're you doing to me?" I screamed, somewhat surprised to hear myself make a sound.

"You are not at peace," a breeze whispered

back. "There is a war inside you that must end. Relax, think of the most beautiful thing in the world, something you wish to be real, and when your storm has calmed, it will be."

"Let me out of here!" The words came out, but they felt less like air escaping my lungs, and more like blood oozing from my soul.

"You are trapped, for now—but do not fret. This is a prison of your own making, Jackson. Free yourself and be at peace."

"How do you know my n a m e . . ."

Lucidity was escaping me, consciousness flickering like a broken light, and it no longer felt like I had a body. In fact, nothing felt at all. Every fiber, every muscle, every nerve, had dissipated into mist, leaving me a cloud of panic and doubt, floating in the dark.

Or perhaps I was the dark, and it was me.

Inkjet Skies

I wonder if this is what it's like to die.

There was the slightest coldness and faint tingle that came with becoming nothing, which is oddly betraying of itself. It's hard to say how much time had passed in my deconstructed state, all of which was spent . . . not really thinking about anything at all, which is ironic, because thinking was the only thing I could do; yet, nothing would stay molded in my mind, as if even my thoughts were dissipating into the void. I was the ashen remains of myself scattered into a breeze, riding a current toward nowhere in particular. There was something blissful about it, which feels unclean to admit, but along with my body and focus, my anxieties and frustrations also melted into the cloud that was me, and I no longer felt them gnawing away.

It was, truly, a numb relaxation; a lucid sleep in which not a single thing mattered.

Until it wasn't.

Sometime between never and forever, I awoke—but not in the ice dungeon or in my bed. A tightness hit me first, something squeezing my forearms, then the kiss of cool air. From the dark haze emerged two inkjet skies, stacked atop each other and dotted with flecks of shimmering silver. One was serene, a picturesque portrait of the night, but the other twinkled and twirled and rippled about without a care. There was a silhouette at the crux between worlds—a woman, I discerned; a starlight dancer, lost in a trance as she tiptoed across light-years. I was lost in her trance, too, for a time.

The tightness spread to my legs, and my mouth, and soon my entire body was being strangled, though I could still breathe somehow. The dark became home to me, and as I settled, the direness of my situation clarified. I was strapped to a chair, not by rope or chains, but something dark and deep that pulsed, as if I'd somehow been bound by an abyss. A pang of panic snaked through my core, and I tried to resist, to scream and rock and move any part of myself, but nothing worked. I couldn't make a sound or move a millimeter.

When next I looked up from my binds, the world was aglow with titanium moonlight, by a moon that was not there previously. The stars shone just as bright as they always had, and I could see her clearly as she danced.

Maya.

She had grace I'd never seen from her, but it

felt natural—it made sense to my eyes. There were not two skies colliding at a horizon, but rather, the night was being devoured by Lake Augr's onyx surface. The castle and armory were carved from darkness, and the courtyard was pristine, as if previous battles had never happened; we were inside the perfect, quiet calm of a snow globe that hasn't been shaken. Her motions were unbroken by the moon's visit, and if I was visible, she paid me no mind.

I wanted so badly to rush over and join her, to rid myself of every worry, every concern, and dance across liquid night. My soul burned with desire, but my body could not match it, and as if it had sensed my want to struggle, the binding tightened further. With the only power I had over myself, I turned my eyes to the dark spire that should have been the armory. Another figure, one that may have always been there, was sitting at its steps, watching the performance with me. It stood, strong and tall, then strode to the lake with a grace to rival Maya's and entangled itself in her rhythm, mocking me with every swoop and swing.

What was once a fire burning in me flickered and wisped, strangled by my own powerlessness, and I went limp in my seat.

Some things just aren't for me.

I melted into the surrounding dark once again, like blood draining from the heart of a man and into the lake he'd been felled in.

◌◌ ◌◌ ◌◌

What is that sound?

It was faint, not quite distant, but muffled through thick walls—something like the staggered sob of a broken heart, perhaps. A hurt, shuddering sound that should've made me feel something.

If I wondered where it came from, or what it was for, the thought came and went idly as I sat there, camouflaged in a crowd of empty pews. The wood was uncomfortable, but it didn't bother me —it felt natural, actually, and I didn't shift. There was a serene numbness to it all, in the holy glow of shattered sunlight spilling through large, stained windows.

It was me, an enormous crucifix, and my dead body beneath vaulted ceilings painted with depictions of godly men and their great struggles. Struggles greater than mine, at least.

His hardened face had lost its lovely tan and rugged beard. The person lying in that casket behind an empty podium was a ghost of the warrior I once was, and I wondered how he met his end. Was it a great battle, where he gave his life to defeat the ultimate evil once and for all? Or did he simply die in his sleep somewhere, where no songs or tales would ever find him?

I suppose he couldn't have been much of a hero, or I wouldn't be the only one sitting here.

Something about the situation should have

struck a chord with me—after all, I was at my own funeral. But as I sat there, free of any bindings, I found that apathy had become a restraint of its own, like my sadness laid with the wails of whatever person was crying out from the other room. There was no eulogy, no speech about what his life meant, and I felt no urge to bother doing it myself.

The silence of his death felt right, and so we both sat in our coffins, unmoved and uncaring.

∞　∞　∞

White—so, so much white that every facet of the cube I was in blended together almost perfectly. It was like the inside of an egg, matte and bright, and the walls could've been ten feet or ten miles away, for all I could tell. Everything was equally lit, with no distinct source.

I flexed my fingers, blinking at them—it was strange, being able to move freely. It didn't feel powerful, per se, but it was nice to have some semblance of control.

"Hello, Jackson."

I spun, reaching for my sword but finding only the cloth of my jeans. What awaited me gave me pause, and I simply stared a while, mouth agape. It was my boss, Mrs. Henderson, dressed in the kind of tired pantsuit she'd wear to work.

"I know, this is an odd place to find me—but, then again, we often cross paths with people at the strangest times, don't we?" Her voice had both a frailty and strength to it at the same time.

"How are you ... no, why are you here?"

She shrugged, then looked around. "I could ask you the same question. Why are *you* here?"

I blinked at the ground by her feet. "I don't really know why I'm here, or where here even is."

"Usually, that means you're lost, doesn't it?" she asked, a weak smile twitching her lips.

"I guess so, yeah."

"And when we're lost, what do we do?" She took a step forward and placed a hand on my shoulder. It looked gaunt and spotted. "Do we stand around, waiting to magically wind up where we're trying to go?"

I shook my head. "No, but where am I trying to go?"

"That's for you to say, isn't it?"

"But how do I even go anywhere? I mean, this place seems like eternal nowhere. Just ... nothing. How do you go somewhere, when you're nowhere?"

Mrs. Henderson smiled a full smile. "Well, now you're asking some of the right questions, aren't you?"

We stared at each other a time, before I shied away, then asked, "Why do you hate me?"

Her face was soft, like that of a consoling mother. "Oh, Jackson, I don't hate you. Why would I?"

"I don't know, it just seems that way. I wouldn't blame you for it."

"You know," she said, looking up to the sky or ceiling or whatever it was, "I see a pain in your eyes, the same kind of look my reflection gives me from time to time. I don't *hate* you, Jackson. I'm a little disappointed, that's all."

I couldn't find anything to respond with.

"You have so much potential," she continued, "that gets wasted away by your apathy. You must hate your job, probably more than I hate mine, but I also never see you trying to break out of the rut you're stuck in. Have you ever come to me and asked if there are other opportunities to pursue, or pitched an idea you thought might help the company? Have you ever tried to show that you're a smart, hard worker—or do you merely accept where you are and wallow in it?"

"I. . . ." The words trailed off in a deep sigh. "I don't know. You'd probably shoot me down if I tried."

"And why would I do that? If you have something to offer, something valuable, and you take the time to show it—how do you know it won't end well for you? If you assume that the only possible outcome is the worst, then that's the only outcome you'll ever get.

"If you don't chase things, you'll never catch them."

My eyes turned to her, but she'd faded into the glowing nothingness, her words lingering like fogged breath—and shortly after, I joined her.

⊗ ⊗ ⊗

The scent of cheap ham and fry grease assaulted my senses first, then a soft sizzling sound, followed by the warm glow of a summer sun slipping through tall windows. Everything had a familiar, comforting feeling, one that I would know with my eyes closed: Harry's Deli.

There were no swirling cupcakes in the display case, nothing was written on the chalkboards that should've contained the daily specials, and only one person was behind the counter. His smile was from ear to ear, his fist clenched around a greasy, brown paper bag that sagged with way too many fries. I walked over and accepted it from him, eating a few and sighing at the taste—who doesn't like fresh fries?

"Is good, Mr. Jax?" Hugo asked, his meaty forearms crossed.

I nodded and grunted through a mouthful of food, then swallowed and said, "Oh, it's delicious, as always, Hugo. And I keep telling you—call me Jax. I'm no one special."

"Ah, but you are number one customer! Special to me." He held his hand over his heart, then bounced with laughter. "Why you always look so doom and gloom? Be happy, friend. Life has many, many things of joy, enough for us all."

Flopping a fry around, I said, "I don't know, Hugo. I think the better question is: how are you always so happy?"

"How am I happy?" he asked, his accent coming through thickly. "Why I not be happy?"

I tussled with the words a moment. "Well, you know . . . I mean, you're not exactly living the dream, right? You're what, forty or fifty? And making sandwiches seems like hard work, and you're always so busy. Not to be rude of course, the food is awesome."

Hugo laughed again, the kind of deep laugh of a man without a care in the world. "Silly Jax, why I not be happy making sandwiches? Is hard work, yes, no doubt. Is no glamour or fame. But every day, thousands of people come into my deli, and they all very hungry, yes? They like you, have long days at hard jobs, and want good food, and I give it to them. Then they smile, and they say, 'Thank you, Hugo!' and I know I make their day better, you know? Life is great, Jax. Is all about sharing things that make us feel better, like hugs, or delicious Hugo Reubens.

"Happiness is just sandwich waiting to be eaten. Don't let it get cold."

I couldn't help but smile back at his continued guffawing, and the smile sparkled into laughter—it was contagious, really. The man had something about him that makes a person feel better, even if they didn't know why.

ⓘ ⓘ ⓘ

The taste of kraut and mustard was still on my tongue when I snapped back into my unattended funeral. I was disappointed—not at myself, or the turnout, but that when I looked down into my hands, a sandwich was not in them.

I was really enjoying that.

It was different, that time, as I sat alone at my own wake—I stood, no longer locked in place, and walked up a few marble steps, past an empty podium, to where my body was lying. It was so cold, so unloved, and I felt no envy for him. A muffled cry sounded from outside the room again, and I took a deep breath, offering silent respect to him; after all, if I didn't, who would?

Nobody deserves to die completely alone— you should at least have yourself.

Something pulled at me, like an invisible hand, and I followed its call to a back hallway with a great oak door, carved with angels and all kinds of other Biblical figures, but it wouldn't budge. I had to plant both feet and pull with my entire body to pry it open, and it groaned with protest for every inch it traveled. Adjacent to the room I was in lied another procession, one that was an entirely different scene. The sound of staggered sniffles and weak sobs echoed through the buttresses flying overhead, dancing with paintings of Moses and Abraham and a dozen others. From a distance, it looked like they, too, were crying.

Nobody noticed me walk in, but I recognized many of them; Maya, Zox, Mike, Diane, Mrs. Henderson, Hugo, various family members, old friends from high school—so many familiar faces, all wretched with sorrow. I was invisible to them, silent, and I used that to my advantage as I crept across the marble floor, past a preacher reading scripture, and peered into the casket.

It was me, again. The real me, even more pallid than usual, but he had a peacefulness to him, too. No bags under the eyes, brows relaxed, and wearing nice clothes in a rare appearance of class.

You, too, huh?

The corpse's eyes snapped open, two eerie pits of darkness, and I stumbled backwards, yelping. "What the—"

I bumped into something else and spooked yet again, scrambling away—it was the priest I'd run into, and when I looked up at him, the same two sockets of night were searing a hole into my soul. In the crowd, there was a cacophony of sniffling, but every single person had the same eyes, tears streaming from them. As I backed away, they slowly raised fingers that pointed through me, and without a single mouth moving, whispers echoed through the apse.

"You."

"You."

"It was you."

I clawed at my face, curling up into a ball on the cold floor, as the voices surrounded me, shrinking me until I became the all-familiar nothingness once more.

⦾ ⦾ ⦾

At first I could only feel it, like a wave of warmth in the dark that tingled and glimmered into green and gold, swallowing me whole. It became bright, so, so bright, with the flickering lantern-light of fading dreams. What I'd thought was warmth was not quite right—it was not a feeling on my skin, but one within me that rose up as if I too had been set ablaze to drift into the heavens. And why did the world look so big? Giants drifted through busy channels full of rising steam and orange glow, sizzling meat and performing arts. The festival was a whirlwind of wonder that drank in my soul, mixing me all up inside of it, and I felt pure awe as I watched from my low perch.

Something squeezed my hand, soft and enveloping; a hand far bigger than mine, yet delicate in its gentle grace. I looked up and saw her shimmering smile between snarling dragons; she was not a giant, but rather, I was small . . . maybe I always had been. I wanted to say something, but the words in my mind could not form on my lips—I was merely a passenger along for the ride.

But she knew. Mothers always know, somehow.

"It's okay, sweetie," she said, kneeling beside me. Her eyes looked so big and bright and full of love. "I know it's scary seeing all these people, but I'm here for you, no matter what."

I wanted to believe it but couldn't. Something welled within me, and I tasted the salt of my own sorrows as I cried.

She shushed me, a comforting hand running through my hair. "I know, love. You might get lost, and the world isn't always kind to us. But no matter how far you stray, no matter how far you fall, I am here. Even at the end of the world, or the bottom of the sea; where there is no moon or sun or stars, and hope is only a dream, I'm never more than a heartbeat away.

"Remember that, Jax, my life, my light. Remember that you are loved, even if it feels like you shouldn't be."

There was a quiet moment of understanding between us as we embraced; I was so small, but in her arms, I felt as though everything would be fine.

Everything was just fine as the dark consumed us.

⦾   ⦾   ⦾

Am I in heaven?

A throne of vine and leaf held me as I sat in paradise, where birds chittered in a thick, emerald canopy that sunlight flickered through. The foliage beneath me should've been bristly or stiff, but instead it seemed to cup my body, floating me in place as I lazed in a jungle peppered with flora of every color. A breeze sifted through that rustled the forest, and it felt like I rocked with it, as if nature and I had intertwined in a peaceful, perfect harmony. It was the kind of place I could get lost in forever. To my left sat a stack of my favorite books, each perfectly placed on the next without even a hair's breadth of divergence. To my right, a garden of plump, succulent vegetables and fruits with glossy coats.

From behind me, a short, greyish-brown monkey with big, black eyes swung in, kicking up a bit of loose soil. It was odd, but not startling, and I smiled at it—I'm fairly sure it smiled back.

"Well, hello, there," I said, waving to it.

The friendly monkey mimicked my motion, then hooted as I chuckled, and ventured deeper into the beyond. Not a single thing was out of place—not even me, for once . . . but an oddness mingled into the open air, a strangeness in the serene setting. It was immaculate, everything I could ever want from a place to hang my head, and yet, something was off.

The air wasn't warm.

Despite being in a tropical slice of bliss, my skin was tight and bumpy, and a chill raced down my spine. No meridian warmth soothed me, no heat lapped at me from the sun's approach, and the air had a still, eerie coldness that became more and more wrong. My throne of greenery turned into a prison as I tried to escape, vines wrapping around me tighter and tighter still as I struggled to break free.

The breeze twisted into a whisper that iced my nerves. *"Relax,"* it said, rather ironically. *"Just be at ease."*

I screamed, yanking with all of my might and stretching the vines, but they would not break.

"Stop fighting that which you want."

"Why don't you stop telling me what I want, asshole?" My muscles felt like they were going to explode, I was straining so hard, and my head turned fuzzy as it filled with blood.

"Do not turn a hand against bliss."

"You know," I grunted between groans and hisses, "I'm getting really tired of these bizarre situations you keep putting me in. Let me out!"

"You are captive only to yourself."

I nearly pulled a hand loose, but a bit of vine refused to slip over my meaty thumb. "That's a load of crap, I didn't lock myself in here!"

Only a gentle rustling of leaves replied.

With one, final shout, pushing the limits of what my body could do, I pulled a hand free of the binds—only for another to shoot out and wrap me even tighter as I squirmed.

"God, this is the worst," I muttered to myself and my chains. "Sorry, Maya—you were right, as usual. I'm sure you'll have a wonderful time rubbing it in my face."

Something stung my cheek, like an invisible hand had slapped me. I was too startled to make a sound, but another strike earned a confused grunt, and another made me shout. There was no one but me in the forest.

A searing pain cried out in my left forearm, and I screamed so loud the world melted into darkness—only, that time, the darkness wasn't total; it was fuzzy, and my heaving breaths echoed against close walls.

I was awake again, and one of my dragons had sunk its teeth into my arm. Warmth spread from the epicenter, and though I knew what it was, it was eerily comforting. Then, another searing pain, but in my ears, then on my eyes. Something crashed and cracked, pelting me with pebbles and the brightest grey I'd ever seen.

Slowly, I realized I'd been set free of my prison.

Maya?

My dragons cocked their heads at me, chittering with annoyance, glittering with beads of moisture, as if to say, "Hurry up already, you idiot."

"Yeah, yeah," I muttered, stumbling toward the shattered opening. "You guys always like to show off."

One latched onto each side of the gap, suspending me in midair, and my stomach dropped at the sight of little green trees dotting the ground. I wanted to protest, but another, smaller crash sounded behind me, and I shot my gaze to it.

"You betray yourself," Alduin said, without a hint of urgency in his voice.

"I don't know why you keep saying weird

things like that, but I'm leaving."

"Leaving, Jackson? To go where, exactly? You would run from utopia, towards what?" He took a step forward.

I glanced back, twitching at the sight. "Nothing about this has been a utopia. It's been a nightmare wrapped in pretty thoughts."

"Only because you are at war with yourself. End the conflict and be at peace." Something deep groaned from beyond the walls, a hard, scraping sound, and I knew what was coming.

"Oh, I think the conflict has just begun." One dragon let go, and the other warped inward, preparing to swing me.

"*You disappoint me.*" The words slammed against my brain like a block of ice, thrumming through my entire being, seizing me, and I clutched at my temples. It was the weight of every failure, every apathetic moment, every time I sat and let life pass me by, packaged into one verbal punch that knocked my soul out of my body. An all-familiar, encompassing misery was left in its place.

"Me too," I muttered, and dropped from the broken edge, curling myself into a ball as I fell, as if that would protect me—but I knew the dragons would do all the work if I held my breath and waited it out. It was a lot easier that way . . . right?

No.

My eyes pried open, immediately clogged by tears as icy wind whipped at me like a cloak of daggers. It wasn't much, but it was a start, and I thrust my arms forward, aiming for the field of pure white that was the ground. My dragons shot out, hitting land with a jolt, and slowed me enough for a rough landing as they bent into arches. I stood, shaking the snow from myself, and like dogs, they whipped themselves clean as well. We shared a glance before they launched me a couple hundred feet over open snow and into the dead forest. Along its edge, maybe a couple hundred yards down, there was a rectangular pillar of snow with birds circling in the sky over it. I resisted the urge to investigate and continued fleeing, though for some reason, Alduin wasn't in pursuit. He simply stood at the castle's burst-open edge, watching me from a distance the way he had when Maya and I first found him, waiting for something. I sped up to escape his gaze.

Where a lush, snow-tipped forest should have faded in, only slick, dead branches awaited—the forest was nothing more than a skeleton. I shuddered, hugged myself, and closed my eyes for the journey home.

Even with the dragons acting as sure-footed stilts taking me home without much thought, I got no rest on the return to Dawnbringer Castle; how could I, with the deep chill and anxiety of being sandwiched in a wooden graveyard between regret and strangled dreams? What if Maya and Zox weren't there when I arrived? What if I'd already burnt every bridge, and there was nothing left to cross the gap with?

How long had I been in that cave for?

No. I have to believe that there's redemption for me, somewhere.

The sky was a sheet of bleak, apathetic grey that stretched to the horizon. As I crossed over the jagged river—which had frozen completely solid, somehow—there still wasn't a sliver of blue in the distance for my hope to cling to, or even the ghost of a sun for comfort. It was like being trapped inside of a stone sphere. Maybe I always had been, but at least the inside of it used to be painted with pretty colors.

As the castle drew closer, for the first time, I felt tired. Physical and mental exhaustion don't typically manifest inside of a dream, but there's a first time for everything, unfortunately. I wanted to stop, build a fire, curl up next to it, and let sleep save me from the uncomfortable future that awaited, but with death reaching its icy tendrils so far from Delirium, I couldn't afford the time. Rest would have to wait.

Thanks to the dragons, that wait wasn't long. High stone walls greeted me through gaps in withered bark, and I vaulted over one just as I had when I'd left—it was certainly more convenient than using the door. *Though, that means nobody re-engaged the shield, which seems strange.*

It was disheartening to see the state of my courtyard after that strange dream I'd had where the damage was all reversed. Grass was upheaved in multiple locations, all patchy and muddy and crushed, and frozen strands of water spanned out of the shrunken icicle toward a crystalline lake. I thought about tossing it into the forest but realized that there'd be a giant pockmark left on the ground afterward, and that would be even harsher on the eyes. At least the shrunken glacier had a chilling beauty to it.

"Maya?" My voice rang through the battered and cracked archways around our lake, tearing through still silence that hung over everything in sight like fog. "Zox?"

Only I bothered to answer myself as my calls bounced off the distant castle walls and returned home.

A chill set in as I walked up the main steps. The air numbed my nose, and the trees within our walls had been desiccated. Vines, once cobalt tinsel, had become old, frayed yarn strung across cracked plaster, like the veins of a fermented corpse. Stone that once felt so full of soul and warmth seemed hollow.

"Maya?" I called, much quieter, once inside the great hall. The interior was dim, and so much space with no one inside of it only magnified the aching loneliness. My home had become an abandoned museum, the plunders and spoils more like memorials tucked away in shadow.

Up far too many stairs, I pressed myself against our bedroom door, feeling wood on my face for a time. Perhaps she was so focused on something, like a puzzle, or playing with some strange stray animal, that she hadn't bothered responding to my calls. That's the kind of desperate hope I clung to, along with the oak, before I took one final, deep breath and pushed forward.

With a deep sigh, I walked in, past our empty bed and empty desk, and shut the sliding balcony doors. Dancing curtains settled to rest from their listless performance, as did I—there was nothing else to do.

I curled up in the bed, tucking myself into a cocoon with the silk comforter, but did not fall asleep when I closed my eyes. Despite that, I kept them shut, hugging myself in the dimness, because opening my eyes would've meant coming terms to the fact that I was alone—that I was completely, utterly lost, and the plaque hanging over my bed was mocking me.

It would've meant coming to terms with the fact that I'd been in that cave for far, far too long, and there was no one left to save me.

Little Gems

Sunrise was not the comfort it once was upon my face—instead, it was a wake-up slap of warmth on my crusty skin, staunchly contrasting the chilled air that soaked into my bones. A cough raked my dry throat and I groaned as I sat up, sighing at the wilted planter on my balcony. The world was a reflection of how I felt inside at that very moment—empty, cold, and dead—and for the first time ever, I actually wished I was back in the real world. Ruthless as it may be, the loneliness of being a loser beats the barren solitude of living in a broken, hollow world. I buried my face in my hands and screamed into them, and though it solved nothing, my hands briefly felt less frozen.

"Reza?"

I screamed, scrambling at the growl, slamming into the headboard.

Zox screamed back.

"Where did you come from?" I shouted, voice wobbling.

"I have been outside all night, waiting for you to awaken. I heard you scream and thought I would come in to check on you."

"Outside? Just sitting there?"

"No. Standing," Zox said flatly. The streaks running down his face seemed brighter than usual in the morning light.

"You—oh, what does it matter? I'm so happy to see you, Zox. Good Lord, I thought there was no one left in this place but me and Alduin." I rubbed at my head—it stung. "Where's Maya?"

"She left shortly after you, shouting something about your intelligence and some other things I didn't quite understand. You did not return with her?"

"No, I—" squinting, thinking hard, I paused. "I didn't see her anywhere. You're sure she came after me? Hard to believe she would, with all the stuff I said to her. She might've left to go somewhere else."

Zox crossed his arms. "No, she absolutely followed you. I recall her saying 'that dumb little bitch better beg on his knees for forgiveness when I bring him back home'." The monotony of his voice dulled the sharp insult into a bludgeon that crashed into my face.

"Thanks for the detail."

"My pleasure."

I scooted to the end of the bed, then rose. "Well, she must have been waiting for an opening when I made my escape. Maybe she missed it, somehow, though that seems odd."

"Odd indeed." There was the faintest hint of judgement in his voice.

I raised an eyebrow. "You disagree?"

"I think you need to find her."

Sighing, I said, "I don't know. I mean, she probably saw me break out and thought, 'well, no need anymore' and left. No way she wants me chasing her."

Zox paused for a moment, then, "You and I have a lot in common."

"What does that mean?" I asked, taken aback.

"A tendency to lean toward obliviousness." He stated it like a fact, not a quip.

I inhaled deeply through my nose. "I don't think it's quite on the same level."

Several slow blinks later, Zox replied, "Don't be so quick to assume. She would not have attempted to rescue you if she wanted nothing to do with you, even despite your questionable choices. Now it's your turn to display a little honor."

I straightened my back. "I have honor. I'm honorable."

More slow blinks.

"Okay, maybe my decisions have been questionable lately. I just—I was scared I'd lose this place if I fought him, and for a while, I legitimately thought staying here forever was the answer to all of my problems anyway. It sounded so nice, and calm, and simple, but I guess nothing good is that simple. You're right; we should go get her. You need anything to get ready?"

"I am confused—why are you assuming that I will be accompanying you?"

"Wow, you are full of unexpected responses today. Are you an eight-ball?"

"Very doubtful."

My face contorted, and I opened my mouth to speak, but got lost in thought.

"I cannot go with you, Reza," he said, unfazed.

"Why is that? I'll need help; that guy is some kind of undying monster, and he's only getting stronger with time. We have a better chance of finding Maya if there's two of us searching, as well."

He shook his head calmly. "What you seek now has no place for me. This is something you must do on your own."

"What is this, some kind of quest in Skyrim? Why are you being so cryptic?"

"I do not know what that means, but our time together has come to an end. You are growing, now, and what you seek, you must obtain. You cannot remain trapped here, nor can you ever come back when you leave."

A chill ran down my spine, and the silly, friendly bear no longer felt like the one I'd known for some time. "How would you know anything about that?"

"You ask the wrong questions. Instead, ask questions to your soul about yourself and who you are. Find Maya, and you will understand more, I believe. This must come to an end, Jackson."

My chest tightened. "Who are you?"

His head shook once more. "Who are *you*?"

I fought with my thoughts to organize them and respond, but he turned to leave. "Where are you going?"

"Away," he said without turning around. "There is no place for me here."

A knot formed in my throat.

He turned to me. "You understand, don't you?"

I nodded, and so did he.

"One more thing—this place is a work of art, a castle of dreams and ode to greater times . . . but it, too, must go. You must break the ties that bind." With that, he left. I ran into the hall with a mouth ready to explode into a thousand jumbled questions, but when I burst through the doorway, it was empty. No feet fell on the stone steps, nothing shuffled in the hall—there was only silence and solitude once more.

Falling back onto the bed, I stared into the ceiling for a time, the way I used to when I was procrastinating going back to the real world. Little networks of grout between the stones formed a mesmerizing pattern that I could just get lost in. My world was falling apart, melting, but those stones were solid and unfazed. I wished I could be more like them, strong, sturdy and built to weather whatever the world would throw at it. Instead, I was more like a tree that wilts in the cold; it shrivels and dies when things become hard, despite all the time spent changing each season to reach peak beauty.

But I suppose that tree hasn't really died, has it? Through the coldest nights it stands tall, a ghost of its spring self but strong in its own way; it braves the creeping dark until one day it can break free and explode with remembered life and color. It does not die.

It endures.

I took a deep breath, sat up, and got to work. The poem plaque overhead came down first —I didn't even bother to unhook it, just ripped it right out of the wall. It seemed like the best place to start. Then a stack of unused parchment, some spare clothes, and all my desiccated plants. They formed a sad pile at the foot of my bed, dead leaves and herbs and dreams, but despite that, they managed to serve a final purpose at the end of their journey. I waited a little while, letting the warmth spread over me and fill me with calm.

Soon, the smoke thickened into slate pillows, and my comforters were a new shade of bright orangey-red. Flames grew, and grew, and reached for the ceiling desperately, dancing their dance to whatever rhythm hides in the natural order of all things. My heart danced with them as I ambled down the stairs, admiring the reaps of my conquests past one last time. There were so many, and they filled me with pride and nostalgia . . . but what were they worth, beyond that? Spoils that served as nothing more than sinkholes for me to get stuck in every now and again, and none of them were even real. Or were they? I couldn't decide, so I continued to descend, stopping at a podium on my way out the doors —the podium with a little, bloodstained dagger sitting atop it. In a moment of indescribable intent, I grabbed it and strapped it to my hip, letting a flap of the shirt cascade over, so that it, too, might also serve a purpose with the end of its life.

The courtyard was an icy mess, dirt spewed and upturned, glaciers lopsided and shrunken but still enormous. Stone archways of the small villa were cracked and crumbled, and I swear the armory looked to lean in the slightest bit. Something crashed behind me, but I kept walking forward, through the graveyard of my dreams and over its gate. Atop it, I breathed deep the cold air, letting it sting my lungs, and offered a final look back to watch the fall of a place I'd worked so hard for—where I'd found glory and something to derive meaning from, and even fierce companionship. I wondered where Maya was and if she'd already slain Alduin as the castle burned. It should've been a horrible, harrowing sight to see the castle smoldering and glowing from the inside, but instead, I felt warmth. In a cold, dead world, something was finally aflame, burning bright against the slate skies; its glow was like a sunrise the horizon so bleakly lacked.

Dawnbringer Castle lived true to its name, delivering the final dawn of our days.

My trek through the forest was far less mesmerizing

than it used to be; ahead, patchy grey of dead wood, and above, veins of icy, withered branch wove blindly across skies of almost the same color. It was like someone had cast a net over the forest, and it felt that way, too.

The journey was quick, but not so quick that the wind chill froze my eyes shut, and about halfway, I encountered a mound of snow in a large clearing. They were faint, but there were signs of commotion—tracks that had been filled in with snow. I approached it carefully, dragons and sword raised, and brushed a bit of piled snow with the blade's tip. Thin, wiry hairs poked out, and as I brushed more, I uncovered legs—spindly, and far too many of them. I recoiled at first, of course, for it was disgusting. That monster had been one of my greatest fears of the forest since I'd first set foot in it, and surely it could eat a man whole.

But sadness quickly replaced it as I realized that not even the worst parts, the parts I feared so greatly, had survived. Alduin had poisoned the land, and there was no good or bad before the blight; nothing and no one escaped it.

Well—I hoped, at least, there was one who had.

I moved with haste after that, filled with a sense of urgency that bit at the back of my mind. *What if she's been injured, and couldn't make it out of the forest? With cold like this, who knows what state she might be in....*

Shaking the thoughts away, I pressed on, my

face numb and sweat icy on my spine. The forest was thinning, the sky darkening, and I knew that it wouldn't be long before I could put an end to it all. I wanted so badly to see the sun again and hear Maya insult me for the mistakes I'd made.

A few hundred yards to the left, I spotted incredibly vague shadows shifting above the tree-line and recalled what I'd seen as I fled from Alduin the day before. The trees were gaunt, but with the storm's permanent haze, it was enough for me to skirt along without worry of being spotted. As I drew closer, the shadows became smudges that grew, and grew, and weaved, and bobbed with a familiar awkwardness.

Please.

Similar to what I'd found earlier, there was a pile of snow near the forest's edge almost to my chest. It spread out and formed a smooth junction with the ground, rounding near the top—it'd been there a while. An anxious bat circled over and over above, against a miserable sky. I took a deep breath, feeling my heart sink into my stomach, and fought the shackles that tried desperately to freeze me in place, churning snow beneath my feet.

You're okay.

You always are.

The perfect coat of snow was dashed about as I dug, not with my swords or dragons, but with my bare hands. They burned, but that was okay. I needed the pain. I deserved it, really. My hands hit something hard and smooth.

A stone? She built a shelter for herself!

My heart leapt from its sunken state, and with haste, I swept the rest of the snow away. She was looking at me, not with a smile, or adoration, or loathing or hurt or fear or anything at all. . .her face was blank. Accepting. Her eyes shone brighter than they ever had, luminescent with their disappointment in me, and I reached to grab her and shake her and let her steal what little warmth I had left to offer.

The ice she'd been encased in was so clear, I hadn't realized it was even there at first. Little trails of water fell from where the surface bit my hands, and I collapsed beside her crystalline tomb. My face had gone so numb that I couldn't let out a pained cry or scream into the slurried skies for vengeance. I simply sat there, crumpled, knowing I'd never get the chance to fix what I'd broken—my final moments with her had been taxidermied, the hurt of which was locked in those two oceanic gems, like fallen glaciers forever gazing across a dead forest.

It was a memorial for her, and for what little hope I'd had left at that point. A monument to my failures.

"I'm so sorry," I whispered, though I knew the words weren't worth a goddamn thing, then wilted beside her.

Awakening

I had been waiting for the cold to carry me into a comfortable oblivion, but it refused to offer even that much. A thick coat of powder sought to entomb me without pause; my bones became ice, and my blood snow, but still my mind would not quiet. My shame, my guilt, would not fade with me, so I rolled closer to Maya and watched her everlasting escape attempt. She was no less beautiful within the frozen glass, and still more of a warrior than I ever was. I could see the fight in her, refusing to let even death stop her from winning—or telling me what hopeless idiot I was, though only the latter was fulfilled.

Something wet and rough smeared across my face, and I grunted, slapping at it with hands like ice cubes. When I unfurled myself, there was a bat looming over me, its beady eyes boring through my soul. The taut, pinkish scar across its belly stood out in the off-white light, and we simply stared at each other for a little while before it took off and left me alone once more. I was left in the agony of wakefulness and leaned my head against the tombstone. It seared my cheek, but the pain quickly faded to numbness.

I don't know if it had been five minutes or five hours, but after a while, her eternal disappointment began to morph into something else—the look she'd give me when I was taking too long. Feet tapped against ice in my head, rhythmic and slow, echoing between the walls of hollow half-thoughts.

"What are you waiting for, dummy?" her eyes asked me, and I realized I had no answer. I wasn't getting any warmer, stronger, or closer to escaping my personal hell, and if there had been any hope of saving her, it had long since passed. If there was any hope of dying quietly in the cold, it seemed I was not deserving of it. Something warmed in my belly, like a deep swig of bourbon, and it burned low for a while, but it grew.

I let this place die.

It grew and grew and grew until I could flex my fingers and move my legs again; a fire raging inside me that melted away the ice on my heart.

I let her die.

Slowly, I stood, and churned through deep snow out of the forest and into the clearing—the once beautiful meadow had been buried under a vast sea of white, icy wind whipped through me like daggers, but still I marched toward the once place I had left to go.

I let you live.

Fueled by pure fury, further forward I trudged through impossibly thick haze, until the faintest smudges of light became visible. They grew bigger, and brighter, but before I made it too close, a massive gust of wind blew me backward. It was like God himself had swooped down and cast me aside, it was so strong, and my dragons tried to latch onto something but found only mouthfuls of fresh powder. By the time I was standing again, the haze had cleared—everything was crystal clear, glowing even, radiant under the pastel sky. About four hundred yards in every direction was a wall of swirling fog; it had not cleared, but simply moved to get out of my way.

To get out of *our* way.

Thunderous rumbling billowed from the icy hand reaching for the sky ahead as tons of spiked ice slithered over it and toward me. Nothing sat atop its sheen, scaly head, or at its back or anywhere else, for that matter—the serpent had been deemed more than I could handle, or perhaps Alduin simply wanted to enjoy the show and get a feel for my movements. Wherever he was, it didn't matter. I drew Somnior slow and measured. Its weight felt welcome and oddly warm in my palms, like strength anew, and my dragons bobbed beside me. I could feel heat on my face from the blade, and the world was warped around it, like the horizon in a desert; as if the blade were forged from dragon's breath, it burned with a passion like mine, its marbled layers almost glowing even in daylight. In that clearing cookie-cut from dead land, I lowered my center of gravity, every muscle in me taut and begging to explode, as a serpent the size of seventy trees barreled towards me.

My mind went blank. Nothing mattered anymore, nothing existed but me and that wretched, overgrown ice sculpture. I must have looked insane, like an ant sitting on railway tracks, waiting for death.

Maybe it will kill me.

I took a deep breath, buried my dragons deep into the snow, finding frozen earth, and rose into the air. The approaching emerald eyes turned from peas to dinner plates.

Nah.

With a scream that carried the weight of a thousand dead dreams, I launched forward, hurtling through the air at break-neck speeds. The snake halted, but could not react in time to my rashness, and I sunk one dragon's teeth into its nose, using the centrifugal force to wheel around and drag Somnior across its right eye. Steam fired out of the false gemstone as I cleaved it like warm butter, and a booming hiss crushed my eardrums as it whipped about, but my momentum swung me up and into the air. A short pause at the peak let me catch a full breath, admiring the insignificance of everything from above, and I fell back down as it turned its head towards me. Icy fangs bigger than the glaciers decorating my old courtyard flared, and glare stung my eyes, but I kept them open anyway. The burn was nothing compared to what burned inside me.

It snapped upward in a desperate and loathing move. I fired a dragon out to each upper fang, breaking my speed, but not enough to stop me from falling into its cave of a throat; with lightning speed, the beast shut its mouth, and I was drowned in deep, frigid darkness.

Exactly as I'd planned.

Latching onto the walls of the serpent's esophagus, winding back until the metal was so tight I feared it would snap, I steadied my nerves—culling not fear, but the excitement eating at me, begging me to rush in without thought. My heart was a well-wound war drum setting the pace for what would come next. I relaxed the rhythm. . . .

And let go of it all—the anger, the fear, the self-doubt and hatred, in a moment of blissful numbness. I exploded forward, immediately swinging the whips around me in a drill-like motion, little flecks of ice dusting my face and cooling my skin. When I burst from the serpent's head, I canceled the drilling and latched a short tether into the ice near where I'd emerged from, swinging up and around in a twisting motion. My sword slid into its head with ease, all the way down to the hilt, and felt smooth as I dragged it around the skull, tracing its curve back to the jaw, where I cut sideways into the mouth and made my way back to the start. At the end of the scoring, I let my momentum carry me into the air once more so I could watch it; the upper jaw cracked and groaned and split with great mist, then fell to the ground as the rest of it writhed around in the snow. An empty eye watched me as I fell back to earth in an explosion of snow.

One snake down, one to go.

I marched toward the hand, which had started to look less like a God reaching for the sky and more like a titan drowning, finding no help. My dragons churned snow, tossing it all over me, but I didn't care. My sight was locked in on the target, with a single goal in mind. I began to understand the flame that seemed to always burn within Maya for the first time; if only it hadn't taken her death to see it clearly.

Rather than attempt a siege, having seen the way the floors and walls could be manipulated with ease, I stopped about fifty yards away and simply waited in silence. There was no sign of Alduin anywhere, but I could feel his eyes. He would have been watching the last fight; in fact, he seemed to spend a lot of time watching me. Perhaps I was always his target, for whatever reason. His endgame. The only thing I wanted was to make him regret that decision.

The air was strangely still, though the distant wall of fog churned angrily. It was like being in the eye of a storm, a perfect calm that was ironically unnerving. Minutes passed like eons, crawling by as I waited in place, eyes dancing in my skull, ears waiting for the slightest disturbance in any direction, but nothing came. I fought off the urge to storm in, as Maya might have done, knowing damn well the shift in power that kind of handicap would offer him. In fact—

Oh. I'm surrounded by snow.

Realization dawned on me too late—Maya, the fog clearing, the serpent; it was all bait. I'd been riled up into thinking my decision was the safe one, when in fact, there was nothing safe at all about the situation. Panicking, I started to pull back, hoping to regain some perspective on the situation, and that turned out to be the worst idea possible. Ice crept up my dragons, thick and layered, reaching for me with hunger. They fought hard to shatter their prison, succeeding just before it reached my hands, and I tasted snow before regaining my balance. A thin thread of glossy blue sparkled in the light, drawn between me and the beast I'd already conquered. My head shot in every direction, but still, there was no sign of Alduin.

Clink.

I shuddered, hesitating to turn toward the sound behind me—it was all too familiar. Another, then another, from all different directions. My dragons saw what I could not and intercepted them. Faster, faster still, the projectiles came from an invisible dome around me. In the distance, snow rose from the ground and formed the next volley. Quicker, wider, my dragons swept until a near-solid dome of gold enshrined me. The grating, chalky sound grew louder and louder as a thousand missiles were destroyed, until it was so loud I felt suffocated. It would have been pitch black if not for the soft glow Somnior emitted. Mist and frozen dust covered me, but I was safe, at least, and I used the break to think a moment.

My defense is near impenetrable, but I have no offense when active. What if....

In a moment of brilliance, I sheathed Somnior and its light, blindly knelt down in the snow and dug like a squirrel on the first day of winter, tossing piles of it aside. He would not be able to see me within the covering, and I knew that if I could get low enough on my own, it'd be safe enough to transition from defensive dome to drill and burrow beneath the earth. Coordinating was something I'd worry about later. Less than a yard down, my hands hit something hard. It was almost impossible to hear anything besides the grating of ice above, but I would've sworn I heard the faintest rustling sound below. Drawing my sword carefully, making sure the hilt had extended enough to give me clearance beneath it, I brushed away at the final layer of snow. I could see my own blade beneath me, like I was staring into a mirror.

That's not good.

There was nothing I could do, really—to let up my defenses would mean certain failure, and that was not an option, so I simply braced myself and let it happen. A massive block of ice crashed into me from below, rising into the sky with me pinned atop it. I released my defense and clamped two golden jaws into it, and, when it reached the vertex of its arc, I launched it back toward the ground. The action sent me reeling backward midair, but it was worth it, and I broke my fall just as the glacier smashed into Alduin's tower in an explosion of frost and snow. The thumb broke off first, the rest barely holding together, cracking and groaning in the distance.

I smiled at the sight of its destruction—partially because it was satisfying to finally smash something of his, but also because it confirmed that the sneaky bastard wasn't in his tower. The sound of rushing snow grew louder behind me, and I turned to find a torrent of it churning beneath a little black speck in the sky.

He was probably waiting somewhere in the snake to catch me off-guard once I'd been swallowed . . . I have to be careful with this guy. No honor in his fighting style.

I widened my stance again, dragons at the ready. He slowed in his final approach, relaxing closer to the ground, and sighed once within earshot. "I hope you don't feel too accomplished—it won't take long to rebuild."

"Good luck rebuilding something as a corpse."

"Ah, yes—because you've done so well to kill me in the past, haven't you? Every time you thought you'd won, it was a lie. Today will be no different than any other day."

I inhaled deep, straightening my back, and raised my sword high. Light streaked across his face, but his eyes did not so much as squint. "You're wrong, Alduin. Today, I change tomorrow and every day beyond."

He shook his head, icy mist condensing on his body to form a thick, glossy armor that was uniform but flexed with his movements. "Tomorrow will be empty if you reject your chance at bliss today, fool. Why can you not see it?"

"I see through your lies—nothing else matters."

Ice formed in his hand, jagged, sharp, and twice the size of any greatsword. It caught light so well it looked to glow from within, and grey vapor trailed from the blade. He stepped toward me, and I matched him. Again. Soon, we were running. He swung over and down on me—the parry was easy, but jets of steam blasted from the connection, fogging our views. They dissipated quickly upon release, and there was the slightest scar on his blade. It healed instantly, however.

Leftover moisture steamed from Somnior's edge as I raised it, tightening the grip. Extended holds were bad for both of us—but also advantageous. A double-edged sword that we each had on hand on the hilt of. I swung left, hitting his blade on the inside, and rolled it flat. Following the path of least resistance, steam exploded toward Alduin's face, and he quickly jumped back.

Good. Now, your turn.

He came at me hard, swinging down, then left. I spun, catching it low, but he pushed toward me and I had no choice other than to sweep it over us both. I stepped back, moisture cool on my face, and he laughed ever so slightly. With his facial protection, the upper hand was his, no doubt. The ice would make steam tolerable for a longer time.

We met again, our swords clashing in maddening dance; up, left, down, behind—neither of us were holding back. Vapor burst from every contact like fireworks with a deep hissing sound. Our blades met high, and my vision clouded. Thankfully, reflexes were my dragon's greatest strength, and one came alive to shatter a shard of ice that flew through the curtain of vapor between us, briefly throwing me off-balance. He laughed, and I cracked my neck.

"It's a shame all this snow has handicapped you," he said, words like sharpened ice.

"It will only make defeating you that much more satisfying." I couldn't see his face, but I felt the grimace he made in my soul, and it was utterly satisfying.

Now we begin.

Our dance in those snowy fields was treacherous; I'd boasted, but Alduin was right. The snow made things much harder for me than it needed to be, and I could barely block surprise attacks, let alone form one myself. I was at a complete disadvantage, caught on the retreat, every meeting of our blades a step back. He pressured harder, harder, knowing I was one mistake away from losing the battle early—which means I was doing my job perfectly.

This is not my first time fighting at a disadvantage, Alduin. I work best as an underdog.

I let him push me, groaning with every hit, getting sloppy and angry with my swings, until finally blocking far too close to myself. A wall of steam formed between us, and immediately I bit into his sword with a dragon to simulate pressure, fell with the other into the snow, then reached for the dagger hidden at my hip—

What?

A shadow formed behind the vapor, and I barely managed to block a nasty projectile. The snow's glare subsided, and a far bigger one was being shredded by my free dragon just as I turned to see it blot out the sun.

"You do not wield trickery as well as I," a slithering voice whispered into my ear, touching my side, and I stumbled back. He stood cross-armed behind me, a new sword forming, and I retracted Somnior—a pillar of ice held his previous blade in place. I straightened, ready for his next attack, but something was off.

What's that in the snow? . . . blood?

I wobbled, warmth spreading over my side, and was drawn to the sparkling of an ornate hilt protruding from it. I touched it with my hand, hissing.

"Don't worry. Leave it in for now, stop fighting, and I can have it fixed in no time at all. There's no need for you to throw all of this away."

Wincing, I raised Somnior again. "Stop pretending like you're here to help me."

Alduin shook his head, sighing. "I speak the

truth. Not only will you lose paradise, you'll lose everything. Surrender, hand your sword over to be destroyed, and you can have anything you've ever dreamed of. Power unlike anything else."

The pain was growing, along with numbness from the battling cold, but I held my ground, using a dragon to brace myself. "Your power isn't real. Your joys are false; your victories are fabricated. You're alone in a world built from lies, Alduin. I understand that now. The satisfaction of filling a hollow life with half-truths and pretty things will never make you truly happy. Maya was right."

"Shut up," he screamed, his hands sprouting claws of ice that left thin vapor trails behind them. He swung, and swung again, each violent and laden with heavy rage, and my parries became painful. "Shut your insolent mouth!" He swung with only one hand once my movements slowed, and a frosted claw latched onto the left side of my head; a deep, icy burn spread from it and over into my eye, and down my neck. I screamed, I think, but could hardly hear it over the crackling of my freezing face. I whipped my dragons around in a futile frenzy, managing to break off a piece of his mask before the pain left me limp. His right eye was visible and burning with hate, and he raised his sword hand. "What satisfaction will your life of failure bring, fool? You have no victories, not even false ones, and yet you cling to the emptiness! How is it even possible to hold onto nothing?"

Numbness melted over my searing nerves,

trickling across my body. Consuming me. I felt at the end of a road which leads nowhere, vision fading in one eye. My words came out slow and slurred, but I forced them through the pain. "I only fail because I've never tried anything else. I've never cared to put in the work because, like you said, I am a failure. I let down everyone around me. But I see now that failure is a fuel, and I'm done pouring it over myself out of pity.

"I'm not holding onto nothing, Alduin—there's never nothing, or I'd have already fallen. I was just too busy looking down, fearing the drop, to see what I'd been holding onto."

"Give up. Give up and let yourself go." I could see the sorrow in the over-packed bags of his exposed eye, the misery he tried to cover with hard words and a life of distractions. It begged for help, despite everything he said. It screamed of misery and lamented the abyss that wouldn't fill no matter what was poured in. False happiness is hollow, and even when painted as a rock, the slightest breeze will send it tumbling toward nowhere in particular.

I fanned the flame lit deep in my soul, knowing it was the end. The fire burned hot enough to keep from freezing solid the slightest bit longer. "No." It felt so good to finally say it. "I'm going to climb back up, now."

His mask repaired itself, hiding him once more. "You can never destroy me, Jackson. I will always return."

Half-smiling, I replied, "I know."

I sent one dragon to his left shoulder, and the other down by my left leg to block, exposing everything above it. His head tilted toward the opening, hungry for the chance to take the win, and he swung hard. With all his might crashed a pillar of ice upon my shoulder, glancing upwards off it as I barely dropped low enough, and surely, just as I'd waited for . . . he overcompensated. The exhaustion, the frustration and sorrow, the glimpse of a victory so close he could taste it—all of it led him astray in a final instant that carried on for an eternity. My left dragon, free of its block, snapped its jaws upon his right torso, across his swing, gold teeth embedding into the thick ice protecting him but unable to burrow further. His eyes lit up, this time with a violent thirst, a want for blood, as false safety was the final thread that unraveled and left him naked before me.

"Have you not learned anything?" his eyes screamed at me in that hanging moment. But I had.

You're always trying to save me, aren't you, Maya?

My right index finger found a tiny bump under Somnior's pommel and a foot of gold fired from the dragon's jaws through Alduin, the tip of which poked out the slightest bit from his other side. For several seconds, we were both still, as if neither of us knew what had happened. His breaths grew sharp and wet as blood seeped into his lungs, dribbling down from the gaps of his mask. Several seconds more and he collapsed.

He was dead by the time he hit the ground.

The wall of surrounding fog retreated, fading like smoke from a dying fire, and sunlight started to poke holes in the thick mass of grey overhead. As the weather cleared, it only made the scene that much more gruesome—the melting remnants of his crumbling tower, crimson snow steaming beside me, and in the distance, an icy tombstone caught creeping sunlight like an ancient gem.

I loomed over Alduin for a moment, every heartbeat a screaming stab in the side. His ice had broken off from me, but the left half of my body was numb—the world totally black on one side—and only a dragon kept me from tipping over. I'd wanted to rattle off a monologue about why I emerged victorious as he died, or hear him have a change of heart in the end, but there was no time for that. There was no fanfare or cheering crowd, no trophy or scroll to seal my win. I wanted it all to mean something. I wanted someone to celebrate with, after overcoming the devil that nearly consumed me, but I was alone in that powdered graveyard; even the forest was dead.

The most terrible victories are born in silence—but, though it hurt, though I was broken and numb, I did well to remember that it was a victory nonetheless.

For that, I was proud.

Dawn broke through a sea of grey, shards of sunrise like orange and magenta flotsam on the horizon.

The dagger in my side caught its light, shining brilliantly, and I couldn't help but laugh weakly at the irony. My dragons had used the last of their power to drag me over to Maya, and returned to their resting place as Somnior's hilt. Though they didn't move, their eyes shone bright, and I rested it blade-down against her. Crimson-coated steel still protruded from one of the dragon's mouths.

I looked into her crystal tombstone—a perfectly translucent monument to my betrayal that somehow made her eyes even more brilliant—and saw a watery reflection of myself in it as more and more sun melted through thinning clouds. It sweat in the blossoming warmth, weeping for Maya.

Weeping for me.

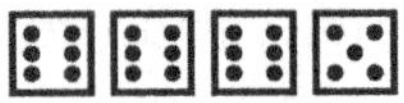

Butterfly

For the first time in a long time, when I woke up in the real world, warm light washed over me, hugging me gently as the blur in my eyes faded. Soon enough, the reason why became clear.

"Ah, you're awake, Mr. Bao." A man I didn't recognize, neatly trimmed and glowing with a welcoming smile, stood over me. Light scattered across the symphony of white filling the room I was in, his coat included. "For a while, we weren't sure if you'd stabilize or not . . . it seems someone up there is your friend."

"Am I—"

"Don't think about it too much," he said. "You were out for a few days, so you're going to be exhausted right now, and probably very hungry any minute. Your vitals seem fine, so let's run through a few quick tests and make sure everything is working the way it should, okay?"

I nodded.

"What's your name?"

"Jackson Bao."

"Good. Address?"

"4839 Allen Avenue, apartment 403."

"Mother's name?"

I hesitated. "She goes by Jade."

His eyes hovered on me a moment, then back to the clipboard. "Your memory seems good, so no concerns there"—he flashed a light in my eye—"and reactions seem solid. We're going to be keeping an eye on you and checking in a lot more before you're released, but for now, let's get some food in you."

I nodded. "Alright. May I have my phone, please?"

He pointed to the nightstand. "Should be charged. Feel free to contact anyone and they can visit with you briefly. Don't spend any more time on the device than that, though."

"Okay."

He turned to leave.

"Doctor?" I called.

"Yes?" he asked, facing me partially.

"Did anyone . . . come by?"

He sighed, pointing across me. There was a vase with bright yellow and red flowers, and a balloon that read 'get well soon'. "People care about you. There were a few who stayed for quite a while, through nights even, but the work week started and we advised them to leave."

My chest tightened, jaw clenched, and I took a few steadying breaths. "Thank you."

"Send your messages and someone else is going to come in and have a chat with you, alright?" He smiled, but I found it hard to look at him. The door shut, and I picked up my phone; the power button revealed a curtain of notifications, so many they didn't fit on my lock screen. There were names I hadn't heard in a while, some I had; the previews showed a lot of the same thing. Concern. Sympathy. Worry. Fear. I felt sick, looking at all of their messages. Some of them were from people I hadn't talked to in months, or years. Relationships I thought I'd burned by being the apathetic pile of shit I was, decayed by neglect—but they still cared about me, for some reason. Happy memories of simpler times spent gaming with friends or playing paintball flooded me, and I cracked. Shattered. Why had all of the good times hidden from me? Why did I repress joy and bury myself in the emptiness?

When did I forget that even behind the thickest, darkest rainclouds, there's still a sun shining?

I didn't know how to deal with some of the others, so I opted to text Mike and Diane back, the two who'd tried so hard to keep me from falling, and let them know I was okay. An older woman entered the room, white hair contrasting darker skin, in a clean, crisp suit. Her smile was as bright and warm as the springtime sun, and she took a seat next to me. I set the phone down.

"Hello, Jackson. My name is Dr. Stroberg."

"Hi."

"How are you feeling?"

I sighed. "Well, I've had better days."

"Yes, I can imagine you're feeling pretty drained right now. Do you feel up to have a little chat?"

"Yeah," I replied, nodding. "Sure."

"Great." Hands neatly folded, she took a deep breath. "Tell me a little bit about yourself."

"Uh, well." I chuckled weakly. "I don't know. I'm a pretty normal guy, I guess."

She nodded. "There's no such thing as normal. Everyone is unique, everyone has talents and weaknesses. Value. So, Jackson—what makes you special?"

"Really, I'm nothing special. Work at a marketing company, don't go out much. Haven't really accomplished anything."

"What about things you love? Hobbies, passions?"

"I like watching some TV, games, that kind of stuff I guess."

Dr. Stroberg took another deep breath. "Can you remember the last time you had fun?"

I started. "Well, I don't know. I don't think about it much."

"When's the last time you were really excited for something?"

"I—"

"Do you typically have much energy?"

"Uh, I guess I'm usually pretty tired, but I work a lot."

Her lips pursed, but she didn't say anything.

"What?" I asked.

"I think you know."

Something strange welled up in me, cold and heavy.

"It's okay, Jackson. It can't get better if it doesn't come out."

"I—I don't know." The words choked, and my throat felt strange and tingly. My lips wavered, and pressure built up in my head.

"You do," she said softly, nodding. "Even if it makes no sense, try to say it. Truth's first words hurt most, but they lift the burdens from our hearts."

I squeezed my eyes shut. "I'm so tired. I . . . I think I'm my own worst enemy."

"Good, good Jackson. Let it out. Drag it out into the sunlight. Don't let it hide anymore."

"I hate myself, and I hate that I hate myself. I hate my life, and I hate that I don't do anything to change it. I hate that I lose people because I let them go, even though I don't want them to. That people try to get closer sometimes but I refuse to let them in because I'm scared they'll hate what they find. And that I'm so bad at making sense of what I feel," I rambled, the words broken and jagged.

"Is this the first time you've been honest with yourself about all of that?"

I nodded. "I think I always knew the truth, but some part of me hoped that if I pretended it wasn't there, then nothing was wrong. Maybe it worked for a while, but now I'm like this."

"It's never too late for a first step. Never."

I still couldn't bring myself to look at her. "Why can't I be normal? My life isn't even that bad. I shouldn't feel this way."

She warmed me with another smile. "I told you already, Jackson—there's no such thing as normal; we're all just trying to make it through, in our own way. The good news is that you're safe. You still have people who care about you. There's still the rest of your life to remember how to love the beauty that there is in this world; remember how to love yourself. It may seem impossible right now, but sorrow, meaninglessness, despair—if life is the Earth, then they're the crust. What we see at first, and all we find if we don't bother to look any further. But beneath is millions of miles of burning-hot passion, and love, and fulfillment. It takes a bit of digging sometimes, that's all."

Another wave rocked me. I hated that she could see me so clearly, vulnerable and weak and mushy. It was exposing, like being naked in front of a stranger with no hands to cover up. But after a few minutes, I forgot the unease. The discomfort grew distant, replaced by something strange I didn't recognize. I felt miserable; tired and heavy eyes blurring, weak arms wiping at a running nose, but for some reason, it wasn't that bad. What had felt like indecent exposure shifted and became a sense of being understood; flipping a light on after sitting in the dark for far too long and realizing, once the burning fades, that it's nice to be able to see things again. To be seen. I must've looked like absolute shit sobbing in that hospital bed, but I felt alive, instead of numb; warm, instead of empty; tired, but for a reason. Something had sprouted from nothing and blossomed in my chest.

I felt real.

The next few hours came and went quickly, and things were mostly a blur. I ate something solid, finally, much to the joy of my doctor, and napped for a while after a few more tests. I didn't dream at all, and it was nice to get some good, clean rest for a change. When I woke up, not necessarily re-freshed but less exhausted, I begrudgingly picked up my phone and held it for a time, staring at my un-flattering reflection. I wondered how long it'd been since the last time I'd gotten more than a spare night or two of proper sleep—six months? A year? It could've been five, for all I knew, the way years worth of memories melted together in my mind like a bag of gummy bears left under the sun.

How long had it been since I'd last talked to her?

With a sigh, I scanned my fingerprint and navigated to the pitiful list of faded acquaint-ances inappropriately stored under 'contacts' and scrolled about halfway down, lingering for a time. In some ways, it's funny—despite all the little voices in my head telling me there's no way she could still love a piece of trash like me, I never de-leted her number. Was that because I was a coward, afraid that deleting it would mean my failures were final? Or did some little part of me hold onto the hope that one day I'd get a call and need to recognize the number?

Whatever the reason, I eventually had to take a deep breath and make the plunge. The water would be ice cold, I knew, the pain crisp and suffocating, but no one can live forever standing at the edge; it's better to test the waters than drown in the anxiety of what lies below.

I clicked on the little green phone icon next to "Mom".

The next few moments were like something from a bad trip, where every second crawled by in agony. My heart sank when the ringing tone began, knowing it was too late to cancel the call and take it back without her knowing. My stomach filled with lead, sickening but too heavy to throw up. Another overdrawn ring, another era of wear on my soul. Another. Another. . . .

What did I expect? That she'd pick up, after all this time?

Another ring—"Hello?"

My body went numb, my mind blank. I didn't know what to say.

"Jackson? Oh, God, Jackson, is that you? Hello?"

"Hi, Mom."

There was a shuffling sound, like cloth against the microphone, and a deep exhale. She needed a moment, of course. I'd blindsided her with the call

—in fact, I hadn't even thought about her at all when I'd dialed the number. It was selfish; what if she had been out at an early dinner with her friends, or staying late at work for a meeting? What if she'd been completely fine with things as they were, and my call ruined that equilibrium she'd reached over the years of getting by with me out of the picture?

There was some commotion on the other end again, and a bit of what sounded like wind. I wanted to say something to break the silence; maybe she was waiting for an apology or something meaningful. I'd called her to try and make things right and overcome years of disconnect, but I couldn't even say anything on the phone. It was painfully ironic, and I felt it.

"I—" she said, the word like a gasp. "I miss you so fucking much, baby." The rest came out as a sob that cut through the numbness, right into my heart. I fell to pieces, and couldn't even hide it from her, crying too hard to coherently respond at first.

To be told I was worthless, or berated for my behavior, or scolded for how little I seemed to care about the people that should matter most to me, or for shutting her out when she'd been the one to try and save me from my loneliness—those were things I'd been prepared to shoulder. I was ready for them to crash into me, tear me to pieces, and scatter them across an empty desert where the shifting sands could consume me. I deserved that, didn't I?

. . .

. . .

. . .

Didn't I?

It was still light out by the time afternoon bled into early evening. The horizon outside was obscured but sunset's crimson waves washed high into the sky. I'd been resting since the phone call with my mother; facing not only her but myself for the first time in a while had drained me, and I'd needed time on my own. I would've stayed alone for a while longer if I could've, but that was never an option. Some people in life are too persistent and refuse to stop caring about you no matter how easy you make it for them. The President will never bestow them with medals, no awards will line their mantles, no trophies for time lost—but they're heroes, nonetheless. The kinds of people who save the world, not with great schemes or grand battles, but simply because each of us is a world of our own worth saving, and they see that.

Voices approached outside the room and I took a deep breath, ready to face whatever would come next, even if part of me wanted to fake being asleep.

The door burst open, and it was not what I'd been expecting. When is it ever, really?

Mike, Mrs. Henderson, Diane, and a few others from work flooded the room with life and conversation, some of it fading into sounds of concern or empathy. They smiled when they saw me, odd as I found that, given how pathetic I must have looked in the hospital bed.

"Oh my God," Diane said, rubbing her face. "I was so—I'm so happy you're awake."

"You scared the shit out of us, man," Mike cut in, weaving in front of her. "I guess you weren't lying about all those headaches."

Well. . . .

Mrs. Henderson didn't say anything, perhaps because she saw how overwhelmed I was, or maybe she simply didn't need to. Her tired smile suddenly seemed so knowing and comforting to me in a way I hadn't ever felt before, as if it said "I see you" in soothing silence. Others from my department, and some new girl Mike had dragged along—the poor girl—didn't know what else to say other than adding to a cacophony of "hi"s and "hey"s.

"Hey guys. I'm okay, I swear, just still really tired." I offered up a half-assed wave that seemed indifferent, but really, I was fighting back tears—if there were any left at that point.

Mike reeled the confused-looking girl around to get a clear view of me, and our eye contact immediately broke. "Jax, you gotta meet my lovely new girl; here, this is Robyn. We—"

"Dude, is this really the best time. . . ." Diane interjected. She widened her eyes and motioned toward the girl with her head.

"I thought we were going to see a movie," Robyn mumbled.

"Well, yeah, we are," Mike replied. "You know,

after this."

Mike took one glance at the awkward face his date was wearing and looked back at Diane. He shrugged, turning his palms up, and she simply shook her head at him.

After a few brief conversations, some of which were more awkward than others, most people filtered out of the building. Once it was down to Mike, his unfortunate date, and Diane, he suddenly made a face of realization and cleared his throat loudly, then made up some half-assed excuse about "being late" and left. Of course, he winked at me on the way out like the moron he is. Maybe that oblivious, uncaring tenacity is why he never stopped inviting me to go out with him. Whatever the reason, I smiled as he left, and something came over me.

"Hey, Mike!" I called out.

He popped his head back in through the doorway. "Sup?"

"Thanks for . . . for always being a good friend. I know it has to be hard sometimes."

"What're you talking about?" he asked, chuckling. "If I were a better friend, maybe you wouldn't be here."

That sickening, hot feeling rose in me again. "No, no, you—"

"I really haven't done anything, man. Nothing to thank me for. We're friends. Now get some rest, Sleeping Beauty." He turned to Diane, who was checking her phone. "Or don't sleep."

Mike was out the door and through the hall before her laser-eyes could catch him. She walked over and shut it, then sat down next to me and smiled, sighing deeply.

"You look terrible," she said with a weak laugh.

"Finally, some honesty."

"But it's nice to see you look terrible—well, I don't mean it like—"

"Wow, thanks a lot." I started to fake cry.

"No, you dummy. Ugh, I'm so bad at this stuff sometimes. I try to be like Caleb, but I'm not very good at it. I just meant that it's good to see you showing what you're feeling instead of hiding it, that's all."

My eyes drifted to the bed sheets, then back to her. "You don't have to be like him, you know. You're amazing in your own ways."

She sighed, smiling. "That's sweet of you, but I know I can be better. I'll never be him, but if I learn from him, and I strive for some of what he offered to the world, then I can carry his legacy on, you know. Or at least a part of it. Or who knows, maybe I won't make a difference at all. But I figure it's worth try-ing."

I chuckled. "You're . . . damn, I don't know. I wish I had some of what you have. That fire, that tenacity. It's incredible."

"You do," she said, her face like stone. "We all do, somewhere. It's not a talent, it's there in all of us. You just have to reach deep down and find it if it's buried."

I took a shaky breath and tuned my eyes on my hand as it fidgeted with the heart rate monitor. Silence hung between us for a little while until Diane finally broke it again.

"So tell me—where have you been?"

"What does that mean?"

"I don't know. You've been different lately. Distant, daydreaming, always staring off into space. Like you're not really in this world."

I laughed, shaking my head. "I don't know."

"C'mon, be honest with me. No matter how stupid it sounds."

"You're gonna think I'm crazy."

She raised an eyebrow, sizing me up as I laid in a hospital bed with fluids running into my arm. "Hmm."

"Yeah, fair enough. Okay." I sighed deep, eyes wandering out the window and toward anything else. It took a few more seconds of laughing and shaking my head to actually find the gall to say it to someone else. "Ah, who cares at this point? I lived another life, basically."

"Another life?"

"Yeah, a world of my own. Somewhere to be in control and live a life bigger than myself."

"Okay," she said, nodding. "So you . . . hallucinated?"

My eyes met hers, then shied away. "No, no, not like that. It was so real, sometimes more real than this place. There were other people, friends of mine, and we took on the world together."

A deep inhale, a slow exhale, and finally she asked, "Well? Did you win? Against the world."

I stared through my sheets, through the concrete and Earth and into the void of space that surrounds us all. "Not really. I mean, yes, but mostly no."

She chewed on my words silently.

"I told you."

"No, Jax. I think a lot of people do things like that, to an extent. Escape somewhere else where it's safer and different. Hell, I drowned myself in tequila the night that Caleb died, after I left your place. Yours is just a little more creative.

"But you need to look at it this way: if you'd spent all that time and effort on your real life, this life, don't you think it'd be better than it is now? Even a little bit?"

My eyes turned to the IV snaked into my forearm.

"Just don't forget that you aren't the only one who isn't the biggest fan of this world. It's got a lot of problems and hurt. But they're best faced, rather than swept under the rug, and it's even better if you don't have to do it alone. And you're *not* alone, Jax. At least, you don't have to be, if you don't want to. Do you?"

Slowly, like the swing of a grandfather clock's pendulum, I shook my head.

"I know," she continued. "I know it's hard. To open up and let someone in. It's funny how the brain works like that. When we break a leg or get pneumonia, the first thing that comes to mind is going to see a doctor because you know it's not something you can handle yourself. I mean, what are you gonna do on your own to fix a broken leg, right? But when you're hurting inside, and something breaks in places you can't see . . . sometimes you try to avoid help. So it festers and gets infected and spreads throughout the rest of you. And in those cases, it's understandable to turn towards other things that make us feel better. Somewhere it doesn't hurt, and where reality becomes the dream. But there are enough monsters and demons that come with being alive, Jax. You don't need to make up new ones."

Our eyes locked, like galaxies colliding in the heavens, sucking in the universe around them. It felt like an eternity before she smiled.

I smiled back. A real one, not some half-assed imitation to meet expectations, or a mask to quell concerns. "Thank you, Diane, for being here."

She rose. "Of course. But don't forget that even without me, or Mike, or whoever else around, you gotta fight for yourself. This is the only life we get, Jax. Don't let it blow past while you're hiding under the covers." She approached the exit, turning to me. "I'm gonna go get something to drink, want anything?"

It felt like I was in a pressure cooker as I stared at her, gathering the gall to say it, to just let the words banging on the inside of my head break out. Bubbling, building, begging to set me free. She started out the door when it finally burst, so much emotion exploding all at once that I half-expected to see blood on the ceiling when it was over.

"I want to be better."

Silence, and a sideways smile. For a moment, or a year, she paused at the door—then, finally, turned back to me. "I've been waiting to hear you say that. Be back in a few; don't go anywhere." The door closed behind her, and I immediately exhaled, like I'd been holding my breath the entire time. Maybe I had been.

I looked through the bedside window into a forest-lined parking lot haloed by a sun-burnt sky. It wasn't Dominaria, not even close, but there was a strange beauty to the surrealism of it all; the almost opulent curtains glowing orange, dancing along a thin breeze, and a series of vibrant potted plants along the windowsill.

From the bedside table, I grabbed my wallet and a cheap pen, then pulled a little scrap of paper out and did what once felt impossible: I finished my crappy poem, despite the tears jamming my vision, leaving the world a misty shadow of itself; silhouette phantoms lurking behind panes of frosted glass.

My penmanship was shaky. The sentence curled toward the end, falling below the line it started on. It didn't matter. I didn't care. It was done; it was a step—the first one on solid ground—and it felt amazing.

If you don't chase things, you'll never catch them.

Sometimes it's a decent start just to chase yourself and catch your fall.

I sat in my seat, hundreds around me.
Ghosts of friends, classmates and teachers.
I wonder, how many would leave home for me?

A thousand teary eyes, my own two among
them, gazing with love and admiration.
Longing, wishful, and proud; silently coveting.
I wonder, how many would shed tears for me?

Snow fell from the heavens; soft, flittery
flakes reaching for Earth.
Delicate and graceful, frozen tears dancing
on wind's gale.
I wonder, would the sky open its heart for me?

I do not believe in God, yet I see something
akin to Him in all those around me.
Soul and heart bound by beautiful
hymn, connecting all as One.
I wonder, would lungs burst song for me?

Yes, it is selfish—incredibly so. Yet, nature takes
hold of us when confronted with such things.
Is my existence meaningful, or momentary? I suppose,

It is I who decides which it should be.

<u>THE ADVENTURES OF A CLUELESS WORM</u>

I, I,
I love my dirt, my modest home
Soil and salt, shit and bone,
No need to ask me why.

Why, why,
I don't know why, or where or how,
I just know of the here and now,
And for that I always try.

Try, try,
My job is simple, my needs are met,
Things are fine; I try my best,
From these duties I won't shy.

Shy, shy,
I shy away, I try to hide
From those who live in heights so wide,
I am not meant to see that sky.

Sky, sky,
What above is held so dear?
Might I know your love or fear,
If I could learn to fly?

Fly, fly,
I'm flying now, I feel so tall!
I fear no heights, I fear no fall!
It's so wonderful to fly.

Fly, fly,
Not forever, not for long,
And none will ever sing my song,
But one day more I'll fly.
A simple step up towards the sky.

ABOUT THE AUTHOR

R. E. Fury

R. E. Fury is an upcoming author who runs several communities dedicated to his own short stories and flash fiction. He received a degree in computer science and has been working in the public sector for several years as a contractor to agencies such as DHS and the VA. He currently lives in sunny Texas, and loves nothing more than writing about himself in third person. Lost in a Dream is his first novel. 

For more information and free access to hundreds of short stories, find the author at:

https://r-e-fury.com/

@r.e.fury on Instagram

/u/resonatingfury

Made in the USA
Coppell, TX
21 December 2020